TOM PAVER

HOW MANY PEOPLE MUST DIE BEFORE AN OLD WRONG IS...

PUT RIGHT

A DELAHUNTY & HEUSTON MYSTERY
THE FIRST IN THE REDEMPTION SERIES, SUCCEEDED BY THE COLONY.

About the author

Tom Paver was born and raised in Liverpool, one of six children in a typically Catholic household.

He has spent his career working in the media industry, winning many awards for his marketing campaigns for clients. He now divides his time between London and Liverpool.

He is a half-decent fly fisherman, has trekked most of the way across the Spanish Pyrenees and is partial to a good Ribero del Duero.

A
Calder House
imprint

A Calder House imprint

Copyright: Tom Paver 2012.
The moral right of the author has been asserted in accordance with the Copyright, Designs and Patents Act 1998.

No part of this book may be reproduced or transmitted in any form or by any means without the permission of the author.

All characters and events in this book – other than those clearly in the public domain – are fictitious or used fictitiously and any resemblance to real persons, living or dead, is coincidental.

Also by Tom Paver

The Colony (Redemption, book 2)
The Blood Puzzle (Redemption, book 3)
The Sanctuary Stone (Redemption, book 4)

Coming November 1st 2012
Take the Soup (Redemption, book 5)

ISBN-13: 978-1478334477
ISBN-10: 1478334479

Amazon author profile and full book list:

https://www.amazon.com/author/tompaver
Book design: Dave Thomas – davetcreative@gmail.com

CHAPTER ONE

He stroked the small of her back as she lay next to him, dozing quietly. Their love-making had been its usual adventurous and sensual affair. He would skim his lips up and down her back, tickling the fine hairs in the nape of her spine and driving her to distraction. Paula Kelly, distracted, was a very fine experience indeed.

Of all the things that could go wrong, her husband Dave walking through the door, surprisingly, was among the least of them. And he didn't think that would happen.

Paula was different from all the others, you see: she didn't want commitment, she didn't judge and she didn't cling. In his line of work, such considerations mattered more than a cuckolded husband – even one as big as Dave. And so he wasn't expecting a kick-off any time soon.

Given the delicate origins of their union and the dangerously fragile nature of his past conquests, her detachment was definitely a good thing. He didn't want a repeat of 'the Newcastle incident.' Christ, no.

His thoughts returned to Dave, nevertheless - a firefighter, and a pretty handy one at that. Joe had first seen the tell-tale bruises at a parish dance when the sleeves on Paula's dress had ridden up her arms. It had made him angry as well as concerned - women should be on pedestals, not gurneys, he thought.

So Joe was part Paula's revenge, part her emotional crutch, he figured - but then, he'd always had a yen for the needier woman, despite being surrounded in his up-bringing by feisty Liverpool girls who had loved without measure and shown him that being strong didn't mean forsaking tenderness.

Paula made full use of her husband's shift patterns to 'keep things interesting', as she put it. And interesting it was. Still, it didn't pay to dwell, he thought. Just get stuck in and take from it what you can – she certainly did. That said, there was a tenderness as well as an adventurousness to their lovemaking. It wasn't just about the act itself and that momentary release. Both had emotional and physical needs they didn't or couldn't fulfil elsewhere and each was prepared to give the other time to explore them.

As Catholics go he had a very healthy, unfettered view of women. They were to be respected, loved, celebrated, gazed upon and, until he lost his innocence at fifteen behind a disco on Marsh Lane, masturbated over endlessly. After that, they were to be pursued and wooed, although his career often made that problematic.

He returned to Paula, who'd fallen into a dream, twitching gently and letting out the odd whimper. Her chest, seemingly unsullied by the need to minister to two hungry babies seven years back, rose and fell temptingly and he couldn't resist rubbing her nipples between finger and thumb. They responded to his gentle touch and he loved that - it reaffirmed that God existed and that he was a bloke. Only a bloke would have invented nipples. And cute little arses, for that matter, of which Paula was the proud owner of a particularly fine example. It felt good to know that God was all around, for sometimes, as with most Catholics, he could doubt his faith.

The thought of God brought him to his senses, as it inevitably would, and guilt wrought predictable havoc with his mood. From the luscious, moist calm of post-coital reverie to angst in a jiffy; such was his lot.

He climbed quietly out of bed and dressed, thinking she'd benefit from the rest. Christ, she deserved it, given the hell that was life with Dave. He couldn't countenance advising divorce, of course, so the best he could do was provide an outlet that brought some relief to her drudgery and fear. That was it, he thought, a key part of his calling: to provide succour to women dealt a harsh hand in God's mysterious way. Doing the Lord's work between the legs of a good woman couldn't be that sinful, could it?

Dave's shift didn't finish for another three hours and the kids were playing at a friend's house for the morning, so Joe made himself a cup of tea and picked up the Daily Mirror from the kitchen table. Everton had just pulled off an incredible 4-4 result away at Manchester United but the headline read 'Utd in 8 goal thriller'. Bloody Mancs – they were as bad as Prods, he thought, before chastising himself for such intemperance.

He heard Paula tossing in her bed, pulled his blazer from the back of the kitchen seat and slipped quietly out the front door. He closed the garden gate and headed east, turning his back to the hulking frame of Dave the fireman just as he came round the corner.

~~~~

Nine o'clock Mass at St Francis of Assisi in Maghull was a bustling, family affair. Parishes in middle class neighbourhoods had survived the collapse in regular worship as parents scrambled to get their kids into the best Catholic schools. Maricourt RC High performed comfortably above average in the area's exam league tables and protected local house prices from the worst effects of any cyclical slump. Families would always want to move to Maghull, whatever the state of the local economy.

Perhaps it wasn't the poshest suburb in the city, but it was clean, safe, people had standards and there was a dignity to the place that Joe liked.

Mass this week would be busier than usual for there was a baptism. Little Kayleigh Kinsella was getting her hair wet and her great matriarchal clan would be turning out in force. Dave Kelly thought as much, too, and it suited his plan.

Joe first saw Paula in the slow, winding queue for communion. She was dressed demurely for Mass, as she always was, but looked stunning nonetheless, her figure accentuated by the cut of her frock and choice of heels. Joe sighed and thought about her tucked into him – spoons – as they lay in bed together, enjoying the warmth of their bodies amidst the after-glow of slow, selfless love-making.

She looked sad he thought as she got closer, and her large sunglasses said why - another slapping. As she drew nearer still he saw the layers of make-up covering the bruising, but it could do nothing about the swelling. Paula was focused on the children and the receipt of the sacrament and she rested her hands on the girls' shoulders as she guided them to the altar rail. They hadn't yet had their first holy communion – that was a year off – but she brought them up with her to get used to proceedings. The priest would always lay his hands gently on their heads and whisper a blessing and the twins liked that.

Paula took her communion wafer and stepped to one side to put it in her mouth before crossing herself, which allowed Dave to come forward. He stepped in close as the priest raised the sacred host, his extra three inches in height combining to provide the perfect angle. He pulled his head back, rejecting the host, then smashed his forehead precisely onto the bridge of the priest's nose, sending him flying backwards in a spray of crimson. It was as quick as it was brutal and the communion chalice, a modern silver affair the priest had chosen himself to represent the forward-looking nature of his ministry, clattered to the floor scattering its contents with it.

Old Mrs Power crossed herself and Michael Kerwin, the head altar boy – blessed with quick reactions that had seen him rise through his school's rugby ranks to senior captain – rushed forward, but not before Dave administered the coup de grace, a full-blooded kick to the priest's knackers that made every bloke in the congregation hold their own and wince.

He leaned back to observe his work. Enough, he thought, then turned on his heels and strode past a stunned congregation and out to his waiting car. It was all over in moments but there was not a man or woman who was witness to it that would ever forget – especially because young Connor Doyle had been absent-mindedly filming proceedings on his iPhone as he awaited the christening of his cousin and, realising he had the YouTube hit of the year on his hands, had it edited, posted and tweeted by midday. By five pm the virality of the web had done its worst and it was a global news sensation. Dave was happy with that: it meant they'd soon know why punishment had been meted out. Meantime, there was that bitch of a wife of his to deal with.

~~~~

Father Joe Delahunty lay in exquisite agony, surrounded at first by communion wafers before being joined by Kerwin, various lay ministers and finally Paula, who sobbed uncontrollably whilst holding his hand. Fr McCready, the auxiliary priest, had the good sense to call proceedings to a close, inviting communicants to the 11am Mass so that they might receive the body and blood of Christ our Lord in a more reverential atmosphere, God-willing.

Sod reverence, thought half the congregation as they scrambled for their iPhones to record proceedings, unaware that young Doyle had trumped them all. People were texting photos furiously as others tutted their disapproval and mothers slapped down their teenagers, for whom all this was the best thing since Paul Bradshaw of 5C had thumped Mr Hynes, the PE teacher, in a row over his dirty football kit.

It was the end, Joe knew. No ministry could survive this sort of scandal and the ignominy of it all, the loss of dignity. It was probably fair punishment in the circumstances. As his testicles ached that unique ache that only someone who has received a boot or a football to them understands, he thought about Paula and what would become of her. How had Dave found out? Did he beat it out of her, he wondered. She'd need to get out of that household pronto; I'll fix her up with a place at the Archdiocese' battered wives shelter, he thought.

He yelped in pain as Dr Barrett stuffed some cotton wool up his nose. Lucky that he was in the congregation, Joe thought, but for fuck's sake, couldn't he be a bit gentler? And who comes to Mass with cotton wool in their pocket?

Kerwin and the doctor yanked Joe to his feet and he surveyed his congregation – these decent, hard-working people of varying degrees of faith, from none whatsoever, like Colin Delacey who only gave a shite about getting his kids into Maricourt, to the widow Williams, who took communion daily and helped with the altar flowers.

Some of the older ladies were in tears, probably at the brutality of it all rather than for Joe, he thought. Others gawped open-mouthed and far too many for his liking were recording it on their phones. A forest of arms topped by winking silver lights greeted his return to his feet and he wanted to smite them all, like Jesus in the temple, but knew it would be for nought. Fuck, this'll be all over YouTube by lunch time. And it was, of course.

Carolyn Kershaw, an old mate from school, wrapped her arms gently around Paula's shoulders and steered her back from the altar towards the girls. They walked quietly down the side aisle, all eyes following them as Paula sobbed gently and people thought, 'Aye, aye, what have you been up to then, young lady?' Tongues were wagging already and Paula wondered how she was going to protect the girls from gossip and teasing at school.

She caught Jenny Cleary's eyes alight with delight, the fucking cow. They were once the firmest of friends until Paula caught her blowing off her boyfriend behind The Grafton after the office party. She bagged Dave on the rebound and had regretted it ever since. Jenny started all this, the bitch, and it was all she could do to stop herself from lunging for her there and then. But the kids were in enough shock and her mind was working furiously over where to go to avoid Dave's wrath.

Back in the vestry Fr Delahunty had removed his blood-stained vestments and was in his jeans, boat shoes and an old rugby shirt from his days at Upholland, the seminary built strategically close to Liverpool to catch the fifth and sixth sons of large families for whom the priesthood was traditionally a career option. His nostrils flared with the cotton wool and his head ached remorselessly. Doctor Barrett sat him down to re-set his nose and Joe fainted at the pain. His day would get worse, still.

He woke a few minutes later to find the vestry cleared save for Fr McCready and Jim Dillon, an off-duty police officer and a kindly man whose daily trawl through the feckless, feral scum of Liverpool hadn't sullied his cheery nature, nor his humanity. Miracles do happen, Joe once thought.

"Do you want to take this further, Father?" he asked. "It's not often we get 300 witnesses to an assault and it might be hard to brush this under the carpet, much as you'll probably want to."

What did he know about the motive, thought Joe. Christ, it doesn't take long for people to get to a man's weaknesses.

"I'll take the Archbishop's advice on that one and if I know him he'll want this buried in the deepest catacomb the Church possesses, and me with it."

Bloody hell, Archbishop O'Halloran. As hard and unforgiving a man as it was possible to find. Not for him the smarm and blandishments of other bishops, nor the schmoozing, brown-nosing and oiling of the Church and civic machinery. His was a hard-line and Joe expected no quarter behind closed doors once all this came out.

The Newcastle Incident, as Joe called it, was already on his file. The full details never emerged and he was swiftly removed from his parish in Tyne Dock to avoid the possibility of scandal. The official line was that a vulnerable woman had taken a fancy to the handsome young priest and allowed her fantasies to get out of hand. She was being given all necessary support to help her through her difficulties and Fr Delahunty had been re-deployed to remove the source of her agitation from view and allow her the space to recover.

The fact of the matter was that he'd been enjoying a highly energetic and imaginative tryst with Karen Robson for four months and it was only her neediness and desire to give the relationship some sort of permanence that had forced his hand. Taking the tabloid approach of putting yourself on the front foot, he told Bishop Wright that he felt his vulnerable parishioner was exhibiting dangerous signs of fixation and requested a transfer.

The Bishop's own investigations suggested there was plenty more to it than met the eye and Karen's offer of evidence gave him the fright of his life. Swift action followed. A deal was struck with his old mate O'Halloran and within two days Fr Delahunty was an auxiliary priest in St Brendan's, a tough inner-city parish in Liverpool's south end, near the old docks. There'll be no young things to distract him in that shit-hole, thought Wright. At least I bloody hope not.

Joe had settled in and kept his nose clean, finding an outlet for his weakness at nightclubs in Chester, where he'd not be recognised and could always afford a room at a local Travelodge if he struck lucky. Which, of course, he did, with happy frequency.

Meanwhile, his energy, looks and enthusiasm won him admirers among the good folk of Dingle and a burgeoning congregation followed in their wake. Missionary work with the kids at the local Catholic primary schools brought more parents – typically just the mums – to Mass, dragged by little Ellie-Mae who wanted them to meet lovely Fr Delahunty who makes her mates laugh.

He could visit Mam and PJ up in the north end and he loved being back in Liverpool. Geordies were friendly, too, but it was the quick-wittedness of Liverpudlians that he had missed and it was only on returning that he realised he was a bit rusty as far as verbal jousting went. He soon sharpened up amidst the merciless piss-taking that passes for discourse in Liverpool.

The revival of St. Brendan's landed him the plum post of parish priest at St. Francis of Assisi when Fr Clarke died. Mam burst with pride. "Maghull? A good job I sent you to school in Blundellsands, lad, or you'd never be able to talk to them," she said, certain of her role in her son's rise through the ranks.

He'd met Paula after his first full Mass as parishioners lined up to introduce themselves to this new fixture in their lives. He sensed her sadness and his old instincts almost overwhelmed him. This woman needs saving, he thought, though from what he didn't know. Past abuse? A bullying husband? Or just the drudgery of life, perhaps? But he knew and he held her gaze long enough to tell her so.

A chance meeting in The Square, the local shopping precinct, saw them settle down to a coffee in the Copper Kettle cafe. Paula slipped into an easy informality in Joe's company and appreciated his empathy. How could a priest understand so much about human relations, she thought? It's not like they know for real, after all.

He knew. He understood. He possessed that magic that few people have when faced with the embarrassment of other people's troubles. Father Joe was the complete man and Paula wanted more of his time as she struggled to deal with the turmoil of an abusive marriage and the need to protect the twins.

It took just eight days before Paula and Joe found themselves in bed together. Not a record by any stretch. Plenty of lasses – in the way of the easy morality of modern Britain – had screwed him senseless on the first date. But she was different and he found himself falling for her, the need to offer comfort and her willingness to take it from him driving them inevitably to some physical union. He was too weak to resist, she too lonely to turn down the chance.

He knew he was committing a grievous sin, but didn't dwell readily on why. Absolution in the form of the confessional sorted that out, with monthly trips to Our Lady of Sorrows in Salford keeping his conscience and his soul on the right side of the balance sheet. That was the beauty of being a Catholic: you were only ever an Act of Contrition away from a clean slate. For a serial shagger like Joseph Delahunty, that was heaven-sent and he allowed himself a smile at the pun.

~~~~

The call from O'Halloran's office came on his mobile at a little after eleven, demanding his immediate presence at the Archbishop's mansion in Mossley Hill. What was that they said about camels and eyes of needles, mused Joe, although he admitted to himself he was in no position to pose a philosophical discussion on O'Halloran's exalted lifestyle. He jumped in his battered VW Polo and braced himself for the imagined shit-storm. O'Halloran's rage was well known in ecclesiastical circles and Joe didn't doubt that he was working himself up into a fury right now in anticipation of tearing a strip off him.

~~~~

Archbishop O'Halloran looked at himself in the full length mirror of his dressing room. Six foot two and still boasting his rugby player's physique at 58, his was a commanding presence and he knew it. It certainly helped in his dealings with local politicians and with community leaders, none of whom was ever a shrinking violet in Liverpool.

He'd come a long way from the bog-lands of Roscommon and he allowed himself the sin of pride at his own achievement. And he was fecked – fecked – if he was going to allow some shag-happy little scrote like Fr Joseph Delahunty, the bastard love child of a raving nymphomaniac, to bring scandal to his diocese. Feck that, he said to himself, I'm going to have that man's balls on a spit before the day is out. God knows they'll be big enough, if what he heard about Dave Kelly's direct hit was anything to go by. Mind, at least he wasn't fiddling with children – he'd seen more than enough of the harm that could cause and it turned his stomach.

The media had already been on for comment and the Archdiocese press office was at full tilt attempting to contain things. Britain's famously prurient tabloids would have a field day with this, thought O'Halloran. The best strategy was to say that it would be inappropriate to comment further until an internal investigation into what had occurred had been concluded. That investigation was already underway, the statement noted, and, whilst police had been made aware of the incident there were no plans to take that any further. Dampen it down, m'laddo, and they'll soon find some bonking politician on which to focus, please God.

O'Halloran spared a thought for the poor woman involved and her twin daughters. What must they be going through? This being 2012, however, he feared a lawsuit and once he'd finished with Delahunty he'd personally intercede with Mr and Mrs Kelly to negotiate a settlement and get this thing buried once and for all. To that end he'd already sent Monsignor Killoran, his trusty emissary, to Maghull to see if he could engage with the family – though not in his dog collar, of course. He didn't want another bloodied priest on the front pages.

The house keeper's bell rang to tell him that his appointment had arrived and the Archbishop closed his eyes and thought about all the potential downsides of Fr Delahunty's indiscretion. In particular, the downsides for O'Halloran himself. The Church could take care of itself. It had sharpened up its act these last few years as far as sexual scandal went. No, it was O'Halloran who was at most risk here and he was bollixed if Delahunty was going to stain his glittering career so close to retirement.

Suitably enraged he stormed down the stairs to his study where he found a bandaged and sheepish Fr Delahunty waiting for him by the marble fireplace. I should feckin' well hope so, thought O'Halloran, as he spied contrition in the man's battered face.

"Father Delahunty," he began, in a show of controlled anger, "am I to understand that you have broken the most sacred of vows in order to satisfy your own filthy desires?"

Joe opened his mouth but then thought better of interrupting. He knew he'd have practised what he wanted to say and that it wouldn't help matters to interrupt.

"I thought that thing in Newcastle was an aberration but you are clearly led by your dick, you stupid little fecker, and I cannot blame Dave Kelly one bit for giving you a thrashing. I'm half a step away from kicking the shite out of you meself." Joe winced. His bollocks were sore enough without the Archbishop's right boot, or something similar, creating yet more discomfort.

"But I could not care less for you because today you leave the priesthood and you leave my Archdiocese. You are as unemployable as the bone-idle eejits that infect parts of this city and the sooner you leave it the better for all concerned. But let me tell you this now: you will not leave until I have tied you in legal knots so feckin' tight you'll be breathless. Nobody, least of all a scrote like you, puts a bomb under my See and gets away with it. Do I make myself clear?" he raged.

Yes, you pompous twat, you do. Joe took it with humility and sorrow, however, keen to play the game so that both he and O'Halloran got what they needed from this and could part quickly, confident that it was done and dusted.

Joe wondered how he would have played it if he were in O'Halloran's shoes. His time was up and he was as keen as the next man to move on. What else could he do? So he nodded acquiescence and asked if he could explain how it all came to pass. He was concerned for Paula and knew that the Archbishop had it within his resources and power to protect her and the children.

"You'd better tell me every last detail," said O'Halloran. "Leave anything out and your bollocks will be in a mangle before you know it."

The Archbishop sat and listened patiently, with a fixed glare that suggested a pending eruption. It never came. Instead he was disarmed by Delahunty's candour and by his calmness. Christ, this fecker either doesn't give a shite or he'd be a good man to have next to me in a bar brawl, he thought.

For his part, Joe was sure he knew how to play O'Halloran and kept to his own plan of matter-of-fact explanation mixed with mild contrition and a dose of fatalism. I can take my kicking and I'll show him I can. But what he really wanted to do was to secure Paula's safety and that of the twins. He explained her position and appealed to the Archbishop's humanity and care for his flock in seeking that he intercede immediately to provide her and the girls with protection from her brute of a husband. Such pastoral concern is core to the Church's mission, after all, and he wouldn't want the media saying he'd abandoned her in her hour of need. Now would he?

The Archbishop nodded and left the room to bark some orders and put wheels in motion. He had resources at his disposal and the Church could move quickly when the chips were down. Five minutes later he returned, the look of thunder replaced by his trade mark scowl – a sign that things were going Joe's way, he thought.

"Delahunty – I refuse to call you Father – you will meet with our lawyers here in forty minutes and sign a compromise agreement that will conclude your employment by my Archdiocese. You will see that it is remarkably fair to you, particularly financially, as my objective is never to see you again. I want you to feck off to some far foreign land and stay there. How many poor woman you bed along the way will be between you and your conscience. Do not ever speak to me again," he said, then turned on his heels and stalked out of the room.

~~~~

The lawyers were all business and Joe found that suited him. They talked him through the compromise agreement, pointing out its overall purpose and that the intention was to bind them both together in a way that they were each compelled to abide by its conditions. He was told to go and find independent legal advice and was pointed to a high street practice down the road in Rose Lane. He suspected they'd been told to expect him as he was immediately hurried through to a side office where a young solicitor awaited him, note pad at the ready.

The Archdiocese would meet up to £300 of his costs, she explained, and as Joe only intended on being in there five minutes he thought it was nice work if you could get it, for he didn't doubt that they'd find a way of billing the full amount. Like rhinos, he thought, these lawyers - they know how to charge.

His phone rang on his way out and the caller id told him to expect Paula. She sounded dreadful but held herself together as she explained that she'd already had a call from a Monsignor Killoran who was going to pick her and the girls up and take them away to a safe house if she could make herself available.

Dave had gone to the pub and was doubtless getting smashed with a few of his fire bobby chums and it bought Paula some time to pack some bags and prep the girls. She was sitting in the living room, she explained, with a couple of bags and the girls' teddies waiting for the Monsignor to arrive.

"Joe, you do know this has to end? I never loved Dave but I didn't love you either. You were just my release, a way for me to find happiness amidst the shite that is living with that...twat," she spat, then apologised to the girls, who must have been sitting next to her on the leather sofa she'd bought last month to cheer herself up.

Joe was happy with that, for all his concern for her wellbeing. He wasn't the marrying kind, vows of celibacy or no vows – and even less so now that he was officially free to screw around. Not that he felt up to much of that, mind, what with his bollocks the size of plums and twice as purple. There must be a few mashed tadpoles in there, he thought. Not much use in the baby-making stakes, then. He'd always used a condom, however, so it wouldn't matter – and then he realised that was another shameful contravention of Catholic teaching. Christ, I'll be heading straight for hell at this rate.

He told Paula that the Church would be taking care of her. He'd seen to that and managed to negotiate the insertion of a monthly stipend of two thousand pounds into his agreement with the help of the not-quite-so-naive young lawyer on Rose Lane. It was to run for two years, he explained, so Paula would be able to build some sort of life away from Dave. The girls would get their birthday presents, school uniforms and everything else that would go towards helping them adjust and she was free to stay in the battered wives home for up to a year, he told her.

"It's not like you'd imagine," Joe offered, by way of reassurance. "You have your own front door to a two bed apartment, but it's in a sheltered, gated development and no-one has a clue what it is. You'll be safe there whilst you sort out what you want to do." She nodded and the conversation petered out. The silence was unbearable.

"Thanks Joe," she sighed. "You take care, too. Don't write or call," and with that she was gone.

~~~~

Maggie Savage, Pamela Smith and Dot Grainger squeezed their ample frames on to Mam's sofa, leaving her to PJ's favourite armchair.

On the coffee table sat Monday morning's Liverpool Echo. 'Husband head-butts randy priest at parish Mass' screamed the headline. There was worse in the nationals, thanks to various YouTube postings.

"Ah, Jaysus," said Maggie. "It's a shame, but he's after proving he's a man and that the calling wasn't for him. So feck 'em all."

"He already has from what I hear," offered Peggy, unable to suppress the smirk.

"Are youse here to help or to gloat, because if it's the latter you can Fuck. Right. Off," said Mam. "I've had enough of this shite already and the pubs have only just opened."

"You'll wanna be avoiding the Caledonia," offered Dot. "Elaine Treanor's in there and I hear she's showing the YouTube stuff on her iPhone thingy."

Ah, fuck. It was going to be a long day, week and month. The bastards would feast on this for a good while because there was nothing else left to feed off. Bootle died not long after the Luftwaffe came calling in the war and all anyone had ever focused on thereafter was the misfortune of others. Maybe Aughton and a nice corner of daughter number four Collette's lovely home wouldn't be so bad, Mam thought. Not that she'd let Collette know that that was how she was thinking. She'd wait until she was asked.

Anyways, the move was a few years off, Mam reckoned, so no need to raise it with her just yet. It'd be tough, Mam knew: Bootle was still home, her tiny little terrace house in which she'd brought up her seven kids and gone through multiple milestones. First holy communions, confirmations, unwanted pregnancies, the lot.

"'They'll carry me out of 'ere in a friggin' box, they will," she'd say.

"It'll need to be a bloody big one," PJ would crack, followed by chuckles from them both.

~~~~

Mam had suspected it would come to this. Joseph was always a charmer and a looker and he joined the seminary, aged 11, because it offered one of the best free educations available and not because she wanted him to take the cloth. Sister Assumpta at his primary school had made strong representations on his behalf, saying that here was a boy of rare insight and charm that would make the perfect modern priest in the missionary lands that had become Britain's Godless inner-cities. Joe was interviewed and in the light of his parents' straightened financial circumstances an application to a trust fund for a bursary was smoothed through the appropriate channels.

The seminary was like a normal high school but with a good deal more God-bothering and instruction designed to tie as many supplicants as possible to the Church. Joe was a sharp Liverpool kid and Mam never thought for a minute that he'd actually opt for the priesthood. That's what the youngest of seven did in the nineteenth century, but not in 1994, for fuck's sake. And not when you clearly had a calling for women as Joe did, and they for him.

But he was adamant and it was novel in Bootle, she had to admit, not that she could figure its appeal. And so it was that, aged 25, he graduated from Upholland in 1999 as Fr Joseph Delahunty and nobody, but nobody, could say that Bernadette had been anything other than a success as a mother. Forgetting that useless streak of piss, Michael, of course. Oh, and Seamus, not that anyone talked about him. Well, not in front of her, anyway.

Strapping lads from Bootle just weren't gay. End of. It's obviously a London thing, she thought: those gobby Cockneys and their liberal ways had infected him with strange yearnings and all he needed to do was come home to Liverpool, find a bonny local lass and that would be that. But it never was, and when he brought Cameron home to meet her and PJ, she admitted defeat, gave him a big hug and encouraged them both back to London. Gay, for Christ's sake. What's that all about?

~~~~

Joe's settlement was good. Five grand a month for a year, tax free, left him with plenty of headroom to decide what an ex-priest could offer a jobs market not exactly brimming with work opportunities. And so he moved back with PJ and Mam to divine what on earth he could do whilst attempting to keep his head down – not easy in a community like that.

PJ took it all in his stride - priests weren't super-human, after all. And the Borgias were all top shaggers, remember. So Joe and PJ fell into an easy accommodation, tip-toeing around Mam as she fumed and fussed about how it all came about. Archbishop O'Halloran emerged as the villain of the piece and Mam withdrew her labour, in the best Scouse tradition, refusing to attend Mass after an unbroken run of around 65 years. That would show them.

A week later, the email arrived from New York that would turn Joe's life on its head once more. Before he went, PJ took him to the Caledonia for one last pint. They stood in silence, each admiring their Guinness as they settled. To them its swirling, swaying firmament was a wonder of technology, culture and history. They let them be for a couple of minutes. Never before the top was white and the bottom black would they ever take a draught.

"A good pint of Guinness is just like any of those women ye've been carryin' on with, son," offered PJ.

"How's that, dad?" asked Joe, warily.

"Easy, son: 'tis a t'ing of beauty."

CHAPTER TWO

Ted froze, after an almost comic double-take. It couldn't be, surely. He hadn't seen his favourite English cousin for a few years but there was no doubting the picture was him. But the headline didn't compute, until he thought about it for a moment. 'Catholic priest disgraced after multiple lovers come forward'. Even Ted had seen, on his one visit to Liverpool, that Joe had a way with women. The dirty little sod – he'd been slotting his parishioners.

He was curled up on his favourite leather armchair in his den, roaring log fire and a generous Jameson's to hand. Todd was studying in his room and Greta was at choir practice. Cindy was in the kitchen with her girlfriends and a bottle or two of Pinot Grigio, leaving him free to catch up with the world via his iPad. He loved it when his time was his own. It wasn't that he was overly selfish, but a busy job running his own real estate business and family life weren't the perfect combination if you liked your own space every now and again.

On screen was the Irish Times, his way of staying in touch with what went on in the auld country, not that it was his auld country, really, more his parents', but he relished his Irish roots and they were a free pass to opportunity in a city as green as New York.

Ted Courtney was Joe's cousin, the eldest son of PJ's sister, Siobhan, and the result of her union to Bill, a sergeant in the 48th precinct in the Bronx. Siobhan, alone in a new city, had fallen immediately for this stocky, handsome Irishman with sandy hair and round, ruddy face. He looked fresh off the fields, she thought, not from fighting a gang war and it wasn't long before her mothering and concern had seem him fall for her in equal measure.

Ted was the elder of their two children, a good ten years older than Joe, but he'd gotten in touch with his Liverpool-based family once the internet made such things easy and, as a Beatles nut, had made the pilgrimage to Strawberry Fields in the millennium on foot of a generous year-end bonus from a grateful boss at the real estate agency where he worked. Joe had been home from Tyne Dock and the two hit it off immediately, Ted taken with this sparky priest and his ready line in wit, which he found remarkably similar to New Yorkers' caustic humour.

He noted then that he had an easy way with women and, like most priests he'd ever met, that he could shift the Guinness like it was his mother's milk. And if he knew his aunty Bernadette, it probably was.

And there he was, his cousin Joe, staring at him from the electronic page of the Irish Times as the story picked up on the feeding frenzy of the British tabloids. The paper offered a more factual and measured reporting style, befitting the house bible of liberal south Dublin, but the facts were the facts: the man was a love machine in a dog collar. Ted had to look up the words 'bonking' and 'shag', having found links to the stories in The Sun and The Mirror and admitted that even New York's salacious Daily News could probably learn a thing or two from Britain's 'red tops', its famous tabloid press that spared no-one. They were brutal.

'Shag-tastic priest the best lover I ever had', said The Sun's front page, above a picture of a demure looking 39 year-old divorcee from a place called Ormskirk, which he presumed was near Liverpool somewhere. 'Perky padre the perfect partner', said The Mirror, introducing its readers to one Jeanette Cody of Wavertree. Ted knew where that was because George Harrison had been brought up there.

The papers were breathless in their reporting, having sent a small team to Liverpool to talk with parishioners and unearth as many conquests as they could. Wads of used notes greased palms in pubs and parish clubs and lasses eager for their fifteen minutes of fame were only too happy to sell their stories. Those deemed sufficiently shapely to merit it were offered extra to pose in their underwear and one or two readily obliged although, Ted thought, a girl called Angela O'Connor was pushing it a little. Didn't they at least have Photoshop in British news rooms?

Joe's inbox on his iPhone had been a lesson in pain and relief in equal measure. Ex-girlfriends e-mailed to offer themselves by way of comfort, whilst others revelled in his comeuppance. Yet another – a Helen, from South Shields – sent him photos of herself in some highly elastic poses and a plea for 'one last go.' Blimey, was his dick that much of a toy?

He also had to contend with some well-aimed arrows from parishioners, let down by a selfish, egotistical and weak man who broke the most sacred of vows in pursuit of his own gratification. How could he think so little of their parish? He had despoiled something at the very heart of their community and would never be welcome back.

It could all have been so different, he imagined, this life of his. Funny how the odd turn here and there can set you on a different course. The youngest of seven – "she took advantage of me after an eight-pinter in the Caledonia," his father grinned – Joe was loved and petted to distraction by his Mam, Bernadette and his four sisters.

Collette, the youngest, was his favourite, but he retained a soft spot for them all: Carmel, Donna and Trish, too, even if he had to develop strategies to avoid them at home so that he could just, well, be. There's only so much hugging a young lad needs to know that he's cherished.

The art of avoidance proved a vital life skill in Bootle, one of the toughest 'old Irish' neighbourhoods in Liverpool; there was always some local hard case spoiling for a scrap. The dislocation that came from it being the most bombed town outside London added an unspoken permission to bare your knuckles which had flowed down the generations since the Blitz. Re-housing had affected entire communities, courtesy of some unerringly inaccurate Luftwaffe pilots, who mistook the tight terraced streets for the nearby docks.

"Couldn't hit a cow's arse with a banjo," his dad noted with mock disgust. What did he know? He came over on a boat from Dublin in 1959 – a city, neighbours were wont to remind him, that, in leaving its lights on, had provided the Luftwaffe with the perfect marker for Liverpool and its miles of docks just fifteen minutes flight time to the east.

Out of the rubble of once proud, tight streets of Victorian red brick terraced housing rose a new Utopia: new-fangled 'estates', designed with an identity so that residents, drawn from all around Bootle, could feel that this new patch of post-war optimism was theirs. Mam's house survived all this madness – all the streets around Cowper Street had, in fact – and there was a continuity in their little corner of St. James's parish that people treasured.

Mam had fought tooth and nail not to send Joe to the local school: "it fuckin' ruined our Mick and I'll not have our Joe turn into the foul-mouthed gobshite he became," she ranted at dad. Joe didn't know what a gobshite was, but it didn't sound promising.

To her surprise she succeeded in keeping young Joe out of St. Ignatius. "He's me last one so I've got to give him me best shot," she'd say, having summoned whatever feminine guile she had to persuade Fr Mallon to put in a good word for her with "the Sisters", who ran one of the poshest primary schools in Liverpool, the Carmelite Convent in ever-so-nice Blundellsands.

So when, in the autumn of 1979 a shiny and nervous Joe Delahunty was dressed for his first day at The Carmelite Convent Roman Catholic Primary School, it was a big event in Cowper Street, Bootle. Neighbours came around to see him in his cap and smart, grey uniform and sweets and coins were thrust in his pocket with reminders 'to speak proper, like' and other advice he failed to understand.

"Jaysus, those nuns'll have a job not huggin' him to death," said Marian McKeating, her hands clasped across her ample bosom.

"They better fuckin' not. That's my job," said Mam and the pair cackled. Carmel, Donna, Trish and Collette, less than resplendent in their hand-me-down uniforms planted great kisses on him and Joe felt warm and happy amidst the hoo-ha. He'd done a trial run on the train from Bootle New Strand station to Blundellsands – just three stops on Liverpool's metro but three miles and an entire world away – and wondered how it would all pan out.

"Get used to this, son. When you're seven you'll be doin' it yerself," Mam had cautioned. When was he seven? How many sleeps was that? He wasn't ready to sit with strangers and do it all on his own just yet, that much he knew.

For now, though, Mam would be taking him. She'd re-arranged her cleaning shifts at the giant Johnson's dry cleaning factory, opened a century earlier to clean the drapes of the city's huge fleet of transatlantic liners and Mrs Coffey from Corinthian Street, a cleaner at the Carmelite, said she'd bring Joe home with her. It meant him hanging around for an hour after school and he'd sit, swinging his legs, outside Sister Assumpta's office gazing at the huge painting of Jesus in graphic agony as a Roman soldier hammered in the final nail for his crucifixion. Sister loved that picture, the majesty and agony of Christ's death. Just marvellous, such sacrifice. 'He knew the nails were coming,' she'd say.

He loved the school with its big grounds and leafy setting, even if the pictures half frightened him to death. It was only a block back from Liverpool Bay and the swimming baths had a huge glass curtain wall that allowed them to watch the ships heading up the Mersey from exotic places like Montreal, Montevideo and the Cape, whatever that was. So he learned to swim and he excelled at football and most other things besides. His was a street-wise, native intelligence borne of living on his wits and the nuns saw that for all his rough edges, here was a lad with potential. 'Charm a-plenty and an everyman's touch,' noted Sister Mary Margaret's report in his Junior 3 review. Sister Assumpta had plans for him, but they could wait a year.

The rough edges were enforced, mind. He only walked home through Bootle the once wearing his school cap. The chase lasted an age and when the three of them caught him the thumping and teasing was merciless. Still, it taught him the value of his knuckles as well as of blending in and whilst he was marked for ever as 'the posh kid', the ambushes became less frequent as the other kids learned that he'd fight back. They stopped entirely when he brought home a stout stub of a chestnut branch that had fallen into the school playground one stormy March morning and twatted Barry Jones square across the jaw with it.

"Good on yer son," said dad. "The Proddy bastard deserved it." Sectarianism wasn't quite dead, then, though neither, thankfully, was Barry Jones. His dad came around to sort it out, meaning to knock seven bells of shite out of PJ. That was until he actually met PJ, at which point a rather more stilted conversation took place. Relative peace descended on to the school run after that and Joe learned to love the independence that the journeys gave him.

Joe's rail fare was paid in advance by the Archdiocese and he had just enough pocket money to buy a bag of crisps from the school tuck shop each day. It was run by Lizzie Cusack – a raven-haired temptress from Junior 4, the top class and a year above Joe when he had his first crush and his first wilful stiffy. She didn't mind kissing the cheeky, good looking rough kid but she was horrified to feel his wooden little member pressing against her thigh. With a screech she ran for the cloak room and straight into the arms of Sister Jude who grabbed Joe by the ear and called him, sotto voce, a "dorty little shite". It always amazed Joe how nuns and priests could swear as much as his Mam who, whilst attending Mass each Sunday, never pretended to be holy or better than anyone else and had a fine line in Anglo-Saxon vernacular.

"Frig off, Sister" was clearly the wrong response and he'd wished he was toe-to-toe with Barry Jones again by the time she'd finished with him. "Yer filthy, friggin' little frigger!" she yelled as she dragged him through the dining hall to Sister Assumpta's office who looked horrified as the story of his sexual impropriety was relayed.

"A stiffy! A feckin' stiffy! Disgustin'!," cried Mary Margaret, all a-flush.

"Joseph Delahunty, you rancid little boy, sit in that corner and I'll deal with you when I have time," she scowled. She let him sweat for an hour, having sent word to Mrs McGrail that he wouldn't be in class, then sat him down in her main office and turned to him with a gentle smile.

"Don't worry, son, it's part of growing up, but do try to leave the girls alone. There's time a-plenty for that." How right she was, though reflecting on the incident now he wished she'd been a little less kind.

And so when Ted's email landed it made him smile, ruefully. What would he have to say on the matter, he thought. In the internet age he didn't doubt the jungle drums would have beaten, however faintly, across the Atlantic.

"Joey, you need a break," it started. "We've got our St Patrick's Day parade coming up in two weeks' time so get your sorry ass over here and take cover in Pearl River. Can't be much fun for you right now and it would be great to see you. Cindy and the kids ain't seen the papers and they'd love to have you over. Email me."

The offer made a lot of sense and Joe could do with a break, Ted was right about that. He'd never been to New York, though Ted had waxed lyrical about Pearl River on his trip to Liverpool twelve years ago.

"Joey, forget Bootle. You ain't never seen nowhere so Irish," he explained, "apart from Ireland." And it was true, to a point. The Irish community in Liverpool had morphed into Catholic Scousers over the years as the number of immigrants from the emerald isle dried to a trickle in the absence of job opportunities. New blood is essential to ethnic identity and confidence but it was lacking in Liverpool in a way it would never be in New York. Its connection to Ireland was as strong as ever, particularly after the demise of the Celtic Tiger and the huge upsurge in emigration that followed. New York, with London, would always remain a favoured destination and so it proved.

But Pearl River wasn't where the new kids turned up. They headed straight for Brooklyn and for neighbourhoods like Bay Ridge, Vinegar Hill or Marine Park. Pearl River boasted a much older Irish community, heavily influenced by the large number of working and retired policemen who lived there. It was twenty miles north of Midtown, away from the city's febrile clamour for law and order and from people browner than your average Paddy. They liked it that way and the way that Pearl River was full of their people - twenty one thousand of them - and they'd been there long enough for it to be a generational thing.

The kids went to Pearl River High School and married peers from within the neighbourhood; dads filled up on full Irish breakfasts at Gildea's at the start of any self-respecting pub crawl, which would always take in Noonan's and Murty's; while stores such as the Danu Gallery gave the streets an added veneer of Irishness. It felt settled and self-sustaining, free from the shifting sands of ethnicity and yuppification in the big city to the south which saw once strong Irish neighbourhoods like Bainbridge given over to Africans or Hell's

Kitchen to gentrification. They just couldn't see that ever happening to Pearl River and its Paddy's Day parade was a huge affair thanks to people like Bill Courtney, whose energy had driven it to bigger and better things, year-by-year. Irish people even came out from New York City to attend, citing its friendlier, less hurried vibe and its authenticity. Sure, ain't they all Plastic Paddies in New York these days, Ted had once said, smugly.

Joe checked out the flights to New York to see what he was in for, cost-wise. He might be on five grand a month, tax free, but he still wanted to watch the pennies. He had two options. Check in with Aer Lingus at Liverpool's John Lennon Airport and go via Dublin, or fly direct from nearby Manchester with American Airlines. There was little in it in terms of price but the three hour lay-over in Dublin looked appealing from the standpoint of enjoying a few pints of proper Guinness whilst watching the aircraft come and go. And so Dublin it was.

Mam and PJ agreed with the plan. They could see that events had knocked the sparkle from Joe and that he was in danger of slipping into a deep melancholy with each tabloid revelation. And they weren't far from it themselves, too. There's only so much piss-taking a man can take down the Caledonia and it was straining Bernadette's nerves delivering ever-sharper ripostes to snide remarks in the Post Office queue.

So, it would be best all round if he quietly slipped away for a while and took the heat out of the media's feeding frenzy. His very availability made him a lightning rod for the further revelations that emerged: the press knew where to find him for comment or a hurried grab shot of him 'sneaking out', as they put it, when in fact he was just going to the corner shop for a pint of milk. He'd turned to the Archdiocese press office for help and advice but they'd cold-shouldered him on O'Halloran's order. Fuck, they really are leaving me to the sharks, he thought.

The girl at the Aer Lingus check-in desk at John Lennon was an object lesson in genetic combination, thought Joe. Her parents were clearly lookers for they'd produced a peach of a lass. Dark, tumbling hair, strong, defined eyebrows below which sat sparkling blue eyes and a button of a nose above blush-red lips. I've just got to flirt, thought Joe. Rude not to. Nothing too heavy, but I need to find a warm smile and to know that it wasn't all for nothing. Salvation lay between the legs of a good woman, he felt, and not the cognitive re-organisation therapy or some such similar bollocks the Church's lawyer had tried to insert into his compromise agreement.

The Liverpool flight was a feeder into the airline's Dublin hub and he'd be checked right through to New York, with American passport control in Liverpool too, for ease. But the Dublin leg would be on a bog-standard 747 with any notion of frippery or comfort stripped out. He knew it would be a different prospect on the transatlantic route, even in cattle class.

His passport still said 'Fr Joe Delahunty' and in line with her training, young Aoife checked the flight's manifest on the Dublin to New York leg before offering a winning smile and saying, "Father, it's always a pleasure to have a member of the Church with us and I've been able to upgrade you to business class from Dublin. I hope you don't mind."

"Will you be joining me?"

"Ach, Father, I'd love to but you're not the marrying kind," said Aoife in a lilting Galway accent.

Blimey, he thought, she's good. "And how would you know that?" he offered.

"It says so in your passport, Father. Enjoy the flight and thanks for choosing Aer Lingus," she said, returning his passport with a beaming smile to close the conversation. Christ-on-a-bike, he thought, if anyone could make me settle down, she could.

~~~~

British music impresarios latched on to Ireland's emerging fashionability in the early nineties and a succession of boy-bands from Dublin had conquered European and, occasionally, global music charts. Good looking young lads with a ready line in wit called Shane, Ronan and Finn had even begun to influence parents' choice of names and it became another strand to the Celtic Tiger. We're all Oirish now, went the theme, and in Britain and America in particular people suddenly found Irish great-great grandparents to justify calling their sons Seamus or similar. Whether Fintan Hepplethwaite from the Yorkshire mill town of Huddersfield would grow up thanking his young mum for such an indulgence may never be known.

The Flow were the latest collection of precocious young men to find their way on to MTV from the back streets of Kimmage and Orla McDade, their equally famous Irish manager, had done a fine job of moulding them in line with current tastes. From haircuts to accents, from romantic interests to the back-stories of their lives, Orla had it all brilliantly mapped out. They'd enrich her and she them and all would be well with the world until they got older and their comeback tours, golden oldies tours and similar eventually faded to nought. Go with The Flow went the marketing blurb and the teenage girls and tabloids lapped it all up.

And so they found themselves striding out of the VIP lounge in Dublin airport's shiny new Terminal 2 to be met with the obligatory clamour of photographers, journalists and pubescent girls, all wanting their slice of celebrity ephemera. Fame, whilst it lasted, was addictive and even the members of The Flow were going with it. Kieran had never had so many girls and Fintan so many boys. It was gas craic, to coin a local phrase.

Tommy Tierney, OK! Magazine's local stringer, was the first to spot Joe at the smart glass-topped bar opposite the entrance to the VIP lounge. Joe had been nursing his Guinness watching the planes take off when he'd spotted the clamour across the way and tuned in with mild amusement. Good to see somebody else getting the treatment, he thought – albeit this would earn them a few extra mil, rather than the opprobrium of a nation.

Tierney peeled away quietly with his camera and notebook, taking a few grab shots of Joe on his digital Nikon D3S, the preferred tool of the modern pap. He reviewed them on the rear screen and realised he had enough crackers to fill a good spread. It wouldn't suit OK! but the UK tabloids would take three or four from him for a couple of grand, so long as he didn't alert all the other sharks with him. Nice work.

He rejoined the mob, playing his part in the charade whilst The Flow pretended to be mildly aggrieved by all the attention. Burly security guards brushed aside the throng and they made it to first class check in and then peace, air-side. The paps and journos stood around comparing notes and quotes and then powered up their lap-tops and wi-fi to send the shots to the news rooms and editorial desks of London's Fleet Street and Soho.

"Yer doin' the right thing," the voice to Joe's left offered. "I'd be after leggin' it, too, in your position. Don't worry, it'll all die down once you're away," he concluded.

"And you would be?" Joe enquired.

"Tommy Tierney, photographer of this parish and the man who can help you set the record straight," he said, offering a hand which Joe took.

"I'm not posing for any photographs, thanks," said Joe.

"A shame, but I've got half a dozen crackers of you looking chilled from five minutes ago so they'll do. But don't you want the chance to defend yourself? To put your side of the story and shut up those slappers comin' out of the woodwork?"

"They weren't slappers," snapped Joe. "Well, not all of them," he conceded, wistfully. "They just needed help and comfort and I felt I could provide them with it."

The touch screen on Tierney's iPhone blinked its 'tell' but Joe missed it. The conversation continued for another five minutes, with Joe apologising once more that he wasn't prepared to be interviewed and Tierney wishing him well. "Good luck," he chimed before heading off, camera slung over his shoulder, phone to his ear.

Joe's naivety would cost him. How was he to know to start by noting that everything was off the record? It's all on the record with a journalist unless instructed otherwise, but even after a week of dealing with Fleet Street's most rapacious hacks he hadn't picked up that simple lesson. He was a priest, after all – or was, once.

When he would arrive at Ted's there'd be one last grand splash in the Daily Star, by-lined 'Ted Tierney and Lisa Holden, investigative reporters' but penned entirely by Lisa, keen to build her coverage book before moving on to better things. Ted got a shag out of her into the bargain after they got pissed celebrating such a good spread and he quietly toasted the Bonking Padre for his good fortune.

'My lovers were no slappers, says Romeo priest' screamed the headline, before a salacious story reprising everything that we already knew but with the headline stacked up by fresh quotes that Joe had naively offered in Dublin airport. Most were taken out of context – deliberately so – but Joe had lost the will to fight and took it on the chin. Things would soon pick up in New York, he hoped.

~~~~

He was unsettled as he sat down at his window seat, despite allowing himself a small smile when he turned left onto the plane towards first and business. It was a novelty as he'd only travelled short-haul in Europe and supply was almost entirely provided by low-cost carriers like Ryanair and easyJet. He thanked the Lord that his passport still had eight years to run. He could get used to this upgrade lark.

Tierney's insistence and probing seemed designed to get something from him – an outburst, maybe – but he felt he'd batted him off well, particularly with his polite but firm insistence that he didn't want to offer a story. Mind, he'd been irritated by the way he fiddled with his iPhone early in their conversation. The first complimentary champagne, acres of leg-room and the very lovely Ciara and Sinead looking after him soon saw a measure of balance return to his mood and he made a mental decision to enjoy the flight for what it was, as he watched the coast of Donegal disappear far below.

Ted had agreed during their email dialogue that he should spend at least a month with them. No point in coming this far for a week, he'd said, and Cindy and the kids were cool – they couldn't wait to meet dad's cousin. Ted's house was a huge white-painted mock-Colonial on North Avenue and the top floor suite would afford him a measure of privacy and freedom whilst avoiding turning the family routine on its head. Ted was nothing if not practical.

He had explained to the family that Joe had decided the priesthood was no longer for him and that his visit to New York was part of helping him adjust to life outside the cloth. Cindy understood: her family were Catholics from Bavaria and she'd had a traditional up-bringing in suburban Minneapolis, seeing for herself the pressures on busy parish priests. And how on earth did they cope with that stupid celibacy rule, she'd said. It's just not normal.

She'd prepared the guest suite for Joe, even shifting up a spare Michelob-branded beer fridge Ted had acquired along the way and filling it with tins of Guinness. She knew that although he was English he was really Irish, being related to Ted, and thought that would be appropriate. Joe was later to doff his cap to her perspicacity, before emptying the fridge a little quicker than Cindy thought was decent. And then she reminded herself he was Irish and got on with refilling it.

A good night's kip under his belt, Joe spent the Friday familiarising himself with his surroundings. Only Cindy was home during the day and she greeted Joe warmly when he staggered downstairs in his boxers and a tatty 'Everton at Wembley' t-shirt from the club's last trip to the national stadium in London.

Cindy took the measure of Joe and wondered what the family was letting itself in for. He wasn't overly tall – about five ten, she reckoned – but was in good nick for a 38 year-old and, she had to admit, darned good looking. Classic Irish looks, at that. Almost black hair, piercing blue eyes and the remnants of freckles to add some piquancy to the relative youthfulness of his face. 'I had an easy paper round', he'd explain. Sheer good luck, those who knew Mam and PJ always thought. All the super-genes that their union could muster had coalesced in Joseph Francis Patrick Delahunty and didn't he milk it? Anyhow, her pal Jenni would have to be kept at arm's length or there'd be sparks, of that Cindy was immediately sure.

But she sensed a sadness too, beneath the introductory bonhomie, and wondered if it was just the turmoil of grappling with his decision to leave the priesthood. Can't have been easy, she acknowledged. People give their whole being to something like that and to find, after thirteen years, that it wasn't the right choice was to realise that you'd just burned up a big chunk of the best years of your life. He should have been out there playing the field and enjoying Liverpool's nightlife, she thought. Even in New York it was known as a party city, but then it had produced The Beatles.

She put a plate of fresh pancakes and syrup in front of him and huge glass of orange juice and settled down for a chat. He scoffed it hungrily, as much for the novelty of pancakes for breakfast as to make up for the lack of any grub since early in the flight. He had been focusing on the champagne poured by the delightful Ciara and not thinking about his stomach, so he had demurred when the next plate of smoked Connemara salmon or some such was proffered. Show me the bubbles, he'd said to himself. They accounted for a good deal of his groggy head, he had to admit.

"Ted's got a session with the boys planned for you at the Horse & Jockey tonight. There's Friday night football on the big screen and there's Guinness and ribs aplenty. You up for that?" she enquired by way of a conversational opener.

Joe could see the effort and doubtless she was keen to stay off the subject of the priesthood, so he reacted with enthusiasm, putting Cindy at ease. She enjoyed his easy banter and his accent, lyrical and vaguely Irish sounding, too. Not at all like the archetypal English voices presented in American popular culture, which were either Cockney or posh country set. He was a charmer, taking a real interest in her family and the comings and goings of her daily routines. She'd set out expecting to be the one asking all the questions but felt like she'd volunteered her life story after just half an hour. This guy would make a great journalist, she thought. Maybe she'd suggest that.

It felt inappropriate showing him around her lovely family home in his underpants and as he walked up the stairs she blushed as she found herself lingering over his tight butt. Joe said he'd pop into the guest quarters and make himself decent and Cindy blushed again, wondering whether she'd been caught in her flagrancy. She was relieved, anyhow. Hers was a happy marriage and she didn't want anything that changed that. And she saw that Joe would be dangerous marital flux in anything other than a settled home.

~~~~

Ted's real estate business, Courtney & Co, was founded in 2004 after he finally threw in the towel with Templeman & Gordon, frustrated at his inability to get to the top and at the cautiousness of his two bosses. They'd assumed he'd make them an offer come the day and had secretly based their retirement plans around it as they headed for their sixties. His news came as a hammer-blow, not just because they doubted any of the other young bucks in the 20-strong firm had the drive or wherewithal to buy them out, but because they knew Ted would take a big chunk of Pearl River's Irish customers with him. His father Bill, a few years dead, had been a big figure thereabouts and his son was a popular chip off that particular community block. With his departure their hopes of a comfortable retirement would go with it, of that they were sure.

The recession of 2008-09 presaged a monumental housing crash but, as with all such things, it was neither universal in reach nor identical in scale. Pearl River was insulated by its status as a settled community propped up by stable public sector salaries and pensions and the recent arrival of some hi-tec employers that had injected some fizz into the housing market with an influx of young families on good salaries.

And so Ted had managed to hold things together, keeping a tight rein on costs and hustling smarter and harder amongst the townsfolk to land the bulk of instructions, especially the prime properties around Laurel Road, grand colonials that could earn him three times in fees what he'd fetch for a three bed Cape Cod. Templeman & Gordon shut down in 2009, unable to compete, and Ted was given almost a clean sweep, enabling him to protect his margins and the firm's profitability.

With the end of the recession and the gradual climb back from the economic brink came greater head room and Ted's domestic economy seemed secure. Cindy had helped out during the dark days, but was able to return to her favoured role of home-maker in May 2011. She was good at it and the routines she drove through each week underpinned the family as an effective unit. She knew that, above all, kids craved routine and boundaries – even teenagers – and that was a job she was made for. Ted was a solid bloke and she was comfortable that he was committed to the team, as she called it.

~~~~

Ted was proud of his achievements and was keen to show Joey what it was all about, being a realtor. He'd persuaded him to join him on a house viewing on Monday morning. Getting the in on instructions was Ted's department, what with his place at the heart of the community, but the real hard work started with the valuations and then the advice on the best tactics for shifting it quickly. For all Pearl River's resilience, it was still a slow market.

In the case of Monday's visit, speed was the real deal. The house was a probate sale and the proceeds would doubtless be distributed to a clutch of eager children or grandchildren who cared more for a quick buck than either full market value or, as was often the case, the memory of the person who'd bequeathed them their good fortune. The possessions had already been removed, which made things easier, from measuring up to allowing visitors to visualise what the rooms might look like with their favoured colour schemes and furniture. Many a time he'd advised a family to invest five thousand bucks in a quick internal re-paint in neutral colours. Gleaming gloss white skirts and oatmeal walls usually did the trick and were worth the investment as they helped get full value as well as speeding up the sale. The smell of fresh paint was a nice subliminal touch too, a bit like the way grocers pipe the smell of fresh bread to their front doors. Clever stuff, that.

The house, on Wildwood Avenue, just off Phillips Lane, was in a pleasant neighbourhood just a few blocks south of East Central Avenue, effectively Pearl River's downtown. It was a popular route to buying into the parish, its modest three and four bedroom clapboard homes being set in small, well-tended plots. Room enough for the toddlers to toddle plus certainty of a quick re-sale when the occupiers' economic circumstances could provide for a move up the ladder. All told, they were as safe a bet as residential property would get and in Ted's world, they spelled easy money. He loved the smell of nothing better, especially now that college fees were hoving into view and Todd having set his sights on a medical degree.

Ted had the keys and threw them at Joe as they got out of his Lincoln MKS. He'd always bought American as the Irish didn't have a car industry and because the rest of Europe never properly acknowledged America's role in saving them from themselves – twice. So he was darned if he was going to support their economies with a big purchase like that. Fine Spanish wine he'd stretch to, but not automobiles.

"Come on buckaroo, let's see what this place has to offer," he said, slapping Joe on the back and striding across the short neatly-mown front yard, up the steps to the patio and the front door. It was a modest house, but detached, neat and well-proportioned. It was in reasonable nick, Joe thought, and the sash windows gave it some semblance of elegance, even if it was seven or eight rooms short of minor grandeur.

The hallway was light and airy, with the staircase up ahead, parallel to the passageway to the kitchen. Ted set to his job of photographing and measuring the rooms, a quick job these days with laser-based point-and-click yardsticks. He excused himself, inviting Joe to wander around at his leisure whilst he set about his tasks.

Joe turned into the main living room, not huge but roomy enough by the cramped standards of your average British semi-detached. There was an attractive original cast-iron fire surround with a grate and stone hearth that had clearly seen plenty of use. Open fires made a home snug, he always thought and he could see himself living in a place like this, away from the gaze of prurient parishioners and enquiring journalists. Maybe he should ask Ted for a job so that he could get his green card, then bide his time whilst he pondered what he really should do with his life.

But he knew now was not the time for rash decision-making and leaned against the window frame, taking in the scene outside. The street was tree-lined, he noticed, and the first buds were just appearing on the branches as the days drifted towards the warmth of spring. It had clearly been developed speculatively as every home was different, unlike the uniformity of many British streets, built in volume by house-builders exploiting grand economies of scale. 'I'll take three hundred of those, my man' would be the sort of conversation guaranteed to drive down the unit price of anything, from bathroom suites to door handles.

The window frame, he noticed, was a generous boxed affair that once must have accommodated shutters. The internal ledge was hinged and he instinctively gave it a lift. It remained fast, bunged with years of paint, but there was some give so he yanked at it again. More give, but the hinges were thick with old emulsion, too. He'd need a jemmy of some sort and looked around to see what he could find. An old screw driver with a broken handle lay abandoned on the floorboards and would do the job, he reckoned.

He found a spot where the paint had parted and jemmied in the screw driver. The lid started to give, but not without gouging a circular groove in the bottom panel. Whoops, he thought, but his curiosity had been piqued and he needed to know what, if anything, was in there.

The lid gave with a start, clattering backwards into the window frame with a loud bang. One of the panes cracked a little and a fine wooden cross-bar lost a flake or two of paint.

"You okay down there, cuz?" shouted Ted. "Don't be reducing my fee, now."

"Fine mate, fine. No worries," said Joe, eager to get on with finding an old stock certificate or bearer bond. Stranger things had happened, he reckoned.

He thrust his left hand into the space, about three feet long, a foot wide and two feet deep, feeling around the floor of the locker. It was empty, but as he withdrew his thick forearm his watch winder gripped something and he heard a faint rip. He turned his body to face the space, looking through the window, and felt his way up the external wall with his fingertips until he hit what seemed to be some sort of parchment. Squeezing both thick arms into the space he used his fingernails to grip the bottom of the document and slowly peeled it away.

It was a delicate job as it seemed to be attached by some sort of glue, but time had calmed its aggressive grip on the wooden casement and he was able to remove it without too much damage to what transpired was a thick envelope, approximately equivalent to A5 in size. On it, in an old hand, it said:

To my loving son, Sean – all I have left to tell my story and right a wrong.

Joe opened the envelope carefully and took his first step towards a dangerous unknown.

CHAPTER THREE

"What's that, pal?" asked Ted, as he poked his head around the door. "Just this room left and we're done. You found something valuable? If so, it's mine," he laughed.

Joe was engrossed and didn't hear him properly. "Sorry, what was that, mate?" he said, in what to Ted was a harsh, guttural accent, a bit like the Dublin one he'd heard when on a side-trip during his millennium Beatles indulgence, but with a lot of the 'ch' sound you get when Sean Connery says 'Loch'. Ted's kids would get Joe to repeat the word 'chicken' in as many contexts as possible around the dinner table and would collapse laughing at the novelty of it all as much as Joe's linguistic inventiveness. Ah, the simple pleasures, he would think.

~~~~

Joe looked up to find Ted hanging over his shoulder, staring at the manuscript, which was dated June 23rd 1938. The hand was almost copperplate and the use of language likewise. The paper, once a reasonable quality white vellum, had faded to nicotine. A bit like the ceiling of the Caledonia, thought Joe.

"What you got, pal?" Ted enquired again.

"Dunno, mate, but something tells me that this is going to be a bit of a read. C'mon, let's get off and we can look at it later." Joe was eager to hole up in his quarters and get to the bottom of what he'd found, but he was mindful, too, not to be an ungracious guest.

But the first sentence was seared in his memory already for it hinted at a great injustice with a link to his home city and a company he'd read about plenty of times in the local press.

June 23rd, 1938.
87th St, Woodhaven, Queens, NY

My darling boy Sean

This story starts and finishes in Liverpool and it begins and ends at the doors of the Bell Line and the charlatans who gave it its name. It is my story, one I shielded from you as your dear father and I sought to build a life for you, away from poverty and the misery that had befallen me in particular, at the hands of Mr Barrington Bell.

I tell you this now so that you may decide whether to pursue the injustice meted out to me by Mr Bell for your own benefit, for you will see that a great fortune should have been yours, rather than the mean and straightened circumstances that were the feature of your earlier years. We have loved you and cherished you, my dear son, and we have ultimately found our corner of the American dream in a quiet and safe parish in which we have watched you flourish into the fine man you have become. But burning beneath me has been a fire, set one fateful day on a ship from Liverpool and, on reading my story, you may feel those same flames flicker into life. That is for you to feel and it will be for you to decide what course to take, from none to using the full might of American justice to put right a grievous wrong.

There is no perfect choice, my dear lovely boy, but at least I can pass from this world knowing that my story may live on and that someone fine and strong and righteous might yet pick up my cudgel and seek justice. Let me tell you what happened.

~~~~

Supper at Ted's that night was the usual fun, noisy family affair. Joe loved the easy banter across the table, admiring these New Yorkers' way with words which he was sure was a genetic thing; he was fairly sure ordinary New Yorkers would lack the loquaciousness of this lot. Irish genes: can't be beaten. He was ignoring Cindy's German heritage, of course. Too inconvenient.

Greta was aglow with pride after reporting that her grade averages had nudged her into the top three in the ninth grade at Pearl River High. She was studious, alright, but sporty too and didn't seem overburdened by the weight of parental expectation that so afflicts some teenagers. And she'd yet to decide what to do with her life – not a crime for a fourteen year-old. Todd had his head down studying, too, and possessed a Trojan work ethic that struck Joe as being standard fare in America. No generous welfare handouts in this country to incentivise sloth, he thought.

Todd had an offer from John Hopkins University in Baltimore to study medicine and nothing, but nothing, would see him flunk that. Girlfriend Demi had been put firmly on ice and Cindy had had to field innumerable tearful phone calls before the deal sunk in and she went on her way to lick her wounds. Cheerleaders, tutted Cindy. She'd never held with the American tradition of females making themselves cute merely as a form of advancement with the jocks.

She may have settled down to motherhood at the expense of her career as a librarian, but it was a calling, a great responsibility at the very heart of the American dream and the nation's view of itself. And as she watched her children flourish she was iron-sure that hers was the right choice. Ted worked hard and earned the bucks; she worked hard to make a happy, comfy home. Friends were always welcome, but when the time came for someone to get their hat so that the Courtney family routines could be observed, Cindy was charming and to the point. Family first, above all else.

"Ted says you found some sort of manuscript down at the survey house this afternoon," said Cindy, looking for a conversational gambit that would bring him back centre stage. As a good hostess she was always mindful of her guests being pushed to the edge of things by the sheer weight of her family's conversational muscle. They were a voluble lot, the Courtneys, and no company for a shrinking violet. Not that the handsome ex-priest was incapable of holding his own, but it always paid to be polite.

"I did and it rather jolted me – or the bit I read did. I haven't got past the first page yet but something tells me it's going to be a bumpy ride."

"I'm a demon researcher if you want any help," offered Cindy. "Librarians: we know where to look. Know where the bodies are often," she laughed.

Joe thought that might be useful. He was an unemployed priest, not a bloody policeman or research major. Scrap that: he was an unemployable priest. Or rather, not a priest at all, but the bonking padre, a tabloid editor's wet dream. Whatever he was in this chastened state, he wasn't a copper if that's where this was leading. The thought that it might be left an odd feeling: why would I think that, he wondered.

"Where is Woodlawn?" he asked. "The lady writing it lived there but it ended up hidden away in a secret casement below a sash window in Pearl River. How did it get there?" mused Joe.

"Woodlawn is a lovely neighbourhood in Queens. It's one of the city's five boroughs, east of Manhattan," explained Ted. "It's always been an Irish neighbourhood. Not exclusively as few neighbourhoods are exclusive to any one group, but each is known for being more than something else. More Hispanic, more Italian or in Woodlawn's case, more Irish."

"Do people move up from a nice neighbourhood like that out to Pearl River? I mean, Queens is part of the big city, right? And if you can stick the city then why move out to woollyback land?" said Joe.

"What are woollybacks?" they asked in unison and Joe found himself explaining this gently mocking term for people from Liverpool's Lancashire hinterland, deemed to be slower-witted, country folk. The term related to the farm-hands who would carry live sheep on their backs through the slaughterhouses in Liverpool's huge wholesale markets and finish their shift with wool all over their shoulders.

Ted ignored the inference that they were slow-witted country folk and picked up the conversation again, enjoying the fact that his knowledge as a realtor could put him in the middle of things. Even someone as rumbustious as him sometimes found he had to compete for attention around his own dinner table.

"Yeah, people move out of town. Even in the better suburbs the Big Apple can grind you down and Pearl River is a nice option, particularly if you're Irish. So it's not unfeasible that someone from Woodlawn would choose it once they'd decided to make the move away. A lot of the guys here are firemen or police officers, but not exclusively by any stretch. Look at me," he added.

Dinner finished in a flurry of clattering plates as the kids cleared and washed up what wouldn't fit in the dishwasher and Ted offered the prospect of a pint in Noonan's. "Best Guinness in the parish," he offered and that sounded tempting, but Joe wanted to return to his manuscript so suggested he was tired and was only up for a few.

Noonan's was busy. It was Monday Night basketball and the Knicks were playing Miami Heat. It was a classic Irish pub in the American mould, rather than a flat-pack version exported from Ireland of the sort that had sprung up everywhere from Prague to Kuala Lumpur.

The ribs were pretty special, Joe recalled from Friday, and in spite of dinner they were tempted. So two plates and four pints each later, they headed off home. A large Jameson's in the den followed, with the two of them picking over the headline details of Joe's fall from grace before heading for bed. With the sidelight on he reached for the letter, but it was 11pm. He was tired – knackered, if truth be told – even if the compulsion to get through the parchment was almost overwhelming. At one point in the evening Ted has asked him if he was okay, he seemed so distant. Foreboding does that to a man.

Letter to Sean, part II

I had made the trip to Liverpool from Dungarvan with your dear grandfather's blessing. He was a practical and sensible man and while the choice was an unusual one, he saw in me characteristics suited to such an endeavour. Ours was a settled dairy farm and though not large at 90 acres, was good enough for a living with hard work and wise trading. Certainly, we had avoided the blight that had afflicted so many of our wretched countrymen a generation before, but with five children there were few options open for me in Waterford. As the youngest it was expected that I join a Holy Order but even mother saw that I was not suited to such a straightened existence, for all my faith in Our Dear Lord.

There was no appetite on my part, I can assure you, for such a lonely and singular life: I had heard tell of the New World and of the opportunities for advancement there and more and more young Irish girls had made the trip and found a life for themselves in domestic service or working in the grand stores in towns like Boston and New York. And so I prevailed upon your dear grandparents to help me emigrate at the tender age of eighteen in the year 1890.

It was clear that I was set upon my course and perhaps it was my determination as much as my level-headedness that saw them bestow their blessing. Passage to Liverpool was arranged via an agent in Dungarvan and I soon found myself aboard the Emerald Wind, a ship of the City of Dublin Steam Packet Company. My plan was to take lodgings in Liverpool with a reliable Irish landlady, arranged with the help of Fr Fanning, and then find for myself the most advantageous passage to either New York or Boston. There were Irish charities aplenty in Liverpool, designed specifically to help souls like me find some form of employ in America before setting sail and it was planned that I should avail of their help fulsomely.

The trip to Liverpool was uneventful for we were blessed with calm weather and I was able to spend much time upon deck. You must understand that the whole venture brought me to a pitch of great excitement for I had never been out of County Waterford. As the mountains of Wales came into view I imagined what my first sight of America might be and as we sailed down the Mersey to Liverpool's famous Landing Stage I had a better sense of what to expect, for here was a giant and bustling metropolis. Grand buildings vied with the huge numbers of ships for my attention and I heard languages and accents from all corners of the world. It did strike me that maybe I should stay here for I could not imagine what New York had that this place didn't. But I had agreed my plans with father and I was not to be deviated from them.

A Mr Davenport met me from the boat by arrangement and took me to Mrs Gilmore's lodging house on Duke Street, a respectable if slightly dowdy home. She was from the county of Sligo and had a slightly stern countenance, as much to keep order I suspected, as by way of nature's hand, for she was helpful with good advice and set me up with meetings with two agents the following day so that I might assess my options.

There were many in terms of lines and routes, classes of carriage and times and dates of departure – not to mention determining where best to make my new life. I settled on Boston for I heard that it was a more civilised city than New York and that there were a good number of our countrymen there. A passage on the Tuesday with the Cunard Line was secured and I began to make my preparations. Then something happened which threw it all into disarray and put in train the most unfortunate set of circumstances; circumstances which almost ruined me and which enriched the rogue Bell beyond measure.

~~~~

Exhaustion – or was it Guinness – had taken Joe and he woke in the morning with the pages of vellum scattered on the floor and a mouth thick from ale and sticky ribs. He was desperate for a pee and his morning glory ached. He realised he needed to deal with both. Joe was beginning to think it was time to make use of his new freedoms.

It was 7.30am and the kids were tucking into breakfast like it was to be their last and Cindy bustled with cheery efficiency, doling out the grub, caffeine and juice.

"Morning Joe," she chirped. "Ooh, you look groggy. Heavy night?" she enquired, as he strode in unshaven and barefoot. At least he had jeans on this time, she thought, and a baggy t-shirt hanging over his butt.

"I've got a gob like the bottom of a budgie's cage. Don't suppose you've got some juice and coffee have you? That husband of yours is a bad influence, you know."

Ah, Ted. He should be up, but who was leading who astray, thought Cindy.

"Todd, go and give your father a dig will you?"

Five minutes later he appeared at the breakfast table, tousled hair, stubbled chin and beery breath suggesting a far heavier session than 4 pints and a generous Jamo's. Crikey, he thought, am I getting too old for this?

Cindy orchestrated things effortlessly and by 08:15 all was quiet, her brood dispatched to their day's work and study, fed, watered and scrubbed with packed lunches and a kiss for each.

"So come on then," she said to Joe, "let's be having a look at this slice of history you've found. Librarians are a bit like historians, you know, and you've got me curious."

On his return to the kitchen – delayed by a shave, a shower and a change of clothes – Joe spread the bundle of faded vellum on the table, a battered old oak affair perfect for the clatter and bang of a busy family. No museum piece, this, but something worthy of acquiring the cheery scars of family life.

Cindy plonked a steaming cafetiere in the middle of the table with two Mets mugs and sat herself to Joe's left. He liked the closeness, although he knew she was strictly – strictly – off limits. She looked good this morning in a single light blue dress and cardigan that told of milder climes ahead, even if it was still chilly outside. God loves an optimist, he thought. There was a nice hint of cleveage, too. Always good for the soul, especially one as tortured as his.

He spread the papers out in front of them, passing the ones he'd read to her before turning to the next instalment.

"Librarians make good speed readers," said Cindy, "I'll have caught up with you in no time."

Great, thought Joe, and then you'll be leaning over me, with your tits weighing on my shoulders and me with a hard-on. Definitely not conducive to concentration. He'd not dealt with his morning glory and didn't fancy having to nip upstairs to do so, but something had to give. Maybe he'd ask Cindy to sort him out with a blind date, or he'd go sharking down at Noonan's. He'd spotted some very fine tabbies down there last night. Early forties, clearly divorced with a good settlement, no doubt, and up for partying. Why else would bonny lasses like that be in a boozer on a Monday night, he figured.

On reflection, Joe thought it best to let Cindy catch up with him so they'd be able to question each other about what unfolded before them, provided she didn't speed read. He'd lay out the pages between them so that she wasn't leaning over him, then the desire to smell her perfume and imagine her astride him might ease. Christ, I need help, he thought.

He relayed his plan to Cindy then headed upstairs for a shower and a shave, returning to find her with her elbows in a washing up bowl.

"I've got as far as her portent of doom," said Cindy. "Thought it wouldn't be fair to start without you and I promise not to speed-read." She'd read his mind, at least.

They settled down to forty minutes that would change countless lives forever.

CHAPTER FOUR

Letter to Sean, part III

A telegram reached Mrs Gilmore's from my dear father via the Post Office in Dungarvan with what was, on the face of it, most interesting news, albeit borne out of sorrow. His brother, my uncle Taigh, had passed away in a place called St. John's in Newfoundland which I knew to be in Canada but no more. He had left some land and waterfront property to my father amounting to some 8 acres, plus a stretch of foreshore on the other side of the peninsula in Maddox Cove.

Dear father could not leave Waterford, of course, and being sure of my determination and thoughtfulness said that he would sign it over to me to see what I could achieve with it. 'It could be the making of you, Theresa,' he said. 'Go and seek that fortune you have dreamed of.' He asked for a response by return but as you can imagine, my head was all a-spin as it meant my existing plans would all be for nought. I walked from Mrs Gilmore's to the free lending library on Seel Street and there a kindly librarian showed me a map of North America and helped me locate St. John's. He told me it was a rough and tumble sort of place, but important to Britain's control of Canada and full of Waterford men who had founded its fishing fleets as long ago as the early sixteenth century. Fortunes were being made there, including by men here in Liverpool, and civic improvements and a sense of the value of culture were driving the town towards a more civilised position, he told me.

A little research showed that ships were bound there regularly from Liverpool and I admitted to myself that my head was turned. If it didn't work out as hoped then at least I was on the right side of the Atlantic and could make my way to Boston on a coastal steamer. I found a ship from the Bell Line, a reputable Liverpool steam ship company, that was sailing on the Tuesday next and bought a ticket in steerage. It was impulsive, but then I was still a young woman and not yet wise to life's challenges nor the weakness or unkindness of others.

I telegraphed father by return and told him of my acceptance of his suggestion and my timescales and Fearon & Co, the principal lawyers in Waterford Town, set about preparing the necessary papers. Title was transferred to me in time for my journey and Messrs Alsop, lawyers in Liverpool, confirmed same and the transfer of twenty pounds, a huge sum, that came with Taigh's settlement. They kindly informed McLachlan & Co in St. John's, Taigh's attorneys and everything was in order. I set sail light of foot, I must say, sure that such good fortune could only presage more to come.

The journey was arduous but the ship's size and the air on deck made things bearable. I would take regular strolls to pass the time and though my status as a single woman caused some unkind folk to comment I cared little for what they thought for I was now a woman of money with title to land and property and I was heading to Canada to see to my business affairs. My confidence grew further as I made conversation with those of a kinder nature and on the third day I was introduced to a Mr Barrington Bell, an unusual enough name, I suppose and which gave me cause to wonder if he was in any way related to the owners of the City of Montreal, upon which we were set sail.

Mr Bell was to inherit the business in due course, he told me, but he had to prove himself capable of sound commercial judgement, good leadership and an ability to add to the family's stock of wealth. He was somewhat aloof but I put that down to his station in life and relative youth, not to mention that he was in lower company, as he and others would see it. But there was a determination to prove himself which appealed for I, too, had found myself in such a place and as we met each day on our strolls – at first by accident – so we came to an accommodation with one another and he softened his tone.

Eight days at sea saw us strike a form of friendship and I admitted to looking forward to our discussions. I sensed that young Mr Bell did, too. I learned much from him and he seemed not to mind my naivety and lack of knowledge, explaining the basics of commerce to me, although father had taught me how to buy and sell cattle well enough by the time I was fourteen. Still, in these mechanised days of manufacture and world trade, commerce was a more complex business than I could ever imagine – certainly more so than at New Ross cattle market.

He was to take over the firm's cod processing and packing business, which sounded substantial enough. It was based in St. John's on its waterfront but he could not expand capacity to meet the scale of the opportunity, as they saw it. The growth of America's major cities presented an almost insatiable demand for cheap fish, he told me, and it was a matter of great frustration that he could not satisfy it.

We landed in St. John's and Master Bell was gracious enough to have telegraphed ahead to his lead man, a John Temple, who brought a carriage with him to take me to my hotel, a modest affair on Barters Hill optimistically called The Metropole. I bade Bell my farewell and reflected fondly on our conversations and his kindness. His was business of some import and I thought not that our paths might cross or that he may take a further interest in me.

I thought it prudent to take my time assessing uncle Taigh's assets so had arranged for seven nights in my lodgings – time enough to see what I had inherited and to gain the measure of St John's. I wasn't sure, of course, if this was to be my home, of that I had made myself certain during the voyage. I had heard much about the trappings of Boston and even my carriage from the harbour to my hotel suggested that perhaps St John's was not to be its match.

Uncle Taigh's property lay on the foreshore at Water Street and my disappointment was complete when setting eyes upon it: a large wooden shipbuilding hall, a slipway and some substantial yardage scattered with scaffolding, planks, ropes, pulleys and other detritus of the trade. There was a separate clapboard house, painted black, out of whose chimney rose dark smoke and a further blacksmiths' workshop with all manner of clanging and clattering that would raise the dead. Men busied themselves about the place and I spied a small boy scooping up the horse manure from the many cart-horses that seemed to bring materials hither and thither.

What was I to do with a boat yard? What did I possibly know about commerce this complicated? Somehow I had allowed myself to entertain the notion that Taigh might be leaving me property with a pleasing rental income; perhaps enough to allow me to take some leisure and assess what menfolk there might be of suitable standing and availability. But a dangerous, dirty, smelly place of manufacture? I am ashamed to say that I wept.

Next to the grandly-titled St. John's Marine Engineering and Boat Building Works lay quite the smelliest place imaginable. It was separated from Taigh's works by an eight foot stone wall behind which was a factory belching out vile smoke and even viler odours. Beyond was a large, u-shaped quay facing east, tied up to which were a fleet of trawlers. I was familiar with them as they were the same design as those in Dungarvan.

I retired, quite despondent, to the Metropole and took an early night, tired as much from the day's disappointment as from the exertions upon the sea. It was the following morning that I thought my luck had changed when I bumped into Mr Bell quite by chance. I suppose I shouldn't have thought that completely unlikely, given the relative size of St. John's – not a Liverpool, by any scale. But it was a pleasant surprise and sensing my melancholy he enquired whether I might take tea with him at the Bristol Hotel on Duckworth Street, an altogether better establishment than my own.

And there I burdened him with my story of sorrow and my wonderment at what I was to do. He listened patiently and kindly and asked questions of me about my inheritance, whilst reassuring me that all would be well. He offered some suggestions about what I might do with the business, seeming certain that there would be a buyer, though not at any great value, for the business, he suspected, would be making little by way of a surplus. Enough, though, he thought, to get me to Boston with a dowry, if that was still my dream. I left feeling lifted by his insights and spent the rest of the day acquainting myself more thoroughly with St. John's.

It was a pleasant enough town, certainly by aspect, and there were signs of prosperity brought about by its position as England's oldest landholding in North America and its modern role as a harbour and fishing port. Many were the Waterford and Wexford accents that I heard and that, too, cheered my spirit. More amazing were the number of our countryfolk still speaking Irish and I learned that they had a name for the place in our fair gaelic tongue: Talamh an Éisc, the Land of the Fish, for this is what had brought them to its shores as early as 1536. They had colonized it in numbers and, for all its roughness compared to the solid, stone-built respectability of Dungarvan or Waterford Town, its homeliness grew upon me in that day. I went to bed renewed at the prospects before me and wanted more of Mr Bell's fair and kind advice to help me in my deliberations.

To my surprise, he awaited me in the Metropole's lounge the following morning and greeted me warmly, asking me not to be alarmed but rather, reassuring me that he had given my situation some considerable thought as well as the benefit of his experience to date and wished to share a proposition with me. He hurried me up the hill to the Bristol and I fair admit I was giddy at the prospect of hearing what he had to say. He asked me to take him by the arm and was most gentlemanly in his demeanour. I caught him giving me a gentle sideways glance and blushed at the attention, for none had been paid to me in that way before.

"My dear lovely Theresa,' he began, 'I must admit to having formed an affection for you during our time on the Montreal but could not, of course, share that with you. Your station and mine are so different and I thought that you, as a Catholic, would not countenance any affections from an Anglican like myself. But I have come to think that in the New World that should not – does not – matter and I realized how much I missed our discourses when I met you yesterday, in such a melancholy state."

By now he was holding my hands and looking sincerely into my eyes and all my instincts were to embrace him, improper as that was. He was handsome, kind – as he had already shown – and a little earnest, too. Gone was the arrogance that had marked him out early in our relationship.

"I have a simple proposal that can make your situation many times better than you imagine it to be. It would be separate from any growing affection I have for you – a proper legal agreement between equals – though I would not want it to curtail any chance we may have of finding where our thoughts for each other may go.

"I wish to propose a business partnership, one that could enrich us both and help us achieve what ambitions we may have in life and provide for those who may find themselves dependent upon us. You own land not particularly worthwhile, producing boats for people who wish to pay you less than they cost to build and for which there is an uncertain market. Next to that land is the cod processing plant that I mentioned to you aboard the Montreal and I have been open with you in already laying forth that, with but extra land to process more fish, I could treble my turnover, for there is but endless demand for salted and frozen cod."

He went on to outline how he would insist on an equal partnership with his board in Liverpool and secure for me an advantageous position in terms of both salary and dividend. And he made it plain, in a most touching fashion, that he would hope all of this might coincidentally lead to some greater closeness between us. A union of equals, prospering and loving together, as he put it. He asked that I would merely consider the matter and thanked me graciously for my time, settling our account and leading me back to the Metropole.

You might easily imagine what that did both to my head and my young, inexperienced heart. Both were aflutter and I lay down in my quarters trying to calm myself and think through what should be done. It was tempting to telegraph my dear father but it struck me that I was here to use my judgment and make what fortune I could out of what befell me, and hadn't he taught me to sell cows and secure a fair deal? Catch a grip of yourself, young lady, I told myself and began to adopt a calmer view of the situation.

He needed my land and I didn't want to run a boat yard so that struck me as about equal. His plant was far more profitable than my yard yet he was offering me a 50% stake in the business, a salary and what I presumed would be equal call on any surplus, the balance going back to Liverpool. That struck me as highly advantageous. Clearly a man of action, I supposed that he might be able to secure some approval for this notion relatively quickly for, whilst £20 remained a fair sum, I did not wish to burn through my inheritance with undue haste whilst I waited for his family to make their decision. I was to be pleasantly surprised.

Two of the most excruciating days of my young life passed with no word from Mr Bell, nor sight of him, either. I visited the boat yard and introduced myself to Willie Greenock, a bear of a Scotsman who was the manager of the enterprise. He was gracious in his condolences and keen to hear of my plans and I promised him that, once I had assessed my options, he would be among the first to know.

I told him I understood his need for certainty and asked him to escort me around the yard and explain the proceedings, which I found surprisingly interesting.

On my return to the Metropole an invitation from Mr Bell to join him for dinner the following evening awaited me. We were to meet at seven pm in the Westminster Lounge at the Caledonia Club and dress was formal. This was to be my first ever such dinner so you might imagine how I set all a-flutter again. The hotel owner's wife, a kindly colonial lady called Dorothy, enquired as to my excitement and offered to help tutor me on the manners and etiquette required at such an establishment as well as to find me a dress appropriate for the venue in Kilbride's, the town's principal outfitters.

The following day passed in a blur but the evening remains scorched in my memory. Not for what happened then, so much as what transpired later and the treachery and deceit that can rest in a man's heart when riches are in prospect.

Mr Bell looked ever the gentlemen in a fetching dinner suit and was complementary about my evening gown, chosen for me by Dorothy but with my own eye on the issue, too. He was solicitous and kind, without being overly formal and I found myself remarkably at ease for such a fish out of her own water. I took that as a measure of the man and wanted to enjoy the experience and the benefit of his gentle enquiries and attention.

We drank fine French wine – only a glass or two for me for I knew not how I may react to it, but was fully aware of what alcohol could do to a man, never mind a woman. At the end of a meal of startling luxury Mr Bell brought the matter to hand: his proposal for the partnership of our mutual interests and his barely concealed excitement at what might be achieved together. He'd make a useless cow salesman, I admitted, and wondered if I should drive some sort of bargain with him. He wouldn't think much of me as a partner if I rolled over and let him tickle me like the farm yard dog, now would he?

The offer was much as I'd anticipated but with an annual salary of £150, which left me breathless. For that I was to help him with the administration of the business, a most unusually exalted position for a woman, he explained, but they did things differently in the colonies and there was a refreshing easiness to their ways.

I remembered my father's coaching and did my best to look thoughtful without being too severe. He feared rejection, I saw immediately, and I drove home my advantage.

"Your proposals seem fair as they stand, Mr Bell," I responded, as gravely as I might, "but you have noted for yourself the weakness inherent in them."

"What? What is there, dear Theresa, that cannot be designed to bring prosperity and happiness to us both, whether in business or some wider, happier union?" he pleaded.

"I care little for the harsh tasks of commerce and shall take your £150 stipend as just that: an annual payment for the pleasure of my land and my company, with no expectation of work in return. I'm sure you'd prefer your partner – of whatever type – to exhibit the most ladylike of lifestyles," I demurred. "And not forgetting the 50% interest in the fish plant, too, of course."

Well, if he didn't swallow the lot and admit that I'd got him. I allowed myself a beaming smile, then excused myself, before jigging around the bathroom in glee.

He told me that he had full authority to proceed and that he could have the legal documentation drafted immediately. He would personally guide me through it and would ensure that everything was properly witnessed at McLachlan & Co, the lawyers that had acted for uncle Taigh. It felt proper and gentlemanly and clear and I admit to embracing Barrington at the conclusion of our negotiations.

He explained that it may take as long as a week to have the necessary paperwork drafted and he invited me to stay at a suite in the company's villa on the shore at Cahill Point. It was far more comfortable than the Metropole and I would have maids to dress me and attend to me whilst he looked after business and I could take walks along the shore or be taken by carriage into town to spend my leisure.

Mr Temple collected me and my meagre belongings and brought me in silence to Woolton House, a most splendid ten bedroom mansion in the latest Victorian fashion. The housekeeper, Mary Carpenter, greeted me and took me to my quarters, a huge suite of rooms on the front of the house, looking north across the sound and north east out to the dark, brooding Atlantic. She explained that she had instructions, immediately, to bring me back into town and to help me choose a complete wardrobe at Kilbride's and by the day's end I was dizzy at the expense and luxury of it all. Bless uncle Taigh and the Good Lord for all my fortune.

Ten whole days into my stay and Mr Bell's attentiveness and solicitudes had left me dizzy and slipping ever more into love with him. We had found time to be alone for walks along the shore and up the steep headland and intimacy was easy to come by. Please remember, my son, that I was young, naïve and in the full flush of my first love. I was rich, too, and suddenly leading the life of a lady at leisure with a man who wanted nothing other than my happiness. And happy I was, deliriously so. Ladies waited upon me and called me 'm'lady' and 'ma'am' and brought me meals and clothes and men tipped their hats at me. It was an extraordinary turn for a farmer's girl from Waterford, not yet nineteen.

I lost my virtue to Barrington Bell and it shames me to say that it fell easily to his entreaties and his charm. Nothing felt more natural and I knew where our love was leading: to a union of business and two matched adults that could only prosper on all levels. He had the papers ready the following day and took me through them, sheet-by-sheet at McLachlan & Co before signing them and engorging the last page with the company's seal and asking for my signature, too, which was witnessed by Mr Alec McLachlan himself.

We went to celebrate at the Caledonia Club, taking a quiet table in the corner and planning our future together in hushed tones. He was a beautiful man, handsome and manly, but with a tenderness that belied his need to be hard in his daily dealings. I respected him immensely for that.

We returned to Woolton House and the night drifted away to pleasure. I awoke the following morning to an empty bed, knowing that he was already hard at work protecting our investment.

The knock on the door was unnecessarily harsh and without any leave Temple walked in with two officers of the law and demanded I be dressed and in the hallway immediately. He threw my old dress at me and I wondered from whence that came since my new wardrobe had replaced it. I dressed in a hurry and in a frightful worry, fearful at what had prompted such rudeness. I was greeted with the sternest of countenances on arrival at the foot of the stairs and my stomach turned.

The first officer grabbed me roughly, spun me around and skilfully attached hand-cuffs to my rearward arms. I yelped as they gripped the knuckle of my wrist and it was all I could do to keep the tears from turning me to wreckage. I was bundled harshly into a horse drawn mariah and taken to Her Majesty's Penitentiary There was no explanation as I was bundled into a straw-covered cell with a wooden bench, a blanket and a drunken Biddy slumped in one corner, muttering profanities in both English and Irish.

I do not recall the days spent in there – too many by half and designed, I know now, to break my spirit and my heart. There was no word from Bell and I could only conclude that my misfortune was at his hand. Eventually, a magistrate called for me and I was brought to his chambers. He was a bluff Englishman by the name of Venmore and lacking in the common courtesies I have learned are the mark of much of that race.

Darling Sean, I was the author of all my misfortune and the responsibility for your hard early life is mine alone. You have risen above all that and my pride is eternal. So please forgive me and be understanding about what I have yet to tell you.

"Young lady, you are in grave trouble," Venmore opened. "You have sought to defraud Mr Barrington Bell in a most cunning plan and almost succeeded. Had our lawyers not unearthed your charade you may yet be in possession of a large fortune and a most advantageous position in our community."

You might imagine, darling boy, that even with a broken spirit this news was an affront to the values your dear grandfather had raised me with and with the facts as I knew them. I would not ever have defrauded anyone, nor had the wit for such a preposterous adventure. I spluttered my objections and Venmore brought them to an abrupt halt with the back of his hand.

"You did not have title to the land you claimed and we have verification of same from Mr McLachlan, who I believe had acted for Taigh Brophy, your alleged uncle. In such circumstances the punishment is normally severe and there is little latitude for me when it comes to imposing lengthy custodial sentences. But in this case one of the town's most important employers and most generous benefactors has asked for clemency and I am to set you free under strict conditions."

I was a trembling wreck, as you may imagine, but my greatest shivers and sobs were brought on by news of my pending release.

"Who, might I ask, has vouched for me for I hardly know anyone in St. John's?" I enquired, puzzled at what or who was the root of my change in fortune.

"That is of no concern to you," Venmore replied, sternly. "You must comply with these conditions for three years and then you will be free to leave St John's and we would expect that you do so. There are too many Irish wretches and whores here anyway without need for detaining them unnecessarily.

"You will work for subsistence at the Bell fish plant and will lodge at the parish poor house. Your date of release will be three years from today, September 12th 1893."

And with that my manacles were removed and I was met at the door by a Mrs Doherty, the parish housekeeper at St John the Baptist where I was taken in shame. I had been feeling fearful sick the mornings of those recent weeks and my condition was soon commented upon in the bunk room at St John's. It was Mrs Doherty who found me collapsed in the privy and determined that I was carrying a child.

There could only be one father, dear lovely Sean and it was not Fergal, I am so sorry to tell you. He brought you up all these years loving you as his own but you are the product of my weakness with Barrington Bell and I need you to know because it can set you free. Surely, there is some means of justice in this great new country of ours that can bequeath to you what was cheated from me all those years ago by your father?

You are comfortable now, a product of our love and your own values and hard work and I know, therefore, that you do not need much greater material sustenance, so view this not as about enriching yourself, but denuding those who cheated you so that you may put their resources to better use. Please pursue that if you can find it in you.

It breaks my heart to tell you like this and you must forgive me my weakness – the second great weakness of my life – for I cannot bear to look upon you as I let you down so.

The rest of the story you know, to a point. The parish helped feed and clothe you as a child and you were not taken from me, as was common elsewhere. Fergal was the parish groundsman, having been an under-gardener at Doneraile, and he saw in me – restored in me – the spark that had taken me to those shores originally.

With my three years up we joined the great migration south to New England that was common among Newfies then, for winters were milder and job opportunities more plentiful. His brother, Anthony, had made something of himself in New York as a restaurant manager at the great Barclay Hotel and beseeched that we join him there. Our early life after that you can probably recall.

You can imagine what it was like watching the great extension to the salting factory and fish quays built on what was rightfully mine. Employment trebled at Bell Cod & Salting, as it became known and young Master Bell returned to England after four years, I'm told, to be embraced for his acumen, his cunning and the vast additional revenues he had helped return to Liverpool. He was given a civic send-off, I learned later, by Mayor Hannigan who regaled all with stories of how his taxes and munificence had enriched the whole community. There is still a Bell Street, all these years later, in St John's, a stain on the town's map.

How he tricked me, dear Sean, I shall not know but I have no doubt that it was with the connivance of Alec McLachlan. Bell was the kingpin of the port's economy and an influential and wealthy man with huge resources at his disposal, off-shore or otherwise. Money will have changed hands, promises of future work made and kept, opportunities for family members to gain employment and build careers proffered and accepted. We call it cronyism now but it was just pure greed and opportunism then. And all that stood between them and the enrichment of an entire circle of contacts was a naïve, silly little Irish girl.

I never saw it coming and I shall die soon, son, regretting my naivety. But I have you and the memory of dear Fergal, so my one wish before I go to my grave is but simple: to know that you had sought to right this wrong. For it must be put right – of that I am certain.

Your loving mother
Theresa Madden.

Cindy and Joe sat staring at the pages, a few of Cindy's tears dropping to smudge the ink before she composed herself with the help of some Charmins.

Joe put his arm around her in comfort and the floodgates opened, the story an emotional catalyst for whatever else may be going on in her life. She sobbed heartily, her head on his shoulders.

This was his trigger; the point at which his natural empathy would normally take him down a road that led to only one place. He could not go there, but the urge was almost unbearable as Cindy's breasts pressed into his side and the smell of her perfume and conditioner filled his nostrils. He reached for more tissues, unwrapping her arms from around his neck and handing her one to dab her eyes. The rest he put in his pocket as she began to compose herself and he eased himself off the sofa and quietly headed to his bathroom.

CHAPTER FIVE

Deep in the bowels of a giant Edwardian office block a bank of screens blinked and flickered. The lights were low and the walls lined and sealed to deter those whose motives were as impure as their own gaining access to their secrets.

Hackers, spooks, environmental campaigners and plenty of others had an interest in their global operations and would try – and fail – to get to the heart of the company's data centre.

The intelligence officer was running a report for the men upstairs when the alert sounded. Nothing dramatic – that was for the movies – just a repeating signature tune that he had selected himself: 'Angels & Devils' by Echo & The Bunnymen. It made him smile, seeing as he was sitting on both sides of the fence. The firm did a lot of good, employing people, paying taxes and funding charities, but it must dance with some interesting devils to weave it all together into a profitable and substantial corporate whole. Overall, he reckoned, the good cancelled out the bad, leaving a large plus on the moral balance sheet.

The alert was on screen four, his web monitoring station. Some rather clever young men had developed the algorithm for him which placed a global watch on any search term they cared to specify. Nothing too general; given the group's activities the Bunnymen would never be off the airwaves otherwise. No: it monitored around eight hundred highly specific search terms, the origins and purpose of which he did not understand. Didn't need to, frankly, though he reckoned each one would relate to toes large and small trodden on in the company's rise to global prominence.

This one seemed innocuous enough: "Theresa Madden AND Bell Line", but he was savvy enough to know that if it made the list then it probably covered a multitude of sins. His job was to identify the IP address which told him specifically which computer at what location had typed the search term. He'd then pass the information upstairs. What happened after that was anyone's guess.

The information went immediately to George Molyneux, who assessed it coldly. They did not yet know it, but somebody had just unleashed a shit-storm. Whatever the connection or reason, they'd sorely wish they hadn't, he thought. And then he picked up the phone and dialed the number.

CHAPTER SIX

Joe came downstairs to find Cindy composed, a fresh pot of coffee on the table and the letter laid out sequentially. She had a pad by her side and was scribbling notes with such concentration that she didn't hear him approach.

"Jesus, Joe, I nearly leapt out of my skin!" she exclaimed, hand to her chest and a minor flush on her face.

"What're you up to, love?" asked Joe, the English endearment one that always made Cindy smile.

She explained that she was building a simple timeline so that she could see graphically people's age, dates of key events and the like. "I work better visually," she explained. "Drawings, boxes, arrows. I'll start with the ages and dates and it'll make it easier to research Mrs Madden – what happened to her when she got to New York, how she ended up in a nice neighbourhood like 87th Street and most importantly, what happened to Sean. "It's doubtful he's still alive, but did he marry and did his wife have any kids? Where are they and what do they now do?" Cindy asked, almost to herself.

"You've missed one key thing," said Joe. "Did he ever pursue any claim against Bell Line?"

Joe doubted it because the firm had prospered long since then – everyone in Liverpool knew that, even a fallen priest.

"There's one way of finding out quickly," said Cindy, turning the family laptop towards her from its position at the end of the kitchen's long work surface. And so they began googling further search terms to see what transpired, but there was nothing: a complete blank. About as likely as if nothing had ever occurred between either party. Or that at least, one of them never even existed.

~~~~

Sean had existed, of course. But a visit one day from two very large men with rough English accents had persuaded him that his interests lay firmly in another direction from his mother's. A large bag of dollars helped oil the conversation, of course, and he was living out the American dream in any event, given his parents' humble origins, so why cause bother? And anyways, like the Englishman had said, they had the resources to bury him, his lawyers and whatever else they chose. And the money would come in handy, getting him up the housing ladder, so the three agreed that would be the end of it. And it was, until now.

~~~~

Back in the basement, Echo & The Bunnymen filled the small room. Someone, somewhere, was on a roll, thought the techie. Molyneux was less impressed.

~~~~

"You'd think there'd be some historical record that's been transcribed to the net, even if it was just a ship's manifest," said Joe. "It's like she's been redacted from history." And then a glaring mistake hit him. "Search under her maiden name, Brophy," he suggested, shaking his head at such an obvious error. But that route proved just as fruitless.

Cindy suggested he leave things to her for a while: as a librarian she had the patience, the organisational bent and the knowledge to dig out information and if there was any out there, she'd find it. Eventually.

Joe agreed and decided to go for a run. He'd let himself go to seed a little since the revelations of a fortnight ago and if he was to get himself back into the dating game to give some relief to his aching nuts he'd need to ensure he was in tip-top condition. He left Cindy to her work and headed for Cherry Brook Park.

~~~~

Richter received the call at 11am local time and took his instructions without much of a word. He noted nothing down, relying on a trained mind and his natural enjoyment of detail to commit his instructions and briefing to memory. And in his line of work, it didn't pay to leave evidence on things like notepads, no matter how many pages you ripped out. Those forensics boys were clever.

He took the Henry Hudson Parkway south from his home in Riverdale before crossing the George Washington Bridge and swinging north up the Pallisades Interstate. He could just see his house across the Hudson, using Mount St Vincent as his reference. It had paid him well, his specialized line of security, but then the clue was in the word specialist – few people focused in on one facet of any profession, which meant that his approach commanded higher premiums.

It was not much more than thirteen miles from door to door, he'd reckoned, and he'd scope out his target before deciding on the best means to identify his foe or foes. His client had already done some of the hard work, identifying the physical address of the computer making some sort of unwelcome noise out in cyberspace. His job was to identify who owned it and used it and then report back. It was the method of his surveillance or rather, some of the methods, that marked him out as amongst the best and he knew his client wasn't the sort of customer that was focused on price. Only ever performance.

He arrived on North Avenue and drove around the neighbourhood at a speed experience told him would not attract attention. He drove a grey Ford Taurus with false New York plates, a pleasingly anonymous combination. He was helped in that regard by his small stature and cheap suits, with a trademark folder under his arm. Photocopier salesman, it said. Definitely not outsourced spook and occasional killer.

The target property was a grand mock-Colonial, well-proportioned and in a half acre lot, with neat lawns, a generous parking bay and flower beds around the patio. There was a two year-old GMC Yukon at a jaunty angle and Richter immediately thought "housewife". Couldn't park straight on an empty acre.

Nice house, nice neighbourhood he surmised - and then he wondered what these good folk in such a pleasant slice of Smallville had done to upset his client. They didn't want to do that. They really didn't.

After assessing his target he headed to Central Avenue East to hit the sidewalks. In a township like Pearl River what passed for a downtown tended to be a lively community hub and he fully expected that he'd soon be trailing household members around the place. It was their small daily tasks that underpinned a community like this through the social contact they brought, he acknowledged, and part of what made Pearl River such a popular and settled place. If he'd had kids he'd have considered it a good place to bring them up.

~~~~

The black Jaguar XJ fringed Sefton Park as it crept silently through the leafy suburbs of south Liverpool. The park, like many in the city, was flanked by mid-Victorian ship owners' and cotton brokers' mansions none of which, he thought, were as pleasing as his own stuccoed pile. A huge slug of Lottery money had helped restore the park and where once it had been a 200 acre den for drug dealers, it was now bustling with families and joggers and the surrounding houses had been converted to luxury apartments.

Sir Meredith Bell smiled as he spied the lovely Palm House through the trees. He'd played his part in its restoration as chair of the fundraising committee and had tapped the upper echelons of Liverpool's moneyed elite for a good few bob. Eight hundred grand was his personal target and he'd reached it in three donations, plus his own, which was just a hundred grand. Nice work. Now people got married in there – possibly the same people who'd pelted it with stones when they were kids. Progress, everywhere you looked in this fine old port, and he had his hand in much of it.

Twenty minutes later Edwards turned the Jag into Sir Meredith's driveway. It was a tricky affair, a tight turn up a steep slope but requiring a hill-start, too, as he'd have to stop in order for the electronic security gates to open. But he'd done it a thousand times and knew the angles by heart.

The house stood atop a sandstone ridge in Woolton in about half an acre of grounds – a huge amount of space by the standards of Britain's cramped cities. It was an early Victorian mansion, still showing vestiges of the Georgian period and certainly avoiding any of the neo-Gothic flourishes of the later Victorian era, which Bell considered vulgar. He was a few doors from Strawberry Fields and it was only three hundred yards as the crow flew down the ridge to John Lennon's home on Menlove Avenue.

That always made him smile. Working class hero? My eye. Aunt Mimi's large semi-detached house was on one of the loveliest roads in Liverpool, a minute's walk from Calderstones Park, one of its largest, most ornate and most verdant spaces. Still, mustn't knock him, he thought. He was good for the tourism industry and Bell had a personal investment in a rather smart boutique hotel that did well out of it.

He had inherited the home and his shares in Bell Group from his father, as was tradition in this most patrician of businesses. It was the responsibility of the eldest son to hand the firm over in better condition than that in which he found it, along with stewardship of the family trusts that were major recipients of its annual dividends. The business had been founded by Robert Bell in 1782 as Liverpool merchants took an unshakeable grip on the slave trade. Late into the market, it hadn't taken long before Liverpool's shipowners had wrested much of it from Bristol and London. They spotted the value of specialism, commissioning ships designed to maximize the amount of human cargo they could carry on the first leg of the notorious triangular trade: trinkets, pottery and guns southwards to Africa to swap with tribal leaders for slaves kidnapped from the interior; slaves sold to work the sugar, cotton and tobacco plantations of the New World; and rum, spices, tobacco, cotton and raw sugar on the return leg back to Liverpool.

It wasn't a wildly profitable enterprise in terms of margin, but by building highly efficient ships, controlling costs and seeking the benefits of scale wherever they could be found the surpluses had been substantial - so much so that the Bell family opened its own bank to lend their spare cash to the ever-growing band of entrepreneurs that headed to Liverpool keen to exploit the opportunities presented by the port's continued growth. By the 1840s forty per cent of world trade passed through Liverpool's vast dock system and in the midst of it all sat the Bell family.

Ever alert to changing trade patterns, the firm was the first to exploit the misery of emigrants fleeing Ireland's potato famine. More than 1.2m headed for Liverpool in search of ships to the New World and the Bell family would be there to meet the demand. Hundreds of thousands stayed, unable to afford passage elsewhere, but for five years there was a hugely profitable trade in transporting the remaining wretched souls to Baltimore, Boston, Philadelphia and New York. Unearthing earlier designs for their slave ships, Henry Bell's engineers crafted a new class of ship using these old principles and a new phrase was born, the coffin ship, such was the profound impact of Bell's cramped, airless conditions on passenger mortality.

Gradually, the trade in emigrants became more settled and the age of steam saw better regulated accommodation in what remained a fiercely competitive market. But before that happened, another golden opportunity emerged that Bell Line would exploit Ruthlessly through its resources and cunning.

On 12th April 1861 the first shot of America's bloody civil war rang out at Fort Sumter from a cannon made in Liverpool, creating turmoil in its place of manufacture. The city's reach spanned the globe, but America was its largest market and the trade in cotton from the southern states one of the biggest sectors of its economy.

Unsure of who would prevail, Joseph Bell, Henry's son, did what instinct told him and backed both sides. He was part of a group of Liverpool businessmen behind a Confederate plan to open a diplomatic mission in the city, in contravention of strict British government orders to observe neutrality. Under cover of a cotton brokerage, Frazer Trenholm on Rumford Place, they provided funds, intelligence and connections to the diplomatic attaché, General Bulloch, who embarked upon a huge ship-building programme in the yards across the Mersey in Birkenhead. Northern Union spies reported their suspicions to Westminster and questions were raised in parliament about the nature of the ships under construction, but bluster and political connections saw the programme continue uninterrupted. Liverpool became the unofficial home of the Confederate fleet, its ships built there and returning there for repair, for fresh crews, for armaments and other supplies.

It was on a bright August morning in 1862 that the CSS Alabama departed John Laird's shipyard for battle in the Atlantic. Bell Line had lent money and technical assistance to the enterprise and Joseph Bell was there to watch it depart. It was a matter of some pride to Sir Meredith that the ship remained the most successful battleship ever built, sinking fifty five Northern Union ships and bonding a further ten.

The Yankees were not to be neglected, of course, and Joseph Bell personally negotiated a deal to provide its army with cheap provisions, particularly salted cod shipped coastwise from the Newfoundland fishing banks. They shipped arms and munitions from Liverpool, too, and ensured that Yankee goods, from the north eastern seaboard's emerging manufacturing sector, could get to Liverpool and to British markets.

It was risky, deft and ultimately hugely profitable as debts – monetary and moral – were cashed in on conclusion of the war. Bell Line was set fair in its largest overseas market and had built political and commercial ties that would endure into the twenty first century.

The chain of inheritance had remained from father to eldest son all that time, but Sir Meredith bore the responsibility with alacrity. It was what he was born for, after all. His standing in Liverpool was unimpeachable, the business community grateful for the firm's and family's loyalty to a city that had seen dark times. He ran a global enterprise from the port's famous Pier Head which gave him one of the most valuable frequent flyers cards anywhere, yet he remained committed to the boards of the city's illustrious Royal Liverpool Philharmonic Orchestra, the world's oldest professional ensemble; and to its famous School of Tropical Medicine, now endowed by Bill and Melinda Gates to support its research into malaria. He never missed a meeting. Bell Group used local suppliers wherever it could and the impact of its presence in the city was worth hundreds of millions of pounds a year to the local economy.

Sir Meredith was not always popular with his staff, he knew. His attempts at playing the benevolent patrician rubbed up against his rather brusque manner and discomfort in certain social situations. He'd learned that his nickname amongst his head office staff was Merry Ding Dong, a typical sobriquet from

Scousers, for whom deference was never a well-fitting cloak. But he won huge respect when he appeared in the firm's annual five-a-side football competition with the letters MDD monogrammed on his shirt and track suit top and he was comfortable that, all told, he was respected by 'his people,' too.

~~~~

The call that evening from the company's head of security, George Molyneux, troubled him. He was hardened to the challenges of a business that spanned shipping, banking, food and, shortly, carbon extraction, but instinct said that something was wrong. George only rang him to tell him of a new challenge or to brief him on a material change to an on-going issue. His style was terse and his boss preferred it that way.

"Some persistent internet searches relating to the Madden Files have been made and we're investigating. I'll keep you posted," he said, then rang off. If he'd wanted anything from the boss then he'd have hung around for a reply. Bell had no problem with such perfunctory behaviour – such issues didn't merit chit-chat after all.

Bell was familiar with the Madden Files, as he was with all the firm's historical dirty secrets, of which there were many, but it set an alarm ringing in his gut and he wasn't sure why. It had been a busy day and the board meeting for his wealth management business, Bell Bertram, had been fractious. He was distracted and decided to leave things to Molyneux.

George, he knew, would sort it. How, where and when was up to him and if he asked no questions he'd be told no lies. But he would fix it, and in a way that could never come back to Sir Meredith's door. For that he was paid handsomely, on top of what he knew was a generous final salary pension after 30 years in the Liverpool police force, where he ended up head of its Special Branch, the anti-terrorist unit. He'd be clearing a quarter of a million pounds a year at least, thought Bell, but that was small change when set against his duty to protect the family's assets. Turnover this year would be £12.4bn, the net profit on which would be around £650m. Of that, roughly three quarters would be parked on the balance sheet to fund future investments and growth and the remainder would be distributed to him as the largest single shareholder, and amongst the family trusts that feather-bedded far too many great-great- grand-children for his liking. Still, it was the way and his cut would be around £19m this year alone, so he wasn't about to rock the boat.

He'd taken a different approach with his own family, following the Paul McCartney model. You could never escape the bloody Beatles in this city, he smiled to himself. Whilst the children followed the family tradition of attending the plush Liverpool College, he wanted them modest in their outlook and sure of the value of hard work. The bugger of it all, though, was that he had not had a son. Three beautiful daughters gave him great joy, but it saddened him that it would be via his loins that the great tradition of male lineage would fall. Only the eldest, Poppy, showed any instinct for commerce or any interest in the family firm and, in these enlightened times, perhaps a lady at the head might be no bad thing. She had an instinct for diplomacy, too, although she was a feisty little madam when it suited her.

He wasn't sure where she got her spark, mind. He was a very measured character, he knew, if a little blunt at times and Caroline, his wife, was a quiet and mumsy soul. He'd met her during his accounting finals and, not wanting to be distracted, had put her evident interest in him to one side. But he'd never been the most comfortable at the art of wooing and so it was a relief to find someone to make the running, of sorts, and two years into their careers they were married. Now 43 years old he accepted that life was set on its course and focused on giving what time he could to the girls, which wasn't much, admittedly. That was Caroline's department.

Meantime, he always had the lovely Anatalia in Moscow to fulfil his wilder fantasies, a bi-product of months of intensive negotiations with NovKos, the Russian energy giant, with which Bell Group had struck a deal for a joint venture in Canada to extract shale gas. When he first met her, running NovKos's reception at its gleaming headquarters in the Presnensky business district in the west of the city, he'd parked her firmly in the spank bank, as he called it to his own mild amusement. One to dwell on in his lonely hotel room later. But she'd shown a genuine interest in him without really knowing who he was and he asked her if she'd show him Moscow from her standpoint and nature, to his surprise, took its course.

She'd exhibited a sexual athleticism – not to mention imagination – that was as addictive as it was entertaining and she was charming company. She knew he was married but said that she had no interest in upsetting that balance back in England. He brought a smile to her face, she said, and she was flattered that he had taken an interest in her. Perhaps it wouldn't last forever but if he was happy she was happy.

Happy? He was bloody ecstatic. Top quality shags every time he went to Moscow with a lass who seemed to worship him, balding pate and all. What's not to like?

And then a cold shiver interrupted his reverie. The Madden File. Canada. How had he missed the connection when Molyneux called? This didn't feel right. At all.

CHAPTER SEVEN

Ted was up to his neck in the finishing touches to the pending St. Patrick's Day parade with his pals in the Hibernians and didn't notice Cindy hard at it on her lap top the following morning. He grabbed a coffee in his go-mug and a cold pop-tart and legged it with a quick peck on Cindy's cheek and a hurried wave to the kids and Joe.

She was a quick worker, Joe conceded, as she laid before him a print-out of Theresa Madden's family tree.

"Genealogical research is big business over here, given that we all came from somewhere else," she offered. "It's taken five hours and just twenty four dollars to find this lot," she said, pointing to the short family tree showing names, dates of birth and death and last known addresses.

Theresa had died just before the outbreak of the war, aged 67, in her home in 87th Street, Woodhaven, Queens, a respectable neighbourhood with pleasant bow-fronted brick-built terraced houses on straight, tree-lined streets. She had only had the one child, the product of her ill-fated union with Barrington Bell, and named him Sean.

Having moved south from the Cod Banks with Fergal Madden she found lodgings in Hell's Kitchen, a rough warehouse and industrial district in lower Manhattan, finding work as a housekeeper in the Upper East Side. They married – 'to make things decent, like' – in May 1894 not long after Fergal had secured a job as a handyman in the Barclay Hotel. With hard work he reached the role of chief engineer, whilst Theresa's energy had seen her rise to a department manager at Macy's, driving her team and her bonus each year. They ended their lives in comfort in a decent neighbourhood with good schools. It was a far cry from a freezing cod packing plant on subsistence wages.

Sean had been 49 when his mother's letter had been left on his credenza at his home in Pearl River and it must have hit him like a hammer-blow, Joe thought. His father had died four years earlier in an accident in the hotel's plant room, but his mother had been provided for by the hotel's generous widows' scheme and her own savings.

Sean had joined the police as an 18 year-old rookie and ended up a divisional commander, moving his young family to Pearl River for the same reason every other copper had: strong Irish links and no scumbags. He'd married an Irish-American, Kathleen De Lacey, and the couple had just two children, James and Margaret, in 1918 and 1920 respectively. James followed his father into the police and had died on duty in 1958 in a shoot-out at a convenience store raid, leaving his childhood sweetheart, Josie, holding baby Kathleen, a blessing they thought they'd been denied. Margaret never married and there was no record of any children. She had died of cancer in 1999.

"You can see where I've hit the buffers," said Cindy. "Where is Kathleen? That's today's job," she said.

"Blimey, you don't mess around," said Joe, a soft hand on her shoulder. She blushed and made to shrug it off. Ted was her only love and it didn't feel right having another man be intimate with her. Okay, she told herself, he's not being intimate, but all the same.

Joe sensed the slight movement in her and shoved his hands in his jeans pockets. The door bell rang, breaking the tension and Joe offered to get it, relieved at the interruption.

A short fellow with a clipboard and a photo id on a lanyard was there, smiling expectantly. American Market Research Society, it said. Bill Kapowski, researcher. Joe looked at it carefully then relaxed. "What can I do for you, Bill?"

"That's kind of you, sir. I only need two minutes of your time for a couple of quick questions on the state of downtown's sidewalks. The borough is considering some new landscaping and wants a quick straw poll."

Joe wasn't really qualified to say, but if it was only a few questions then he'd just pretend, frankly. A bit of British reserve – unusual in Liverpudlians, admittedly – made him think it would be impolite to turn him away and he didn't want to interrupt Cindy.

"First up, just to confirm who lives here, I presume you're Mr Courtney?"

Joe put him right on that score, explaining, with a smile, that he was Ted's cousin just over from Liverpool for a few weeks' break. Bill asked him, deadpan, if he knew Ringo Starr, then cracked a beaming smile and got on with his survey.

"Well, thank you for your time Mr Delahunty – and enjoy the rest of your stay in Pearl River," offered Bill, before heading back down the path. From the kitchen Joe watched him head for next door, then returned to see what else Cindy had found.

~~~~

Molyneux's inbox chirped the arrival of an email, spelling something important. There was no small talk, funnies and sports banter on his email address – strictly business. Whoever was interrupting his day would have a good reason for doing so.

It was late lunchtime in Liverpool and Molyneux was demolishing a bacon, stilton and black pudding sandwich. Wholegrain bread, wholegrain mustard, bit of salad, no butter. He saw that the mail was from Richter. Quick work, though he knew it wasn't the most challenging assignment as it was pretty straightforward to find out who lived somewhere. The brief was not just to confirm that, though, but to offer a view on anything unusual or noteworthy and to unearth it required a little more guile. And guile was what Richter had in spades, that much he knew.

The report was to the point – no value in being anything else of course. It listed the names and ages of the householders and their occupations, provided a physical description of the home and its setting with some photographs and a Google Earth and Google Maps image attached. It listed Ted's workplace, with a photograph, and noted Cindy's status as a housewife. The kids' school forms at Pearl River High had also been unearthed. There were grab shots, probably taken from a car across the street, of the family, plus Joe, heading off on another run.

The word Liverpool jumped off the page and Molyneux's double-take was pronounced. What was that about? As a seasoned copper Molyneux was no believer in coincidences, even when something patently was one. He was suspicious of everything and every one, a general state of being that had served him well.

"Also in residence is a Mr Joe Delahunty, from Liverpool, cousin of Ted Courtney. He will be in residence for a further fortnight, according to his claim. He is not related to Ringo Starr."

Richter's attempt at humour fell on stony ground, but Molyneux let it pass – his brain was already working overtime. Something about that name was familiar, meaning the alarm sounding in his head would only get louder. What was the connection?

Google, as was often the way, had the answer. The bonking priest. He compared the photograph on The Sun's web site with Richter's grab shot and there was no doubting it. What the fuck was that horrible Paddy twat doing in New York and what was his connection, if at all, to the worryingly precise Google queries that had been pouring, these last two days, from an IP where he was staying?

Molyneux loathed the Irish. Years grappling IRA terrorists had conditioned him to condemn the lot of them as disloyal, bog-trotting half-wits. His upbringing had a bit to do with it, too: his father had been a city councillor for the Protestant Party whose seven seats on Liverpool council kept a minority Tory party in power until 1973, when the city finally cut them loose in favour of the Liberals and Labour. Politically-inspired sectarianism gasped its last, but not everyone was happy with it, Molyneux amongst them. He'd marched with the Orange Lodge for years and was still a member of the Masons, not given to letting left-footers in, even nowadays, when everyone was meant to be cuddling everybody else. Sod that.

Molyneux's reply was concise: Thank you. Payment sent. Await further instructions, but advise if pending capacity is an issue. He always liked to have his ducks in a row, did Molyneux, and if Richter was off helping someone else he'd want to know now.

His instinct told him Delahunty must be behind this. Had to be, given that Liverpool was the common denominator.

He moved quickly. The first job was to get a pencil sketch of Delahunty's life to see what that would tell him, then to decide his first move with the aim of putting an end to all this. Bill McWilliam, a reliable former colleague and a highly diligent detective, was put on the case: "Four hours only. Pencil sketch, please, from the moment he emerged from his whore of a mother to today," he growled, urgency and contempt dripping in equal measure.

He then returned to the Sun's coverage, spending half an hour reading a variety of news links about the saucy priest, the bonking padre or whatever else you wanted to call the shag-happy Paddy bastard. What was clear immediately was why he'd legged it to New York – wouldn't you want to lie low somewhere far away after a shit-storm like that? Yes you would, particularly if you ever wanted another shag. Hard to woo a bird if she's read that she'll be notch number 126 on your bedstead.

And then Molyneux had an idea. A very good one indeed.

~~~~

"Found her!" yelled Cindy triumphantly as Joe came through the door, panting from a fast run. He'd been putting himself through it as these Yanks knew how to ply you with calories. What's with all this pancake and syrup stuff every morning? Any wonder half of them are the size of a mountain.

"Who?" said Joe, hands on his knees and sweat pouring down his nose.

"Kathleen, you eejit!", squealed Cindy, showing him that living with a Mick had rubbed off on her.

"Where is she? What does she do?"

"She's a very brave girl, that's what she is," said Cindy, with obvious admiration. "She's head teacher of Parkway High in the South Bronx. That's a war zone. Oh, and she's Kathleen Fabrini these days."

"What else do you know?" asked Joe, seeing Cindy's face fall, before kicking himself. "Sorry love. Let me start again: Great work, thank you. Have we got an address or any more on her? I think we should be paying her a visit."

Cindy smiled. "Give me half an hour and I'll have it."

"You should be a cop like everyone else around here," Joe offered, with a beaming smile of approval. Cindy blushed, then watched him head upstairs in his tight Lycra running shorts.

~~~~

The head teacher's secretary was old school and not given to passing any personal information about anyone, ever, to anyone, at all, unless it was her mother or husband. And then only under advisement.

"Look, sweetheart, I don't care if you're John Lennon's brother, you ain't getting her to the phone." The Beatles again, not that he'd mentioned Liverpool, before remembering Lennon spent a good chunk of his adult life in New York.

"Can I leave her a contact number and a name, then?" pleaded Joe. "Just tell her that it is about her great-grandmother Theresa Madden and that it's important."

He left the number – Cindy's cell – and waited for the call. By the time it came the following morning Joe's life was back upside down again.

CHAPTER EIGHT

Ted was up first, what with Paddy's day just a few days away and things still to do. He pinched a hot pop tart from the toaster and swigged a long draft of fresh orange straight from the carton whilst putting his jacket on with his free hand. He grabbed his briefcase, shouted his farewells to whoever the bathroom-bound person on the landing was and flung open the front door.

The flash of cameras and the flurry of questions almost sent him reeling. Who the hell were this lot?

"Whoah, whoah, whoah, guys!" he shouted, with his palm out front. "What's this all about? You," he said, pointing at a pretty female reporter in the middle of the small scrum, "tell me, slowly."

"Jenna Rosenhart, PRBC radio, sir. Can you tell our listeners why you're harbouring a sex-pest priest? Is this normal for the Ancient Order of Hibernians in the run up to St. Patrick's Day?" she asked as she thrust her microphone towards him.

Shit, thought Ted, that's blown it. Cindy will do her nut. He'd omitted to share Joe's moral difficulties with her, reckoning there was little point as she was hardly likely to find out and she'd only worry anyhow.

"Guys, guys, he's family. I'm just helping out, not judging. Give me ten minutes will you?" he pleaded as he dipped back inside.

Ted thought quickly because, to be honest, he hadn't the first clue about what to do next. Then he remembered: this year's Parade Committee had decided to retain the services of a PR agency, Linford Santini. A very pretty little number by the name of Anna Heuston was his account manager and she was due in his office this morning. She'd know what to do, surely? Although looking at the size of the scrum, maybe not. But what other choice was there? He searched his cell, found her number and made the call. She was up and ready for her day. There is a God, he thought.

He explained the problem, outlining briefly the tabloid's feeding frenzy in the UK and Joe's fall from grace. Somehow they'd found him here in Pearl River and he wanted to know what he needed to do to get them off his front lawn.

Anna's advice was straightforward. Get Joe out of bed, comb his hair and get him in front of the cameras there and then. If he attempted to hide then they'd camp out until they had word from him. Give them what they wanted now and the storm would pass over – albeit not without further embarrassment to Joe. And, thought Ted, not without a severe kicking from Cindy.

"Can you get here now?" asked Ted. "You'll know how to handle a mob like this and I'll owe you one. Make this problem go away and I'll see to it that the next three years' PR work for the parade is yours."

"Give me twenty minutes," said Anna. "Go tell the journalists that there'll be a press conference in around 35 minutes on your doorstep and that will keep them happy. Meantime, get Fr Delahunty out of bed and scrubbed up, will you?" And with that, the line went dead.

~~~~

Molyneux was in the security bunker tuned into Channel O, the local cable network news channel for Orange County, watching the press conference beamed live via a private satellite feed Richter had secured. Delahunty looked hunted but held himself together well enough, he thought. To his side was a pretty little lass who was bossing the journalists and running the show, it seemed. Where the fuck had the greasy little Mick found her at such short notice, he wondered. Something else that didn't fit.

The questions were as planned: cutting, intrusive and partly aimed at Ted's family for being complicit in harbouring a defrocked, sex-pest priest. Christ, I'm even beginning to sound like a journalist myself, Molyneux admitted.

It was all highly uncomfortable and designed to drive a wedge between Joe and his cousin. Molyneux reckoned that there was no way a morally-upstanding suburban soccer mom would tolerate having Joe in her home, or the media intrusion. What would it do for her reputation? Never mind that: the kids? They had important exams to study for and she couldn't have Joe get in the way of them. And wasn't the daughter fourteen and starting to blossom? An easy target for a pervert like Delahunty, any mom would see that.

If, as he suspected, it was the librarian doing Joe's research bidding, then at least this would put a temporary stop to proceedings whilst he worked out what to do next. It may even bring it all to a juddering stop, which would be the ideal result.

Anna's intercession had worked and the pack retreated with enough quotes and soundbites to fill some good space, what with all the other background that had been printed over in Britain. She wouldn't want to be in Joe's shoes, but hey, priests shouldn't go around sleeping with their parishioners.

Cindy looked ashen as the grown-ups gathered for a conference around the kitchen table. The kids had been kept upstairs whilst it all played out, then sent hurrying to school on their bikes.

"Don't ever blindside me like that again," she growled at Ted. "We'll talk about this tonight when you get in. Joe? You're out of here. You understand why, I know. I have children that need to focus and this sort of circus is just too much of a distraction."

Joe hung his head and the awkwardness was excruciating. "Let me help," Anna chimed. "Get your stuff Joe and I'll take you to this B&B I know."

He looked over at her and stopped, mid-thought. He simply hadn't noticed, amidst the furore, just how lovely this girl was. Petite, about five four, a boyish blonde bob tucked behind her ears with long lashes and milky blue eyes. Better still, she had small, pert breasts and a peach of an arse just like Paula Kelly's and he wondered how he'd missed her. This shit must be getting to me, he thought, as he sprang upstairs alive at the thought of getting to spend a little time with her. The feeling wasn't mutual.

~~~~

The message in Molyneux's in-box was typically brief: 'First objective met. Will follow target.'

He smiled at his own cleverness and tried to imagine the kicking Ted Courtney was in for. If his calculations were right, this should end here.

The scale of that miscalculation was to prove devastating for Molyneux.

~~~~

Joe packed his bags and thanked Cindy and Ted for their kindness, whilst apologizing profusely, once again, for putting them in the firing line. He had one last request of Cindy. "If Kathleen Fabrini calls, can you pass on my cell phone number to her?" He gave Cindy his UK cell number, having altered the permissions with his network provider to allow global roaming, and jumped into Anna's car after hugging them both.

He was off to Rattigan's guest house in downtown, Anna had told him – a good place to lie low for a few days. That suited him as he wanted to be around for the parade, after all, and to be on hand should Kathleen give him a call.

As Anna pulled away a grey Ford Taurus slowly eased out from three cars behind and settled into a well-drilled tail routine.

~~~~

Kathleen made her phone call during morning break. She was naturally curious to know why an Englishman had called with news about her great-grandmother but was short and to the point, New York style.

"What can you tell me? What do you want?" she asked, taking business-like to an altogether new level.

Joe gave her a well-rehearsed summary of what he knew and she listened patiently, giving verbal nods down the phone to confirm that she was listening and that he should carry on.

"Can you be at the school at 4pm?" she asked. "Pick me up in a cab and we can go to a nice café I know in Woodlawn."

Joe spent the rest of the day holed up in his room, watching cable and pondering his predicament. It was three days until the parade and then he'd take stock. He wanted to know what Kathleen would do with his news, though he wasn't sure himself what she should or could do. This was well out of his league, when he thought about it. What on earth had possessed him to pursue it?

And then, for the first time, he asked himself the most obvious question of all: how did the local media pack get wind of him? Only Ted had known and he knew from Ted's shocked reaction and the sure-fire bollocking he was getting from Cindy that it couldn't have been from him. Something wasn't right.

~~~~

Parkway High School was a bleak, four story Victorian block with a playground on its roof, not unlike how they used to be in Liverpool, thought Joe. The surrounding district could only be described as a post-apocalyptic battle zone. He'd seen some rough neighbourhoods in his time as a priest, but this was on another scale. He asked the cab to wait and headed for the entrance.

The security guard at the gate was expecting him and, as was routine, scanned him for weapons before stamping his hand with a blue ink 'V' for visitor and pointing him to the correct entrance. Another guard – Delroy, according to the badge – greeted him cheerily and offered to walk him to Mrs Fabrini's office.

Kathleen Fabrini was a tall, elegant red-head in her early fifties. Slim, with an immediate physical presence and an aura that smacked of charisma, she stood up to greet him with a firm handshake and an even firmer gaze. I'd love to have met you when you were twenty one, Joe thought. That said, it would be a pleasure getting to know you now, he thought. Very much so.

"Welcome, Mr Delahunty. Or is it still Father Delahunty?"

Okay, so you want to be in charge, he thought. I can live with that. But the low blow winded him, nonetheless.

"Joe will do these days," he said, holding her gaze and her handshake. After a long moment's silence Kathleen let go and indicated for him to sit down.

"I dedicate my life to this school, Mr Delahunty, and to the kids of this neighbourhood, for whom my staff and this institution are the only stability many of them know. We hold them together and we show them that they can achieve great things if they want to."

"Our methods are unorthodox, but they work," she went on, expanding on her theme. "We insist on cast iron discipline to provide the calm they need to study. No exceptions. We provide after-school study so that they can do their homework in an environment conducive to it and most kids stay on until past 6pm to succeed and to avoid the disruption that goes with their home lives. And we have holiday clubs to keep them off the streets and to stop them forgetting what they've learned through the year." It sounded impressive, Joe had to admit.

"Some businesses are waking up to what we're achieving, but we still struggle for resources. We force our kids to focus on employability as well as academic performance. No trousers around their butt-cheeks here; no stupid email addresses; learn how to greet adults and shake their hands. That kind of stuff. It's drilled into them, and all the while we tell them they're valued, that they can contribute and that their worth is the same as anyone else's worth. And you know what? Most of them get it and our grade averages and our job placement record are the top of our peer range and better than many schools in much better neighbourhoods. And still we're largely ignored by the education chiefs. What the hell else do they want?" she bristled.

Not getting their balls broken, possibly?

"So if you come in here wanting to take me on a wild goose chase about my great-grandmother you best be aware that goose-chases don't figure in my life. Helping these poor kids is my world, you got that?"

Joe nodded silently, absorbing the whirlwind and admitting that he was hugely impressed. Looking out of the window to the war zone outside he could appreciate just what an achievement it was to get the kids to turn up and study, never mind succeed, and he started taking more of a shine to the feisty Mrs Fabrini.

"You promised me a coffee and I've got a cab waiting outside. You still up for one?" And with his prompt she rose, smiled, and ushered him out of the room.

~~~~

Molyneux's email beeped again. It was Richter, still on Delahunty's tail. Why had he gone to a school in the South Bronx? What was he up to? How was it related to Bell?

Richter would know what he needed and he had, after all, asked him to update him on anything – anything – that he might consider out of the ordinary. And some slimeball Paddy priest with a wayward dick does not turn up to a school in the South Bronx without good reason – especially when he's never been to New York before. God, I hate Catholics, Molyneux thought. Irish Catholics even more.

Richter sat in his car, iPad and iPhone working overtime as he sought to find the connection that he knew Molyneux would crave. He'd have it soon and if he was a betting man it would have something to do with Theresa Madden. Molyneux had given him her name and explained that she had caused the firm difficulties in the 1890s and that was it – need to know, but he needed to know that much. Relatives have a habit of springing up out of nowhere at the first mention of money and, this being Bell Group, that's all it could mean.

~~~~

Waiting for them at the Hub Café on Katonah Avenue was a diminutive lady in a plain white blouse and navy suit that was on the edge of tatty. Frizzy brown hair, a Roman nose and swarthy skin: got to be a four-by-two, thought Joe. She jumped to her feet, crushed his hand and introduced herself in a comic-book Noo Yoik accent. Christ, do people still speak like that? Yes, they do.

"Roz Goldstein," she barked, "lawyer." A Jew it is then, he thought, not that it had been the hardest anthropological test of the day. Jesus was a Jew, he reminded himself, in a rare reflection on the fact that until recently he had a calling; a ministry sworn to help others, do good and preach the Word of the Lord. He sighed, banished the thought, then looked up.

"She's also an inseparable friend, great adviser and a mean poker player," added Kathleen.

Blimey, thought Joe, I might not get out alive.

"I took the liberty of sharing your summary with Roz when I went to the bathroom," said Kathleen. Ah yes, she'd popped to the loo before they'd returned to the waiting cab.

"She shares everything with me," Roz butted in. "Well, almost everything," and the two laughed, or rather Kathleen did whilst Roz cackled.

"I want Roz to know everything you know and for you to fill in what gaps you can with me, then we can decide what, if anything, we do."

Joe pulled out Theresa Madden's letter from his backpack just as the waitress came over to take their order and they got down to business.

CHAPTER NINE

Sir Meredith had personally overseen the deal with the Russians. Slippery customers, he knew, and he wanted to see the whites of their eyes every step of the way - not to mention agreement up front that the courts of England & Wales would have jurisdiction in the event of any dispute. Sorry chaps, he'd said, but it's fair to say commercial law is a bit more reliable back home.

He needed their technical expertise, their access to cheap money and their distribution channels; they lacked his drilling licence and land ownership and knew that if Bell Resources didn't select them then they'd be locked out of the opportunity completely. It was a step into the North American market and a prize very much worth having.

So Sir Meredith had the whip hand and had agreed a stepped deal. Fifteen per cent share ownership in a new energy subsidiary in return for £200m to fund geological surveys, test drilling and capital equipment, with a further 35% shareholding once a viable supply of at least a billion cubic metres had been confirmed. To the Russians the uplift in shareholding equated to about £450m in immediate capital value and at least £95m a year in clear profit over the remaining twenty three years of the drilling licences' lifetime.

So, all told, it was a good deal and the provincial government of Newfoundland and Labrador had given it their blessing. Bell had spare land and quaysides at its old cod processing plant, largely moth-balled since the last of the cod fleet had been bought out to preserve what was left of stocks in 1993.

The truth was that they'd never got around to selling it off – other fish to fry, Bell had cracked, smiling at his own joke. So, no great strategic insight, then. Just happenstance, but a very profitable one at that. There were a few examples of that in the illustrious history of Bell Group.

It was one half of the Madden legacy, as those few who knew the real story called it. The other was a fairly worthless chunk of exposed foreshore at Maddox Cove on the eastern, Atlantic-facing shoreline of the St. John's peninsula. They'd never made use of it – too exposed to build a harbour for small trawlers and a bit of a hike over impassable hills or around an unreliable coastal track for anything else. But the Bell philosophy in such circumstances was that the Good Lord wasn't making any more land so best keep hold of it.

And then came the great leap forward in gas drilling technology which allowed prospectors to extract, profitably, carbon trapped within hard shale. The process, known as fracking, involved sending a drill pipe down into the shale and injecting water, sand and chemicals at incredible pressure to fracture the shale and release the gas. The same pipe would then gather it and bring it to the surface for processing. The best bit, thought Bell, was the fact that the drill pipes could bend, meaning that you could come into the shale horizontally, if need be, rather than just vertically with the traditional method. This opened up even more shale beds for exploration and exploitation because of the angle at which sedimentary beds lay.

The early technology was flawed but rising gas and oil prices saw a wall of cash get behind the boffins and some very clever folk indeed had perfected the technology. Well, relative to earlier attempts, anyway. War in the middle east and the rapid growth of the BRIC economies was a toxic combination for western economies used to low cost energy. Speculation married with high demand saw the price of both oil and gas rocket and stay there.

Worse, the bulk of known recoverable stocks were in countries best described by diplomats as 'challenging', meaning run by nut-jobs on a short fuse who liked to stone women, hang gays and suppress just about every freedom the West took for granted. Or the stuff was buried beneath Russia, which liked to throw its weight about and could prove an especially unreliable partner.

And so, in spite of concerns among environmentalists, fracking was greeted enthusiastically by western governments as a means of becoming self-sufficient in energy, reducing huge capital flows to despots. In the case of the USA the country generated such a surplus that it became, for the first time in its history, a net exporter of energy. Clean gas, a boost to a nation's balance of payments position and less reliance on grouchy Ruskis and crazed towel-heads. There was a lot to like in that for your average government.

Better still, geological calculations showed that there was oodles of the stuff in the West. Hundreds and hundreds of years' supply, even based on projections showing continued growth in demand. The yoghurt-knitters, as Bell called them, didn't like this at all. For a moment they thought they'd succeeded in putting us on a trajectory back to caves, but science always wins out and solves our problems, he noted, smugly.

All of which got him thinking. Canada was already awash with oil sand so what about shale gas? He'd seen how Alberta was swimming in money from exploration licenses and a handy tax or two on recovered stocks and he thought it worth a punt to see what lay off Newfoundland.

He brought in GeoCore, a geological surveying and mapping business to provide an elementary assessment of his chances. Just tell me if the rock strata out there gives me a prayer, he'd said. If it didn't, it was a thirty grand punt, but if it did then he was into a different ball game altogether.

The report was disappointingly thin when it landed on his desk and, rich as he was, he began to ponder what else he could have spent thirty thousand quid on. The hairs on the ears of a good racehorse, perhaps? Half a hospitality box at Liverpool's famous Anfield stadium? Or six of the best days' grouse shooting imaginable. It was the latter thought that made him most gloomy.

Still, that was the nature of his business. You took risks and calculated the odds and 4.9% growth in turnover this year during a global slump told him he wasn't making too poor a fist of it. So bollocks to all that, he thought, and he cheered himself up.

Pulling the report from the brown manila envelope marked 'STRICTLY CONFIDENTIAL – TO BE OPENED BY ADDRESSEE ONLY' his pulse ticked up a notch when he saw the words Executive Summary – so not the full thing then. He brightened up further as he read on and within two minutes he was grinning wildly.

Beneath the preliminary guff and some deft arse-covering was the professionals' view that not only was the rock off St John's highly likely to contain shale gas, but that it was relatively close to the shallow in-shore sea-bed and also on-shore. They could not predict likely volume – that'd be another three million quid, please – but their professional opinion was that the cost of any further assessment was a better than evens risk. Moreover, the nearest landfall was Maddox Cove, which, at a cursory glance, would prove an ideal landfall for the pipelines and associated storage and distribution infrastructure. With no neighbours and a sloping shoreline perfect for constructing piers, marshalling yards and jetties, it was as near to ideal as it got. 'Did the client know who owned it?' the report asked.

Bell sat back and pondered his place in the pantheon of his illustrious relatives and suddenly realized that if he pulled this off no-one would give a flying fig that he hadn't sired a son. So he called an extraordinary board meeting and put things in train. That was three years ago.

His business had always sought close and cordial relations with any government of any political stripe in any territory where they had strategic assets. Their line into the British government's Foreign & Commonwealth Office had been oiled assiduously since the late eighteenth century and, together with the Department for Trade & Industry, they had supported Bell Resources' quiet diplomacy with the Newfoundland & Labrador provincial government. After two years' negotiation they helped them seal four 25 year drilling licences along the St. John's coastline.

Sir Meredith was grouse shooting when he was introduced to Nikolas Adaksin by Sir Quentin Fanshaugh, permanent aid to the foreign secretary. Nikolas was CEO of the giant NovKos Holdings, a £40bn turnover Russian oil and gas major, Sir Quentin explained, before leaving them to it.

On the steep walk up the heather-covered moor to the fourth drive, Sir Quentin engineered himself next to Sir Meredith and explained that the FCO was keen to improve links with the Russians and that assisting it in its commercial interests, where it could, was part of that.

"You've just got those licenses off Newfoundland, Merry, and these chaps would love a dig at the North American market. We could engineer it so that you got their expertise and cheap money in exchange for a piece of the action. Lots of technical help from our guys and some big diplomatic brownie points along the way. Think about it, will you?"

Which, in diplomatic speak, meant 'jolly well play ball or we'll screw you over the next three times you ask for help.'

The shooting party retired to the Inn at Whitewell to enjoy the sort of sumptuous accommodation and food you'd expect in the Queen's own boozer. It tickled Adaksin to think that the Queen of England should own a pub and he proved to be well-read on British history and rather jolly company too, Bell noted. He watched him carefully amidst the mix of bankers, lawyers and industrialists and saw a man at ease with himself. He was bright and opinionated, but had facts and figures at his fingertips to back up his case too. A man who stays on top of the detail, Bell saw. Excellent.

Back at the firm's Liverpool base, Bell had Molyneux prepare a briefing note on Adaksin and NovKos and studied its contents thoroughly before deciding what to do. Adaksin had proven an astute operator, exploiting the chaos of the Soviet Union's disintegration to snap up disparate, under-valued exploration rights and seemingly tired old wells and refineries. He'd greased a lot of palms – still greased them – and there was more than a whiff of criminal derring-do about the chap. He'd have done well in Bell Group, Sir Meredith thought, reflecting on the firm's skullduggery during the slave trade, the potato famine and, of course, Great-great grandfather Barrington's neat little shuffle with the Madden woman.

So, the fellow was sharp, astute and clearly had balls of steel to thrive in the bandit-infested lands of post-revolutionary Russia. Eyes wide open, old chap, he said to himself. Eyes wide open.

The FCO and in particular Sir Quentin proved highly useful in helping them smooth through the negotiations with the Russians. As of course did Barlow Hayes, the firm's enormous legal advisers, whose Liverpool office was the second oldest in a global network spanning 161 cities, Moscow included. A six and a half million pound fee note will fund a few nice bonuses come year end, Sir Meredith thought. Better get an invite to the Christmas party.

It was on the second of his trips to Moscow that Sir Meredith caught the eye of the very lovely Anatalia and the year of to-ing and fro-ing proved tiring but worthwhile. 'That thing she did with her right forefinger…' His mind trailed off. He'd never experienced anything like that before. He should have to have a word with Caroline. On second thoughts, maybe not.

The Ruskis had proven tough negotiators yet were keen to do the deal and always made that clear, "but you have to understand, Sir Meredith, that I have issues in my back yard that require me to secure value and to reach my margin targets," Nikolas had explained. Yes, like bunging the president a few bob, I don't doubt, thought Bell.

The spirit of partnership had prevailed. The deal was struck and celebrated in Moscow and Liverpool with lavish entertaining. Whilst the Liverpool party opted not to invest in a raft of African prostitutes and half a kilo of cocaine, it was a jolly affair nonetheless.

An expensively-recruited team at Bell Resources was assembled to play their part in the test drills. They had gone surprisingly well and preliminary results, just in, had proven that at least 200m cubic metres of gas reserves were available for immediate extraction. There were three more test drills to do within their first licence zone and the expectation was that the recoverable stocks would tip them over the billion cubic metres mark and NovKos would see their stake ratcheted up to 50% and with it huge capital growth and a much more substantial flow of annual dividends. A lot rode on the outcome and the Russian chief engineer and his bluff Texan counterpart, Marley Clitheroe, felt the pressure from on high.

~~~~

Sir Meredith made the call personally to Nikolas. It wasn't a big deal, he felt, but it was clearly the right thing to do. Partnerships often went through rocky patches, but they recovered if the men at the top were straight with one another and wanted it to succeed. So he must tell him about the Madden file – albeit a gilded version – for it wasn't something he'd want him to find out from a third party, that's for sure.

Nikolas listened carefully as Sir Meredith explained that there had always been some small doubt about elements of their title to the land deal struck in 1890 for Maddox Cove. Their monitoring of the situation identified that someone was digging around the subject and his private security people had intercepted them and were dealing with them right now. He expected the problem to disappear, one way or another, but felt it prudent as Nikolas's partner on the venture, to raise it with him.

The silence was unsettling – just the faintest sound of Adaksin breathing and, doubtless, his brain whirring away.

"You will understand that we expect you to deal with this conclusively," said Adaksin, with a steel in his voice that Bell had not heard before, even in the tougher moments of their negotiation.

"In our experience, people like this want too heavy a price to melt away, but melt away they must. I trust your people are of the right type to ensure that happens?" he asked. "Tell me now, because if they are not I shall have my team see to it."

Bell didn't like the way this conversation was going. It was all well and good him being tough when he needed to be around the board room table and it was all jolly good having an easy accommodation with the dark stains on the company's past, but he'd never committed any wrong-doing and wasn't about to sanction what he felt Adaksin was implying. No way.

"Nikolas, I can assure you that my people are the very best and are, in fact, in the middle of settling this matter as I speak. It has moved quickly, as these things often do, and this has been the first and I hope the last time that I will need to brief you on it."

"See to it that it is," Adaksin growled. "I have £200m invested in this," and with that the phone went dead.

CHAPTER TEN

Roz, Joe and Kathleen were on their third refill at the Hub Café and were starting to get a little wired, but the conversation, at Roz's instigating, had taken a very interesting turn.

Kathleen's initial stance had been sorrow that her dear great-grandmother Theresa had been treated so badly, but she took heart that her life's course recovered well through her partnership with Fergal and that subsequent generations had climbed up the ladder, living out the American Dream of ever-increasing prosperity as they went. 'So thanks for the great story, Joe, and can I keep the letter as an heirloom?' went her conclusion.

Roz's jaw hit the floor.

"Are you absolutely fuckin' nuts?" she asked, incredulous. "Let me spell it out to you, lady. You have spent your career refining your model until you hit on something that is genuinely changing the lives of some of the city's poorest kids. Okay, so no Nobel Prize winners yet, but by the standards of their peers your guys are in clover – and you don't normally find clover fields in the South Bronx. You're their ticket out and by keepin' 'em on the straight and narrow you're saving the country a fortune. A fortune," she emphasized, thinking how the cost of the judicial systems weighed heavily on the nation.

"The big thing is that government ain't noticed yet. They ain't bothered enough and they oughtta be. But business is noticing and where they go, the government follows. Your school, your methods: they should be state-wide, even nationwide. Wherever there's a ghetto, there's a need for The Fabrini Method."

Kathleen was listening, and clearly flattered, Joe thought. But she was interested too and thoughts were forming behind her furrowed brow.

"So listen up, lady, because here's the big opportunity. We screw these limey bastards…"

"Steady-on," Joe interrupted, feigning insult and raising a smile.

"Hey, you're supposed to be a Mick, so leave it out," cracked Roz with a push on his shoulder.

"Look, here's where it's at: you gotta golden chance to leverage some serious investment out of these Brits to help you deliver your dream. Whether it's just better – and more of better – out there in the South Bronx, or a chain of schools in every ghetto in the country, they owe you and the law says they should pay."

Roz puffed her tiny frame and outsized chest upwards and she looked for affirmation that hers was a plan. The plan, in fact.

Kathleen didn't buy it. "How the hell do we prove this? That letter could be from anyone and the absence of anything on the internet suggests all this could be a load of baloney. And who's gonna take on their attorneys? They'll have the biggest Wall Street hot-shots money can buy."

Roz looked hurt. "You don't think I can handle this? You think the little Jewish girl ain't got daddy's balls or brains to put one over these preppy Wall Street types? Let me tell you, my end of the law sharpens you up for anything. It ain't the soft-hand, penny loafer shit that makes pussies out of men. My stuff is for real and I ain't afraid of their offices. The law works for all folks and I know how the law works," she said, riding indignantly on her caffeine wave.

"There are too many problems," Kathleen argued, after a few moments' silence. "First up, money. They'll fight long, hard and dirty to beat us and none of us has the resources for that."

Joe nodded his assent on that score. Even in Liverpool they'd eat his monthly £5,000 pay-off in the blink of an eye, and office space there cost a fraction of Wall Street's.

"Second, we need something more than this letter. Other evidence. Something that would back them into a firmer corner and force them to parley with us. I just don't see where that is coming from. Yes, I'd love to see my dream funded and more of my kids given the chances we all had, but howling at the moon ain't gonna get me there." She sounded deflated, as though Roz's performance had lifted her. But she saw no way through it all and made to change the subject.

And then Joe's cell rang and George Molyneux made a mistake that would ultimately cost him his life.

~~~~

It hadn't taken Richter long to identify that the elegant red haired lady heading out with Joe Delahunty was the school Principal, Kathleen Fabrini. The red hair was the giveaway. Gotta be Irish. Can't be an Italian, he thought to himself. And how many Italians do you know called Kathleen, for fuck's sake. He should have spotted it sooner. He'd been trying to figure what the connection was with Theresa Madden and two related Paddies up in Pearl River and it had now finally twigged.

He hit the genealogy websites with a vengeance, focusing first on those for Irish Americans, and his second hit came up trumps. Well, well, well. If she wasn't Theresa Madden's great-granddaughter.

~~~~

Molyneux took the news down in the bunker with his usual terse gratitude but, out of sight, allowed himself a small smile. I'll have that shag-nasty Paddy bastard now, he thought.

The connection to Joe's cell phone was immediate and clear as a bell, even at that distance. He was only made to wait two rings when the call picked up.

"Hello," came a cautious voice at the other end. I'm not surprised, thought Molyneux, after the roasting you've had from the tabloids. And serves you right.

"Delahunty, you don't know me, and you don't ever want to." Joe was taken aback at hearing a Liverpool accent again after nearly two weeks and he wondered why the call number was blocked.

The threat put him on alert and he put his finger to his lips before laying the iPhone on the table and putting it on loudspeaker as well as 'record'.

"What is it, pal?" Joe asked, with a harshness to his accent the ladies didn't recognize.

"Look, I'll keep this brief, you half-witted Fenian. Stop me if I'm talking too quickly, will you?"

"You've got it part right so far, though who are you calling a Fenian? I'm from Bootle," Joe quipped. Whoever this eejit was, Joe was up for some verbal jousting. That was the Liverpool way.

"My name is Molyneux and I want you to listen. Whatever it is you think you are doing with that Theresa Madden thing stops now. Right now. You walk away from it and we all get on with our lives. If you do not I will unleash a shit-storm on you and your two lady friends so bad you'd wish you'd stayed in bed."

They all shot each other glances and looked around, before Joe put his fingers to his lips again. He wanted him to carry on. Apart from incriminating himself, Joe sensed some fear in his voice and Kathleen did, too.

"That media ambush the other day? That was just a starter for ten. Your reputations will be ruined and your lives with it by the time we've finished with you. Am I making myself clear?" Molyneux asked, rhetorically.

"If I am not, let me spell it out further. That Fabrini bird you've been eyeing up, she's head teacher of Parkway High, right? Well you can tell her from me that unless she drops this now her school and her precious fuckin' kids will rue the day."

Kathleen bristled at the threat and suppressed a yelp as Roz clasped a firm hand over her mouth and held her back.

"No-one wants anyone to get hurt, but they will if this doesn't end now," said Molyneux. "You are all out of your depth. Way out of it in fact," he added, softening his tone, "so just let it lie."

"Okay mate, if that's how you want it," said Joe, entreating the ladies with a look to stay with him on this.

"It is."

"Then we'll keep out of your hair," said Joe.

"Good," came Molyneux's reply, although the ambiguity in Joe's response nagged him. Surely these amateurs wouldn't carry on after a warning like that, he thought. A priest who's had enough shit to shovel for a lifetime and female teacher in her fifties? Nah, they wouldn't be up for what I'd throw at them and he'd bet his life that they'd never before faced a conversation like that. If menace could do the job – and it usually did with people like this – then perfect. No bloodshed, no personal visits, no evidence. Just some silly people scared witless and ruing the day they'd ever got involved.

"We'll leave it at that then," said Molyneux and the line clicked to signal the end of their conversation.

He turned immediately to his PC and began typing a briefing note to Sir Meredith. His professional conclusion was that that would be the end of it, but he would keep Richter on standby for another day or two just in case.

Bell was relieved and, still rattled from his earlier conversation with Adaksin, decided to put his mind at rest, too. He didn't fancy a night tossing and turning any more than Nikolas would, he was sure.

"Nikolas, I am assured that the matter we discussed earlier has now gone away," purred Sir Meredith. "I am sorry I troubled you with it, but partners share these things or it isn't much of a partnership, is it?"

"A proper partner would have told us at the beginning. I hope for everyone's sake there are no more skeletons in the Bell cupboard," he replied, coldly.

There are bloody grave yards full of 'em, thought Sir Meredith, but this was the only Canadian one so that should be that.

"No, you can sleep well tonight on that score," said Bell.

"Oh, I would have anyway," said Nikolas, airily, before bidding good night and putting down the phone. Bell blanched and took a slug of his Scotch, a fine single malt. But it didn't hit the mark.

~~~~

The three of them looked at each other dumb-founded. Joe fiddled with his iPhone until he could replay the conversation and they sat, in silence, as they listened to it again.

"Email that to me now so we have another copy," barked Roz. "Belt and braces. You got another email account so that you can send it to that too?" she asked. Joe nodded and the audio track headed out several ways into cyberspace.

Roz jumped up and headed for the door. "Wanna see who's been following us." She marched out to the pavement and looked up and down the street but, try as she might, there was nothing out of the ordinary. A bloke with a clipboard was taking down details from the parking metres and an old lady was walking with her dog. Other pedestrians came and went in the way of normal suburban main streets and she sighed before retreating back indoors.

"He threatened us," Kathleen said, quietly. It got their attention. "That means he's scared." She'd seen enough school yard bullies in her time to know that threats are almost always underscored by fear.

"It means there's truth in the letter. We have a case, although we've still got to prove it," she added. "And nobody threatens my kids and my school," she whispered as she gazed across Katona Street.

~~~~

The press conference was timed for 10:45am the next morning. That way they would hit the lunchtime news bulletins as well as the rolling news feeds beforehand. It would be on the web in a flash too, and, if their calculations were right, social media networks as well.

The financial reporters at Bloomberg, Reuters and the Financial Times had been told that they'd be particularly interested in what was to be discussed and papers with an investigative reputation in the UK, such as The Guardian and Sunday Times, tipped the wink.

If the business editor at the Liverpool Echo was taken aback at receiving a call from New York telling him he would absolutely want to tune into the press conference via his office satellite feed, he hid it well. What was going on over there with a Liverpool connection, he wondered. It would be nearly 4pm by then and they'd be working on the next morning's first edition, so if the story was a big one then it left them plenty of time to gain supplementary quotes from whomever was affected by it, whilst posting a truncated version on their massive web site immediately. The paper had a daily readership of a quarter of a million and an equally large following amongst ex-pat Liverpudlians on its web site and however this news affected the city, it would be the talk of the town by tea-time, he was sure of that.

A room had been hurriedly booked at the Marriott, a few blocks west of Wall Street in the heart of Lower Manhattan's financial district. Might as well bring Mohammed to the mountain, they thought. Park your tanks on their lawn, they agreed. That would rattle them.

Anna Heuston had been brought into their plan the evening before and had listened carefully to the issues before setting out a strategy for Roz to refine. Staying on the right side of the law was critical so long as it left them room to fulfil their principal objective: cause maximum mayhem. And they were absolutely confident that this would cause mayhem – so much so that this was her sell-in line to the harassed news desks of New York's newspapers and TV stations.

"Believe me when I tell you I am happy to stake my entire reputation with you going forward when I say that this will cause mayhem. You do not want to be taking someone else's feed by the time we've finished," she said, over and over again. And from the responses she was getting, she figured on a fairly busy room.

There were no promises, she explained to her 'team' as she now called them. If Mayor Bloomberg announces he has a terminal illness or Prince Charles drops dead then all eyes will be turned elsewhere, but if famous people manage not to die, then we should be okay, she assured them all. They were in her hands. What did they know about such things?

Each of them was prepared to overlook Anna's tender years and it proved to be a good call.

~~~~

Richter stayed with them all evening, wondering what was detaining them so long in a place like Hub. Okay, it was funky, in the way of these independent cafes, but it hardly had the largest of menus. 'Left wing food' like lentil salad, as he dismissed it – and those chairs didn't look like places you'd want to park your butt all night. He'd popped into the café after a while to see if he could overhear their conversation, but it was busy with evening diners and the nearest table turned out to be in the far corner. The clatter and buzz defeated him, just as his disguise defeated Joe. "Crikey, those market researchers get about," was a response he didn't want to hear.

They were leaned in close to one another with their heads down so lip-reading any of them to get an approximate take on the discussion was out of the question and his view was partially obscured by a large pillar, in any event.

He couldn't figure out who the short, feisty looking lady with the big chest was so he decided that she'd be his tail that night. He knew where Joe and Kathleen would be going, not having reckoned on their reaction to Molyneux's unhelpful phone call, so it was the Ay-talian looking broad he'd go for. Or was she Jewish? Didn't both those races wave their arms around a lot? He flipped a mental coin and settled on Ay-talian.

~~~~

Anna Heuston had been at Linford Santini three years since majoring in PR from Columbia University. She was a sharp cookie, a born hustler and as ambitious as they get. She'd risen from intern to junior account executive and upwards to account manager. She was a year ahead of the curve, she thought, for a firm of this size and standing, so she was happy that she was delivering on her career goals and career was where she was at right now.

All aspects of normal life were on hold whilst she climbed the greasy pole. No boyfriend, no pet, too little contact with her mom in Woodside and never enough partying. But the plan was on track and that was all that counted. By twenty eight she hoped to be an account director overseeing three or four of the firm's big business-to-business clients. She preferred corporate work to consumer PR, but was more than happy to steal good ideas from her consumer colleagues and mould them to suit the shipping company, pet-food wholesaler and airline maintenance outfit at JFK on whose accounts she worked. She was popular, this diminutive Irish kid – no heads or toes were being trampled on during her rise to the top and she was a team player as well as a leader when she needed to be. It was working out, she knew, and men could wait.

The Paddy's Day parade thing was a distraction, albeit an enjoyable one. The firm's CTO was born in Dublin not that you could tell from his accent, she thought. He was a bit of a cheese in the Hibernians, wangling them on to the pitch list as a result. They'd low-balled on the fee to win it, figuring that the rest of the board would allow him this one indulgence, and it proved correct. There were so many influential Irish Americans around New York that it was worth almost going pro bono. Anna was brought on to the team because of her own heritage: Grandpa Eamonn was from Dundalk and had been in the Hibernians' NYFD branch.

Joe had caught her wrapped in a towel, sitting at her desk in her small Windsor Terrace apartment on Prospect Park, producing a plan for next week's client review at Foxwell Pet Products. She didn't need reminding of who he was and he had her ear when he said they had a major issue with Bell Group and would welcome her advice. She worked for one of Bell's major rivals in the trans-atlantic container market and instantly calculated the brownie points that might flow from putting a spoke in her rival's wheels. She always felt that level of ownership of clients: it was as though she worked for them directly and she would immerse herself in their industries so that she could hold her own in any conversation as well as spot the opportunities for out-gunning the opposition. It was always the way in trade PR – a lot of players in any market would be asleep on the job, leaving the sharper cookies room to run rings around them.

Joe explained that she was on loud-speaker and introduced Kathleen and Roz. He believed they were being followed or monitored in some way so it wasn't safe or sensible for her to come out and meet them, nor was there time. After what she'd done for him on Ted's doorstep the other day he knew she could help them and she was the only person they could turn to. Would she help?

Anna saw the possibilities immediately. She had no client meetings the following morning and hers was a firm that gave staff latitude to re-arrange diaries and even take 'duvet days' if they wanted. The bosses knew how hard everyone worked and cutting them some slack in a structured way just made sense. Especially if they wanted to keep rising stars like Anna Heuston – the majors like Hill & Knowlton were always hovering, trying to steal the brightest from the smaller practices like Linford Santini.

And so she put her work on Foxwell's campaign review to one side, sent an email to her boss requesting emergency leave and began what would turn out to be a career-defining conversation.

~~~~

"One last thing," cautioned Anna, having sought and secured agreement on her final summation of tomorrow's plan, "you're not going home."

The three of them looked at each other, puzzled.

"This may sound paranoid, but it isn't when you think about it. Someone has been tailing you and digging around into your background for Molyneux and the likelihood is they'll still be watching you now."

Their heads and eyes swivelled. They had been so engrossed in working through the details of their plan that they'd forgotten the circumstances around the need for a conference call. Where was he, this super-sleuth who'd gone unnoticed? There was a man in the corner who'd spent an inordinate amount of time on a crossword and the lady two tables down had seemed overly interested in what her neighbouring tables were up to before she left.

It wasn't a comfortable feeling at all. How the hell had they all got embroiled in this, Kathleen thought, until she remembered the letter. Ah, yes, her dear great-grandmother whom she'd never met.

"I'll check you in now to the Marriott. We've got a corporate rate with them and they've got the laundry facilities to clean your clothes for tomorrow morning. You're not going home, that's for certain," she said, enjoying taking control.

~~~~

Richter reported back to his client in England that his subjects had left the Hub café after almost three hours, hailing separate cabs. He'd opted to tail the one person he didn't know to try and get a handle on how she figured in this group and something didn't feel right about all this. He hated second-guessing, much as it was inevitable in his job. But he had to concentrate on what he knew, and finding the facts on what he didn't. Speculation was only helpful in so much as it gave him pointers to consider that might help him unearth the truth.

Molyneux's response was characteristically terse as he agreed to Richter's assessment. What were they up to, he wondered. He wouldn't trouble the boss with this yet – only substantive things, not every beat of an operation. That's what he was paid to deal with. And paid handsomely, he had to admit. Good bloody job after that grasping cow of a wife of his had taken him to the cleaners during their divorce. 'Unreasonable behaviour and neglect' her writ had cited. The ungrateful bitch. He'd bust his bollocks providing for her and the kids and that was his reward. If there was any compensation it was that he was able to play the field, when time allowed and he'd enjoyed 'a bit of different', too, bedding, at the last count Chinese, French and West Indian girls. But he wasn't like that shag-happy priest he was chasing. That guy had no morals whatsoever.

~~~~

The cab wove in and out of the traffic as it headed south through Manhattan. Richter was practised at staying in touch without drawing attention to himself and, in any event, the cab driver wouldn't be expecting a tail. The greatest threat lay in falling the wrong side of a red light and watching his target disappear in the distance so he stayed just two cars back and only had to gun the accelerator twice to stay in touch.

Roz had explained her instructions from Anna to the driver and paid him upfront, with a more than generous estimation of the cost thrown in for good measure. Speed and surprise would be the essence if they were to lose their tail. One of them would be followed if the logic of what had happened that evening was correct and if they were to stand a chance of putting their plan into place without disruption, then they had to play their man at his own game, argued Anna.

Christ, thought Joe, what sort of up-bringing did this kid have to know all this stuff? Was her dad a mafia boss, he wondered? Unlikely, given her surname. Surely a diet of Law & Order didn't teacher her all this shit?

Anna was to have one last card up her sleeve that was to prove the ace in her pack. And it was just intuitive - common sense, even – she told herself.

~~~~

The cab lurched to the right across two lanes of traffic, horns blaring as cars skidded to avoid it. A beat cop a block away raised his head as he heard the skids and started walking toward the source of the noise. The traffic wasn't too heavy at that time of the night but that was the problem: it was flowing at a reasonable speed, meaning any immediate response from Richter was fraught with danger. If he got into a fender-bender then he'd have some explaining to do about those false plates. His senses went into overdrive, eyes darting between rear view mirror and side mirrors whilst trying to work out his options. He needed to park up and follow his target but his rear view told him she was already heading down the steps of the 6th Avenue subway station.

Richter's mental map of the subway network was as good as any hardened New Yorker's and it told him he was doomed if he didn't get in sight of the little lady quickly. With trains every one hundred and twenty seconds she'd be beyond his reach within about sixty seconds.

A space presented itself to him thirty yards ahead to the left and he swerved across a lane, cutting up a cab and prompting a long, angry blast on the horn as he nosed into his possible salvation. His dash across the traffic was equally fraught and Officer Garcia quickened his pace as another cacophony of horns rang out.

Where the hell was she? He knew it would be impossible but he had to try. Give her her due, she'd thought about this. Sixth Avenue allowed her to go north or south on the 6 Avenue Express or to connect through to the 14th Street subway to go east/west on the 14 Street-Canarsie Local. A few stops in any direction and she could change to another line and be lost forever. If she was on a train now then she'd won, but he had a four to one chance of picking the right platform if he'd managed to get there in time.

He saw her frizzy hair disappearing behind the closing doors as he turned on to the platform. The train was heading north to Central Park, but that signified nothing. The network's inter-connectivity meant direction of travel could have no bearing on your ultimate destination if you were in a situation like this. Doubling back on yourself was easy, even for a tourist, provided they could read a subway map. And she didn't look like a visitor, something told him.

He gave up the chase. Futility wasn't his thing. He had other options to investigate now and he exited the way he came and froze as he reached the street, forced yet again to re-calculate. A police officer was walking around the grey Ford Taurus and radioing in a message of some sort, probably checking its plates as the quickest way of establishing who the driver may be.

It had caught his attention, parked at an odd angle. Someone had been in a hurry and a series of sharply-sounded horns, spaced out in two blasts added up to the right scenario. Garcia knew he could make the grade as a detective and this was the sort of instinct and savvy that was already getting him noticed by the brass beyond his desk sergeant.

Richter knew it would be moments before the news that they were hooky plates was radioed back to the officer and he turned on his heels, blending in with the crowd as he worked out what to do next. The plates couldn't lead back to home in Riverdale and as he wasn't in the system personally, either print-wise or for DNA. His habit of using leather driver's gloves gave the police less to work with, too. The car had been stolen from New Jersey to order so the chassis number couldn't lead back to him. Its loss was an occupational hazard and on his pay rates a new one was comfortably within his business budget. Good job he'd grabbed his iPad off the front seat, mind.

~~~~

Roz's heart was beating furiously and she admitted to herself that she was no Michelle Pfeiffer. But forget being a heroine: just getting through this in one piece would do her. If she could make that press conference then her career was on a new trajectory altogether, of that she was sure. Her time as a main street hustler in the South Bronx for low-life scum and hard-done-to traders would be over. It had served her well enough – a nice apartment in Washington Heights, a BMW 3 series and a pension that was the right side of the line, but truth be told she'd love to spend her days dealing with what was at hand rather than defending poor families from eviction notices.

She'd met Kathleen Fabrini representing one of her pupils accused of stabbing his drunk of a father who had taken his belt to him once too often. DeShaun Campbell was facing a manslaughter rap and possibly 12 years inside and once in the system there was little left of life for a poor black boy from his side of the tracks.

Roz and Kathleen had fought tooth and nail for the kid, using their knowledge of the system to pull an impressive array of character witnesses and offers of agency support to sway the judge and DA. He'd been advised to plead guilty on a plea bargain whilst they negotiated the best deal they could and the DA had settled on 18 months in a youth detention centre, with time off for good behaviour and commitment to various educational and corrective training programmes.

Six months later Kathleen had wept endlessly on Roz's shoulders when they had shared the news that he'd been stabbed to death in a petty squabble on the prison's recreation yard, and their bond was sealed. They were the only white folk at his sparsely attended funeral and the misery and hopelessness of their clients' lives had weighed heavily on the pair of them. But Kathleen had resolve and she wasn't for giving up and where the hell was I going to go, thought Roz. Her practice was established and well-respected and whilst she could only dream of the money the big-shots earned in Manhattan, it gave her a reasonable-enough middle class living and she was drawn to fighting for the under-dog. Her father, Manny, had drilled that into her: "You gotta fight for what's right. It's the only way," he'd say, and her career scrapping for the little guy was cast in stone.

The commute from Brooklyn was a ball-ache, but that was another story altogether. It gave her time and space and she liked both, even if she did long for a relationship. But men weren't stickers with her and she never could fathom it, so she grabbed sex and comfort where and when she could, without going out looking for it. It was less and less frequent at her age and she'd resigned herself to spinsterhood, focusing instead on other comforts – like good whisky and the best Chinese in Chinatown, which was definitely at Wong's. Not that the two went together, of course.

She did as Anna had instructed and headed north to 34th Street before catching the Broadway Local south to Courtlandt Street in the Financial District. She was sure she wasn't being followed, having scanned the passengers and platforms feverishly and her heart rate settled down from near-cardiac malfunction to something approaching normal. This was too much excitement for a woman of her age, she thought, although why she thought forty eight was old she wasn't sure.

~~~~

They met in the lobby of the Marriott on West Street to find that Anna had booked them in as promised. Not under their own names and also as three couples, to confuse the trail. The third couple was fictitious, of course, but Anna knew the girl in reservations who agreed that she'd just re-allocate the rooms should she get any walk-up business that evening. That girl was good, they admitted.

They gathered in Kathleen's room and hammered the mini-bar whilst sharing news of the routes they'd adopted. Anna had left it to them to find their way there, figuring that there was too much risk in over-planning it. For such a cheery thing she had depths of paranoia they hoped they'd never fathom.

They reviewed the plans for the following morning and Roz excused herself, using the hotel's free internet terminals to research her position and ensure she was on the right side of the law. They agreed they'd meet Anna at 8am, after breakfast, and go over their plan for the press conference one more time.

~~~~

Richter returned to his home in Riverdale by two cabs and a bus, clear about his plan. He needed to get to the door of the guiding hand that instinct told him was behind the trio's odd movements. They were too choreographed and effective for people not used to this sort of event and he suspected a peer behind it all. But who? How would they know a spook or a detective?

His den, he reckoned, probably matched anything Molyneux could muster in terms of technology. The internet and corporate networks were a boon for people like him and his strategy was clear. If he could break into Delahunty's UK cell account then he'd be able to identify whom he had called and go from there. He was certain they must have been on the phone to someone during that long period in the Hub Café and realized his error in not figuring on a speaker-phone discussion. So whoever Delahunty had called – or whoever had called him – held the key.

The UK angle presented a few issues but he was seasoned enough at this to think his way through the problem and it took him thirty seven minutes precisely to bring Delahunty's call record up on screen. No wonder the tabloids found it so easy to scoop celebrities with gossip and tittle-tattle, he thought.

The New York cell number and the time and date told him he'd hit jackpot and it took just one minute and twenty seven seconds before he was staring coldly at the address and call history of one Anna Heuston in Windsor Terrace. Now he just needed to know if she had called anyone to keep his trail alive. The suspects had clearly agreed to split and congregate again, either tonight or tomorrow and as the lady with the frizzy hair hadn't headed for her home in Queens he'd assumed they were holed up somewhere. One of them must have booked it and, having watched the others all evening in the café on Katonah Avenue, his money was on Miss Heuston .

Nothing. The last call out had been at 7:34pm and that turned out to be what he assumed from the name on the records was her mother in Woodside. Why had the trail gone cold? He set to work on Kathleen Fabrini and within fifteen minutes he'd worked out from the pattern of her calls that, whilst she hadn't placed any that were potentially incriminating that evening, she did make an inordinate number during the average week to a Roz Goldstein. Women and their girlfriends - they couldn't half yabber.

One click on Google Images and a quick stroll downwards and he found himself staring at a photograph from the New York Daily News of Roz Goldstein on the steps of the Bronx County Courthouse, doubtless pronouncing about how her shit-head of a client didn't really mean to mug the 84 year old pensioner and that he, too, was a victim. She was the lady he was tailing, alright, and once again he found himself wondering what was going on. A PR girl, a lawyer and the fallen priest – an unlikely combination that could only spell trouble for someone. His was not to reason why and Molyneux didn't pay him to ponder those connections – just to find them, join the dots and keep tabs on them until instructed otherwise.

Then a bell rang faintly inside Richter's head and he stopped, closing his eyes and concentrating so that he could follow the trail as his synapses flickered and sparked and led him through his memory until the circuit was joined. He'd heard that name in the last few days and then it hit him: of course, the PR girl on Ted Courtney's steps. Whatever was going on, it was picking up a head of steam and he knew Molyneux wouldn't like it one bit.

With a cold trail there was nothing left to do but to report in and await further instructions. Back at the Marriott, Anna quietly congratulated herself on switching from her cell to a public pay phone to make the bookings. Just in case, she'd told herself. If they can follow us they can trace our calls, too – that's what these people do. So don't give them the ammo. No more outbound calls, she'd told the team, then thought better of it, held out her hand and collected their phones to meek protest.

~~~~

Molyneux's alarm bells were anything but faint. They were ringing like a peel from Liverpool's giant cathedral and his head ached as he entertained the possibilities ahead. He had foolishly accepted that his threatening phone call had put the issue to bed – such things normally did, in his experience – but the arrival of a lawyer and a PR girl on the scene opened up scenarios almost too awful to contemplate. And when he saw that it was the same PR girl that had taken some of the sting out of what should have been Delahunty's final humiliation in Ted Courtney's front garden, he knew he was in trouble. The fact that they had disappeared in concert meant only one thing. They were in cahoots and that this was going to blow up in his face quite horribly. Far from dropping the whole Madden thing, he knew the opposite must be true: they were up to something and the ramifications would be extremely damaging.

Even for a grizzled old cop like him his stomach took a nervous turn and he let out a bilious fart, the stench of which would take a full ten minutes to dissipate in his airless security room. I'd have been proud of that as a teenager, he thought, and he allowed the humour of it to return him to something approaching equilibrium. Think, he said, think, even if it was just 5am and he'd been raised from his slumber just twenty minutes earlier. He lived in a huge condo in one of the refurbished historic warehouses in Liverpool's tourist honey trap, the Albert Dock, and it was just a three minute stroll to the office. He'd chosen it for eventualities such as this as much for the security it afforded him from those who bore grudges from Liverpool and Ireland's underworlds.

It was against his better judgment but he decided to let this play out, assuming they couldn't find the targets. He'd instructed Richter to bring in however many freelancers he needed to track them down but there could be no guarantees. Though they should be no match for his team he had to admit that they'd shown remarkable resourcefulness this far and who was to tell what lay ahead?

~~~~

Richter took another slug of Red Bull as he settled down for an all-nighter. His freelancers, one an ex-hacker and only 24, the other a retired member of the NYPD's cyber crime division looking to supplement his meagre police pension, had a very simple brief: to hack into Manhattan hotels' reservation systems and find either the names or the pattern – four people, late booking – that would lead them to their targets.

They divided up the routes that would lead them to their goal: on-line clearers such as latebookings.com; calls made direct to the hotel; corporate travel bookers such as American Express; and corporate accounts from the huge number of Manhattan firms that entertained clients or suppliers keen to enjoy a slice of the Big Apple. It was a huge task but the algorithms and query codes at their disposal would foreshorten it. And at seven hundred bucks an hour, he hoped they worked quickly, although the success bonus he'd agreed with Molyneux was certainly an incentive to them to do so. A ten thousand dollar pot if they'd cracked it before 10am and which led to their targets' door. Nice work in anyone's book.

The three of them set to the task and agreed to review progress after the first and third hours, assuming they'd get as far as that without finding what they needed. That would be unusual, even with a search field as large as this. There were four hundred and ten hotels in Manhattan representing more than fifty thousand rooms but technology meant that the needles were a good deal more visible in the concrete haystack than they might once have been.

At the second review, a little after 3am, Richter had to hide his growing sense of unease. He had always entertained the notion that they may be bedded down in a friend's apartment but the circumstances and hour of their meeting, the fact that they didn't know one another – Goldstein and Fabrini aside – and the need for security and a base for whatever they were planning pointed to a hotel. They would have to plough on but he feared disappointment, not that the finger would be pointed at him – sometimes things worked against you in this trade.

CHAPTER ELEVEN

The phone rang at precisely twenty one minutes to four in the afternoon as a spring squall came in off the Irish Sea and battered the windows of the Cunard Line's famous old headquarters. It would pass in twenty minutes, the sting taken out of it by the Welsh mountains thirty miles to the west. The sky in Liverpool was rarely a uniform grey – more a constant flux of giant white cumulonimbus and deep blue. It was just weather and the natives were inured to it, the only thing tending to change during the year being the temperature.

Forshaw, the young PR executive on the first floor, was breathless as he dialled Molyneux's number. He'd received the oddest of calls and had a feeling that he'd put his foot in it but couldn't be sure how or why.

After establishing that she was through to Bell Group's PR department the voice, a young-ish sounding American lady, had grabbed Forshaw's attention from the off:

"We need you to tune into Bloomberg TV at 3:45pm your time. As a professional courtesy I am putting you on notice to get your whole PR team on stand-by because your phone lines will be red hot. Warn your switchboard operators and tell your boss. Am I making myself clear?"

Forshaw, just a few years out of Manchester Met's post-graduate PR programme and still pinching himself at landing one of the plummest jobs of his peer group, gulped and offered a meek "Yes, you are."

"Good. Now is Molyneux there, please?"

That threw him. Molyneux, it was made abundantly clear, was an off-the-books resource, never to be quoted or acknowledged because his role was too sensitive. There were strict protocols about who could speak with him, plus how matters were escalated up to him. Forshaw paused then stammered, but felt he recovered well.

"I'm not sure who you mean, madam. My name is Rikki Forshaw, can I help further?"

He'd given him all she needed and Anna Heuston thanked him, reminded him that he didn't have much time and rang off.

Forshaw looked around the marketing and media department for Angela Godber, the rather prim and joyless head of department, but he'd seen her head out of the office earlier and, realizing the gravity of the situation, took the initiative. That was what she always told him: 'Take initiative, lad. You've got a degree and a brain. Use both of them, you won't be criticized for it.'

So he picked the phone up and rang Molyneux who listened to his news in stony silence, realizing that the expected storm had finally arrived and that Richter's efforts had failed. They had simply disappeared and extending their search reference to credit card transactions and such like had proven equally fruitless.

He had realized that he had best get the firm's crisis response ready and has asked Godber to come and see him. Something was brewing, he was in the process of telling her, when Forshaw rang. She saw Molyneux's normally imperturbable face flash with momentary anger and then, with a narrowing of his eyes, he began to think. Godber knew that whatever was about to hit her was not going to be pleasant.

Within four minutes Godber, Molyneux and Sir Meredith Bell had gathered in the board room. The firm's head of legal services, Peter Middlewood, was taking three steps at a time up from the first floor and stumbled through the office door, breathless, as a young reporter looked earnestly into the camera.

"We are here at the Marriott Hotel in the New York's financial district to hear claims that the giant Bell Group may not have title to the huge shale gas resources it has discovered off the Newfoundland coast. The deal to extract the reserves, estimated to be worth up to fifteen billion dollars, may now be under threat, I can confirm, from sources close to the company."

Anna had needed to provide Bloomberg with a strict off-the-record briefing in order to land the TV coverage that was key to the leverage she wanted over Bell Group. Having assessed the gravity of the news, they had asked for, and got, exclusivity in terms of TV coverage. She'd blown a few credits with the other channels but the reality was that they understood the necessary horse-trading that was a PR consultant's stock in trade. Whilst Bell Group wasn't a quoted stock, they were a huge business spanning the globe and the scale of their reserves in Newfoundland was bound to have an impact on the energy markets. In an era of huge price volatility and concerns over energy security, this was a big story whatever way you looked at it.

Bloomberg cashed in on their privileged position, as Anna hoped they would, by selling a feed from the conference to other business and news channels, anticipating that they'd slice and dice the best bits in time for their own news updates on the hour – that, or head live straight to the conference and put a screen ident saying 'pictures courtesy of Bloomberg TV'.

Sir Meredith shot Molyneux a look of sheer thunder, but remained stock still, eyes returned to the screen. He knew that cool heads must prevail in a crisis and he could deal with George later.

Molyneux, who had Richter on standby, walked to the corner of the giant office overlooking the Mersey and issued him with a series of coded instructions. Godber, who was recording the TV coverage, had her trusted number two, Jenkins, on the phone and he was in Sir Meredith's office inside the minute.

"Ladies and gentlemen, thank you for coming today. My name is Anna Heuston and my client, Kathleen Fabrini, has discovered evidence which leads us to believe that she is the rightful heir not just to a proportion of the revenues that will flow from Bell Resources' Canadian mineral rights, but to half of the profits of Bell Group's fish canning operations for just over a century.

"We have evidence to show that her great-grandmother, Theresa Madden, then Theresa Brophy, was tricked out of the land-holdings that formed the basis not only of 101 years of highly profitable cod processing in St. John's, Newfoundland, but also the land at Maddox Cove which is the cornerstone of Bell Resources' entire Canadian drilling operations.

"Without those seemingly ill-gotten landholdings we can prove that Bell Group would not be the huge force it is today and nor would it be able to exploit, without huge additional cost, the Newfoundland gas rights that look set to underpin decades of further growth and enrichment of the family shareholders.

"My colleagues will now hand you a transcript and photocopy of a testimony from Theresa Madden laying forth her story. Many of you will find it heartrending; it is certainly a very sad tale indeed. If it is true – and we believe that it is – then it represents one of the greatest frauds in the history of commerce and we are here, in the words of Theresa Madden, to ensure it is put right."

As she continued speaking three Marriott employees brought in for the purpose handed out photocopies of Theresa Madden's letter to her son, Sean, plus typed transcripts to save news editors the job of straining to read her copper-plate handwriting. There was also a full statement from the Fabrini team outlining their view on the legal issues the letter presented, quotes from Kathleen Fabrini herself, plus further commentary from her attorney, Roz Goldstein.

"In the process of investigating this story somebody, corporate or singular, put us under surveillance and threatened not just our team but innocent New York school children – children from among the most deprived communities in our city, given hope by Kathleen Fabrini and her outstanding teaching methods. Just how low will these people sink – whoever they are – to stop the truth from emerging? Let me play you a tape and you can decide for yourselves," and with that the room fell into stunned silence as George Molyneux was heard threatening dire consequences for Kathleen Fabrini and the children under her care at Parkway High unless she backed off from her claim.

A barrage of questions followed, all of which Anna ignored as she sought to quieten the melee. She then proceeded to lob another bomb into proceedings.

"Having spoken to the PR team at Bell Group's Liverpool headquarters today, we believe that there is a Mr Molyneux in their employ, but they would not confirm or deny that for us." She was bending the truth a little on that one but she'd taped her conversation with Forshaw and she wasn't a journalist so her scruples didn't have to be so, well, scrupulous.

"We therefore have a few simple questions for Bell Group's board: Do you employ a Mr Molyneux directly or as a contractor? If so, is it in any security, investigative or public relations capacity? And is this his voice? I know that you, my colleagues in the media, will have many more questions you would want to ask," and with that she stepped aside to a clamour of enquiry.

Calming the room again, she introduced Roz Goldstein, Attorney-at-Law and a close personal friend of Mrs Fabrini who had decided to represent her. Beside her stood Kathleen Fabrini, an arm each around two solemn looking school children, in their tired and worn uniforms. Most families had struggled to afford them, but Kathleen had insisted that every child wore one: it was core to discipline, respect and to the sense of the collective that she wanted to engender and sacrifices were made accordingly. Then a local refrigeration business had heard of what she was achieving and she got her biggest boost yet, a $10,000 endowment to subsidise all new school uniform purchases.

"Ladies, gentlemen, thank you for your patience," Goldstein offered after she had regained the room's silence.

"We know you will have many questions. I am here so that you can see that my client is properly represented, does not take threats to her life and those of her charges lying down, and that we have no fear in taking on any corporate interest that seeks to trample on the rights of the individual. We can only imagine a corporate interest would make such a threat and as far as we can see only one corporation had any material dealings with Theresa Madden and that was Bell Group. That is why we are seeking their help in getting to the bottom of this whole issue."

In a bid for American opinion in what was a battle against a distant, British business, she added: "It is not the American way to allow the powerful unfettered rights over those too meek to fight them, too poor to represent themselves or too distant from the source of their injustice. So I am standing up for my friend and the children of Parkway High and together we will take this issue directly to Bell Group in Liverpool and ask them for every assistance in proving our case."

"This morning I have lodged a subpoena in the New York district court seeking access to Bell Group's entire historical archive so that we may assess for ourselves what was known about this injustice at the time and what, if anything, has ever been attempted by past or current boards to put it right."

And in what even Godber later admitted was a PR master-stroke designed to give the current board of Bell Group some wiggle room, Goldstein concluded by saying "Instinct says that we cannot hold the company's current directors personally responsible for a fraud seemingly perpetrated more than a hundred and twenty years ago and, as befits a major employer and patron of charities and the arts, I fully expect them to join us in wanting to settle, amicably, a patent injustice, committed in their name, by people they could not know, a very long time ago."

Then, in a move worthy of Columbo, Roz, having made to step back from the hotel's branded podium, returned:

"Central to Theresa Madden's claim is that she fathered the child of Barrington Bell. If that is the case then DNA evidence from the current Bell family will prove that conclusively, one way or another. I ask that Sir Meredith Bell, the great-grandson of Barrington, come forward and offer us a sample of his DNA so that this simple test can be completed and the matter settled. I would fully hope that he would want to comply but let me make it clear: we will not hesitate to seek recourse to the courts to compel him to do so should he seek not to co-operate.

"To help, I have included in your press packs Kathleen's own DNA profile. Now let's see Sir Meredith's."

It was an unexpected flourish and it set the room alight. It was Roz's idea, something she'd picked up from the various paternity suits she'd filed.

A whole industry of quick turnaround DNA labs had sprung up following improvements in analysis techniques and for a hefty premium they could offer overnight results. Anna realized that it could become the lightning rod for their whole strategy of forcing Bell out into the open, beyond legal manouevre and firmly into the court of public opinion and moral obligation. Once again Godber was forced to make a mental concession to the sharpness of these damn Yanks.

~~~~

The senior Bell team stood in stunned silence as a battery of questions from the journalists bombarded Heuston , Goldstein and Fabrini herself. Then phones began ringing, almost in unison. First to Sir Meredith's private mobile number was Cameron Moncrieff, the bluff Glasgwegian editor of the Liverpool Echo, who had a direct line to all of Liverpool's corporate, political and civic royalty.

"Sir Meredith, just one question at this stage. Will you co-operate?"

The phone was snatched from his hand by Godber who poured honey down the line and asked for a little time to assess their options in what was a set of grave allegations that came completely out of the blue from an unknown source.

"Cameron, you know we'll be absolutely open with you and offer you a full response. Just let me line my ducks up," she asked.

Aye, there'll be plenty of things getting shot after this, thought Moncrieff, before saying that if he hadn't heard back in an hour he'd be printing that no-one was available for comment, which, by implication meant that they had something to hide. By extension, it was an effective threat. Meanwhile, he set three of his best reporters to the task of digging out supplementary quotes from any local business luminary foolish enough to offer one, to assessing the energy market's reaction, and to the task of finding out what they could about this Theresa Madden, including obtaining a copy of her statement. The last bit turned out to be easier than he thought: one had just been sent from the back office of the Marriott hotel in Lower Manhattan, marked for his attention. These guys really do mean business, thought Montcrieff.

Sir Meredith took charge. He had faced plenty of difficult negotiations and business decisions in his time at the helm of Bell Group and, whilst none was as explosive as this, he knew that firmness of action, a clear mind and a willingness to listen to those he trusted would see them through it.

Godber was to co-ordinate the media response, offering a holding statement which said that they would co-operate with any official requests but that until such time as they were forthcoming they would not comment until their own internal investigations brought anything to light that might help. These were serious allegations and needed investigating thoroughly, they said. That would buy them a little time to allow the senior figures – Bell, Middlewood and Godber – to debate their options in more detail. One thing was for sure: Sir Meredith would be facing the cameras before the day was out.

Middlewood called Peter Hale, Barlow Hayes's head of litigation and instructed him to drop everything and bring a team straight down to the Pier Head. Bell Group's investment with Barlow Hayes' Liverpool office amounted to more than £20m in fees in the average year so drop everything he would. He had a team of seven there in under eight minutes, helped by the fact that they were based only four hundred yards away on Castle Street in the heart of Liverpool's historic business district.

~~~~

Bell took Molyneux through the grand mahogany doors that led from the boardroom to his office. A huge wooden desk sat in front of three grand windows and the room was lined with portraits of generations of Bells, men who had risked all and more besides to build the business into the giant it was today. Men who had buried secrets – and people – along the way in a time when deployment and interpretation of the law and a man's standing often coincided in mutual interest.

The grand marble fireplace had long since ceased to function in a welter of health and safety concerns, so it was filled each day with a huge fresh floral bouquet. Bell's PA, Mo Rimmer, had the task of distributing the still fresh flowers each evening to employees on an entirely random basis and she was respected for her even-handedness. At more than seventy quid a go, it was a treat that would last the lucky recipient more than a week by any stretch.

Bell had his back to Molyneux, looking out across the Mersey to two large ferries moored on the Birkenhead landing stage disgorging trucks from Belfast and Dublin respectively. The Irish Sea trade had been a mainstay of the port for centuries and Liverpool, with its extensive deep-sea connections, still handled more than 50% of Ireland's exports.

"The problem here is not whether one of my feckless relatives porked some poor Irish servant girl," said Bell, looking thoughtful and pensive, "it's the bloody Russians. They'll kick up merry hell and there are some pretty stringent performance guarantees in our JV agreement. If this gets out of hand it could impose some heavy penalties on us related to reputational harm - a bit rich, frankly, given what we suspect they get up to on a daily basis.

"I want you over there, tonight, to smooth their furrowed brows. But I want you to rein them in a little, too: there's no knowing what these buggers will get up to if we let them. You've got to reassure them that we're on top of this. Barlow Hayes will deal with it, they'll see.

"And we need you out of the country, too – you're going to be the target of some pretty intrusive media activity and if you're not here then we can't put you in front of the cameras now can we?"

Molyneux was about to find out how intrusive, in a move that brought some rare satisfaction to Joe Delahunty.

~~~~

The price of shale gas rose 4% as news of a likely delay to Bell Resources' drilling activities off Newfoundland was absorbed by traders and the wider market. The problem was compounded when the Newfoundland and Labrador government announced that they would be asking for early talks with the board of Bell to seek answers to the allegations and by close of trading on London's International Petroleum Exchange prices had jumped 5.2%.

~~~~

Anna had rung Karl Chung in Linford Santini's social media team late the night before to ask for a favour. A big favour. She winced as she ladled on the charm because she knew she was being unfair. Karl had professed his undying love to her at the office Christmas party three months before and his longing would remain unrequited if she had anything to do with it.

But she needed him now and calculated that he'd do anything to help. Which, of course, he would.

And so, when her mobile phone beeped at 11:40 she smiled as she got the answer she'd prayed for. It was all good to go.

"Ladies and gentlemen," she had said in the midst of the Q&A session. "I can confirm for you that we have set up a facebook group called 'Justice for Theresa Madden' and that we have a twitter feed, @TessMadden, from which we will update you each day. The hashtags, #findMolyneux and #WhoIsMolyneux? will, I predict, be trending on twitter by the end of the day and we are asking for people's help, particularly in Liverpool, in meeting those two challenges."

The response was electric, in the way that can only happen in the internet age, helped by Chung's carefully-planned seeding of questions on key chatrooms and web sites of a rag-tag alliance of left wing groups, global warming campaigners, anti-capitalism demonstrators and, of course, via key twitter influencers – mostly gullible celebrities that would hop on any bandwagon in order to look hip.

And then, of course, there was the Irish ex-pat community. Anna had primed the global Irish media via her firm's on-line journalist and media targeting systems to expect 'the biggest story to hit the Irish diaspora since Paddy first learned to sail' and she hadn't disappointed. She'd calculated they'd see the humour in that subject line and it paid off. By 1pm Eastern Standard Time there wasn't an ex-pat chatroom, web site, news organization or social club that wasn't alive with news of Theresa Madden's great loss and a link to – or the full text of – Theresa's heart-rending letter to her dear son, Sean. Friends were sending each other links via email, text message and through their facebook pages, as well as twitter, and Godber sat in awe as her on-line reputation monitoring system, offering real-time coverage of all on-line chatter, went into melt-down.

Each entry showed the first half of a sentence or headline and they ticked up on to the screen relentlessly, second by second. It was a reputational car crash and she knew that she had to get hold of the story immediately, or be swamped by it, never to regain the initiative.

~~~~

Bill Goodbody, the school's trusty caretaker, took Shaniya and Timber back to Parkway High, leaving the Fabrini team to gather after countless individual interviews and briefings that lasted almost two hours. Anna had prioritized the more immediate news sources, such as TV and radio, so that they could get on air as quickly as possible with real voices to add further human interest to what was a tale awash with the stuff. After that were the daily newspapers and key bloggers, then the feature writers. In all, more than 60 journalists had attended on the promise that they were about to witness a reputational car crash of staggering magnitude. And they weren't to be disappointed.

She'd primed Kathleen and Roz carefully about how to talk to the journalists, what was factual and what was heresay, and when to call a halt and ask for clarification if they were unsure of their ground. "I'll be right next to you," Anna had assured them.

It was one of the most terrifying yet exhilarating experiences of their professional lives and at the heart of it was this remarkably confident and competent young lady who seemed utterly fearless. Joe Delahunty, by contrast, was in the shadows. Anna had reckoned, rightly, that putting a serial philanderer – and one wearing a dog collar at that – in the middle of the story would distract the media from the real issue and he was more than happy to keep well out of it. Joe figured he'd had his fill of self-righteous moralizing and wouldn't be unhappy if he never saw a journalist again.

It wasn't long before Sir Meredith Bell felt much the same – and for broadly similar reasons.

~~~~

It was 6pm before they all retired to McKeown's Bar near Battery Park on the southern tip of Manhattan, amused at overhearing conversations about themselves and tempted to step in and correct any inaccuracies. But all they really wanted was a pint and to take stock.

It was Paddy's Day the day after tomorrow and Joe had invited them all up to Pearl River to see his cousin Ted's parade. Anna had promised herself that she'd make a long over-due visit to her mom and and Roz had belly-laughed at the notion of a good Jewish gal attending something so overtly Catholic.

"I can do integration and harmony with the best of 'em," she laughed, "but that does not extend to drinking green beer and wearing a false red beard. You Micks go have your day in the sun. I've got work to do," hinting at the storm that lay off-shore as she prepared for the return salvo from Bell's lawyers. She'd heard they were a feisty lot, those Liverpudlians, and she expected every dirty manouevre imaginable to try and frustrate Team Fabrini. But she had the weight of public opinion behind her and a story that was firing up the imagination of feature-writers and the liberal commentariat as she sat there. It was an uneven battle and she knew it – and that was before she pressed home the question of the DNA test. Right now the media were doing that for her, speculating, mostly wildly, at the legalities of it all and the PR implications for Sir Meredith Bell if he declined to respond positively to the challenge. By happy accident the image of Kathleen's DNA string, like a sort of fat-fingered bar code, became the visual cue for the story itself and papers across the world were to carry it over the following week as first the French, then the Germans and onwards via the London correspondents of their major media groups, latched on to a human interest story that had, for them, everything that was quintessentially British: minor nobility, family dynasties, slave trading, old money, greed, sex and much, much more.

The stupidity of Bell's business partners only fuelled that particular fire as the week unfolded, throwing into the dynamic an archetypal Russian bully boy with more than the whiff of criminality about him.

~~~~

By seven pm local time Angela Godber had conceded defeat. Not only was the firm's holding statement not holding, but the sheer weight of media and internet speculation – much of it seemingly slanderous – was ripping to shreds nearly two and a half centuries of carefully cultivated political, social, economic and media ties.

There was nothing for it but to put Sir Meredith, figuratively, on the steps of the Cunard Building to face the media in an attempt to get back on the front foot, take some of the heat out of the wilder speculation and to deflect attention back to the motives and integrity of the counter-party. She knew the latter was highly risky. Her reading of public and media opinion at this juncture was that here was a brave and modest woman who had come out of the shadows to put right a terrible wrong, only to find herself and innocent children in her care threatened.

Godber was wondering how on earth she was going to find a chink in Fabrini's seemingly impregnable armour when the call came from Molyneux, who was in Manchester airport awaiting his eight pm flight to Moscow. It was a sparse and pointed conversation in the way that they always were with that horrible man. God knows how many poor Irishmen he probably framed while he was in Special Branch, she often thought.

But all that could wait, for Molyneux had unearthed a gem and, reflecting on Heuston's and Goldstein's peerless performance, she smiled as she realized she might have something that could match them. At the very least it would put the media on a different scent and confuse the story. With any luck she could put the brakes on the unfolding detective rush that felt like a journalistic Klondyke: find the gold to complete the story. That would be a sample of Bell's DNA.

And so the media call went out announcing a press conference the following morning at 9am in the Crowne Plaza hotel, 75 yards from the Cunard Building. Sir Meredith Bell would be taking questions and seeking to reassure the firm's business partners, partner governments and the people of Liverpool, who relied on him for so much employment and who were fearful of harm to one of its few remaining corporate leviathans.

CHAPTER TWELVE

The TV trucks arrived from 8am, setting up in the generous hotel car park in the shadow of the giant Liver Building, the symbol of Liverpool and the very essence of its muscular, self-confident swagger – a trait that had not made it universally popular among many of its country-folk in the past.

The photographers, journalists and bloggers came later, though early enough for the coffee and bacon butty that had been promised and by 9am it was a veritable scrum. There were more than 150 people in the main function room, with a stage set to centre and a table bearing three names: Peter Middlewood, Sir Meredith Bell and to his right Angela Godber.

The three came in via a door to the rear of the stage to be greeted with a barrage of flashes and the TV crews' arc lights. It was an uncomfortable experience for Bell, who'd always preferred a more discreet approach to media relations. One-to-ones in his club over a nice dinner with his driver at the journalist's disposal to take him home. Or elsewhere should the siren call of the city's lap-dancing clubs be too great, which was often the case.

Over in New York a small team gathered in front of their Sky News feed to assess what they were dealing with and to plan their response accordingly.

"Ladies and gentleman, thank you all for taking the trouble to join us this morning. I know that many of you had early rises to be here and I hope the bacon butties filled a gap."

There was a murmur of laughter and consent which helped Sir Meredith to relax and Godber, to his relief, kept things moving.

"We all know why we're here. Allegations have been made which go to the very heart of the ethics, probity and values that have guided our business over two hundred and thirty years of trading across borders, cultures and time zones. We want to answer the questions yesterday's New York press conference posed as well as those that you will have. Some we may not be able to answer for legal reasons, though not for wont of openness, and I know you will understand that."

Godber paused and it was fatal.

"Bill Watkins, The Sun," he announced. "Sir Meredith, have you brought your DNA analysis with you?"

It was a sucker punch, but anticipated to come up at some point so it was only the timing that fazed them. Bell had been prepped and his calmness was aimed at taking the heat out of proceedings. The brief was to appear open, reasonable, almost non-plussed by this news of something that may have happened more than one hundred and twenty years ago. Nobody could blame him for the sins of his father, never mind his great-grandfather. He was here to help as much as he could.

"A person's DNA is a unique fingerprint that can be used, nowadays, in all manner of ways, both legal and nefarious. It would be highly naïve of me to publish mine and I think Mrs Fabrini was poorly advised by her lawyers to release something so personal."

Round one to us, thought Godber, but she knew this was going to be a slugfest so no point in totting up the points just yet.

"Will you privately compare your DNA in that case?" Watkins fired back.

"Our first aim is to investigate the veracity of these claims. You and I are not so naïve as to think that a business like ours, involved in areas as sensitive as carbon extraction, is not open to scams and blackmail. We are, all the time, it's just that most of the time our detractors don't announce their intentions in a flurry of publicity. I'll be more than happy to work personally with Mrs Fabrini and her advisors to assess their allegations but I see no value in playing it out in front of the world's media. If they'll meet me here in Liverpool then I'll work with them. I am happy to pay their airfares and make them my guest in our fine city whilst we get to the bottom of this."

He was cool, thought Watkins. Fair play to the fella. Imply that they may be scammers, be reasonable and co-operative. That Godber was good, too, he admitted. Bell had even suggested that they were naïve and poorly advised. Better turn the heat up, he reckoned, otherwise we'll get played for patsies here.

But then Julian De La Valle from The Guardian stepped in and did his work for him.

"Sir Meredith, will you resign if these allegations are proven? I mean, the loss in shareholder value will be significant and it will take a different person to bring the business back from something as catastrophic as this."

"There has been and will be no catastrophe so you can look forward to me at future annual results announcements for a good few years yet, Julian," he replied, raising another gentle laugh and taking more heat out of the situation.

"Ciaran Harte, Irish Times. Your firm was famous for its coffin ships, Sir Meredith. Was what happened to Theresa Brophy symptomatic of your views towards the Irish?"

"My views of my Irish friends and neighbours are the same as most people's in this room – they're valued friends and neighbours. What my great-great and my great-grandfather thought of them I don't know and is for their conscience alone."

This was Liverpool, so everyone knew he was highly likely to have Irish friends and neighbours, so it sounded sincere as well as credible. The tally of credits was clocking up nicely, thought Godber.

The Echo's business editor, Paul Harrington, was watching with concern. He was unique among the throng in not wanting to see a crucifixion. Liverpool could do without losing another corporate giant and he knew Sir Meredith to be a decent enough skin. He'd certainly always given him more than the time of day and he had a couple of mates who worked at Bell's, as it was known, who vouched for the healthy corporate culture in the place. Not outstanding, but decent and they did things properly they'd told him the night before in the pub. Time to jump in.

"Paul Harrington, Liverpool Echo business desk. Sir Meredith, you have a well known policy of donating one per cent of profits every year to good causes. If these allegations are proven to be true, how will that be affected? Will the numerous charities you support in Liverpool be affected? Will the battle against malaria be lost?" It was a soft ball and every one in the room knew it, but there was a game to be played out and they'd all go with the ebb and flow.

"If my forebears were proven to be less than honourable then I and my family will prove to be the opposite, of that you have my word." A good promise, but not one with specific bills attached. The tension was leaving the air with every answer, thought Godber. Time for someone to jump in and turn the tables decisively and she nodded her assent down the table.

"Folks, I think you can get a sense that ours is a business built on a strong sense of ethics. We do not run away from our responsibilities and nor do we seek to denigrate others. But we have to draw a line when those who seek to harm us are themselves proven to be of highly dubious morals and character." It was Middlewood, the firm's pin-striped enforcer, a former corporate lawyer and a man known for his street-fighting qualities.

The room went silent. Coming from Middlewood they sensed a hand grenade and that was, of course, what they got. The slings and arrows of commercial imperative, brutally played out in front of them and hang the collateral damage.

"We have discovered that the driving force behind yesterday's allegations was Joseph Delahunty, who most of you will recall was splashed across your front pages less than a month ago for having broken his sacred vow of celibacy as a priest on multiple occasions. We do not know his motivation but we do know that he is a man whom even the fairest-minded among us would hesitate to describe as trustworthy. It's not clear whether his partners in this enterprise know of his background, but even they can't all be relied upon."

The room fell back into silence, having gone into a frenzy of hushed phone calls, text messages and internet searches, particularly among the foreign press corps for whom Joseph Delahunty was off-radar, having been a tabloid plaything. They only followed the broadsheets and missed much about modern Britain as a result.

Everyone knew and expected that a department of dirty tricks would be hard at it until this game came to a conclusion, but whoever they were had excelled themselves with the Delahunty revelation, they acknowledged.

"The lawyer representing Mrs Fabrini, Roz Goldstein, is currently being rehabilitated for chronic alcoholism and Mrs Fabrini herself married the son of a mid-league New York mafia boss until he was shot dead as part of a suspected criminal dispute eight years ago. As far as we can see we have an unholy Trinity of people in need of help and what we need to do is to get to the bottom of their motives, I suspect, as much as the veracity of their claims," said Middlewood, as the journalists once again began a scramble to their phones and iPads.

When it was agreed that Middlewood was the man to deliver the conference's coup de grace they knew it would have the ring of authenticity. But he surpassed that; it was a killer blow.

The conference broke up quickly as the journalists scrambled to beat one another to get the first response from Bell's adversaries. Most of them had the relevant numbers – they'd been handed out by Heuston the day before – but their efforts were helped by unattributable briefing notes handed out by Godber's team as Middlewood was lobbing his grenade. It was a clever move, calculated to disrupt the flow of things and focus each media outlet on the necessarily selfish task of pipping their opponents to the post as far as quotes and comment went. And it meant they didn't ask the most obvious question of all – the one about Molyneux.

Before they broke up Sir Meredith called for order, looking the BBC's camera straight in the eye, having calculated that they would have the greatest global reach, and making a direct appeal to Team Fabrini.

"My door is wide open to discuss this issue with you all. I will send our corporate jet out to collect you from New York and you are welcome to stay in my hotel in Liverpool as my guest. I want to resolve this to your and my satisfaction and, if we get time, perhaps we can have a pint in the Philharmonic, too."

The reference to Liverpool's most famously ornate pub was another winning blow – a man with the common touch, at ease with a pint and civilized enough to offer the hand of friendship to his adversaries. How very British and not how it would have played out in America. Game, set and absolute fucking match, said Middlewood to himself. We'll have these twats by the day's end.

~~~~

Roz had wiped the tears from her cheeks and sat sullenly on the sofa, eyeing the mini-bar. Fuck it, one won't hurt. Joe was pacing around the room, muttering under his breath whilst Kathleen stared out of the window of the fourteenth floor room in the Marriott, lost in her thoughts. She'd asked Myrtle Van Hoogard, her deputy, to cover for her that day and the whole school knew why. She was owed at least a year's paid leave in lieu and no-one was about to gainsay the request.

Anna sat in the corner, thoughtful. Never mind the bruised egos, what counted now was the riposte. They had to get back on the front foot, and quick. This was brutal, hard-ball stuff and you couldn't fold at the first flurry of punches. There were twelve rounds of this shit and you'd better be prepared to stick with it, she'd warned them. She was some corner girl and she drew them back to the task in hand.

"Right team, round three is coming, so what are we going to do?"

It was a rhetorical question, of course, not that they saw it that way. What's next? Curl up and hide frankly, thought Roz.

"I'll tell you what we're doing, we're on a flight to Liverpool, that's what," said Anna.

They looked at her with tired eyes, tearful, bruised and incredulous. Like shite we are, thought the former priest, the Scouse voice in his head emphasizing that the last place he wanted to be right now was his home city.

"No, this thing ends here," said Kathleen. "I never knew Theresa, I never wanted this battle. What spare energy I have goes on the kids in my school and getting past my own demons."

Joe and Roz stayed silent, as did the phones. Anna had ordered them to remain off until they'd agreed their response to the morning's press conference and it was to prove another prescient move.

"No guys, it does not end here. It cannot end here. We are in the right. They have threatened you, Kathleen, and the kids you care so much about. They would only do that if they knew you had a case. The evidence is in their archives. Bound to be. Roz's subpoena could get us in there, in their library, or whatever it is." She was impassioned and Joe stopped pacing.

"Look, they'll play dirty, but that's because their secret is dirtier than anything we may have. So you like a drink?" she said, looking at Roz. "And a few billion others too. And you fell in love with a man and married him, like billions of women before you," she offered, looking at Kathleen. "The only fly in our ointment is Joe."

She let that hang for a moment, before continuing.

"The evidence is there somewhere. Let's play them at their own game. They extended that invitation precisely to put us on our back foot, to make it look like they are the voice of reason and it worked. So let's just play their cards right back at them. Roz, you get that subpoena nailed and I'll get on to Bell's office and get that jet over here. We'll show them that we're as ballsy as they are because they have the ace that will turn our hand into a winner. Somewhere in their archive is proof of Barrington Bell's crime."

She could see that she'd won the argument, but she wanted to drive it home. No waverers or backsliders in her team, thank you very much. "And they still haven't answered the most important question of all: who is Molyneux? So we're going to ask them again and again until we get our answer."

~~~~

There was no press conference this time, just a blanket emailed press statement welcoming Bell Group's offer of conciliation and confirmation that they would, indeed, be flying from New York to Liverpool. She repeated her questions about Molyneux and knew the press would be kicking themselves for letting the heat of the press conference deflect them from that. Before the day was out Bell Group would have to issue a statement in that regard, surely.

#findMolyneux and #WhoIsMolyneux? had stopped trending but were still clocking up nicely on Anna's tweet deck so all was not lost, despite a solid points win for the opposition. And she still had the DNA card to play. How was Bell going to wriggle out of that one, she wondered?

~~~~

Molyneux was met at Moscow's Sheremetyevo airport by what he took as standard issue Russian muscle. Big, silent and intimidating. Except that he'd been on that side of the fence for most of his professional life and it didn't trouble him one bit.

The Mercedes E-class purred effortlessly through the city's early morning traffic and Molyneux focused on the discussion ahead, which he knew would not be easy. They headed from the north west of the city south down the western leg of the MKAD, the city's notorious outer ring road, cutting into the Presnensky financial district after only thirty five minutes. NovKos's offices were text book new money, all steel and glass and phallic exceptionalism. Tacky, thought Molyneux. No class and no quality.

Waiting for him in the huge, galleried main reception was a short, stocky man in a smart, dark woollen suit and brogues – the epitomy of subdued English taste. No gold chains, signet rings or blingy Rolex for this chap, which immediately put Molyneux on the defensive.

"Anatoly Pugin," said the man, extending a hand, "I am what you call your counterpart, I think."

Head of security, eh? At the door. This was going to be interesting.

He was all bonhomie, confirming that they had taken care of his hotel booking and that they would drive him there after their discussions. If he was free after dinner then a few of the lads were up for showing him proper Russian hospitality, if he knew what he meant? Yes, he did. Severe liver damage and coming perilously close to catching something nasty, no doubt. He'd pass on both when the time came.

Pugin whisked him up to the chairman's suite on the 48th floor which afforded predictably spectacular views over a cold and crisp Moscow. He wondered if there were any Irish pubs in the city so that he could have a decent pint and enjoy the Paddy's Day celebration the following day. St. Patrick wasn't just a Catholic saint, of course. He's ours, too, Molyneux reminded himself with a snort.

They sat in the chairman's luxurious suite and waited until a leggy blonde had finished serving them tea. It was surprisingly tasteful, thought Molyneux. Someone with an eye had gotten hold of it, clearly. Couldn't have been any of the muckleheads he'd seen on his way in, but then interior designers were as mobile as the next profession and a remunerative gig in Moscow could be fun.

They sat down, Molyneux placing his slim briefcase to his side on the seat beside him and carefully folding his jacket, pocket upwards, on the sofa arm before pulling up his trouser legs and sitting down.

"George," said Pugin, "May I call you George?"

"Yeah, go'ead mate," said Molyneux, flexing his accent to put the guy on the back foot and not make it too easy for him.

"Our employers are not too different, yours and mine, and certainly their aims will be broadly similar. Make money, have fun, get through life. So we have some common ground that will help us solve this problem, no?"

Look pal, thought Molyneux, I've been on the same psychology courses as you have so you can cut the empathy shite and get to the point. Something in his scowl registered with Pugin and he sighed, having detected the mood shift and decided to bring things to an immediate head.

"We do not think you have been decisive enough – that much is evident. You reassured us this was dealt with, then it all blows up in your face. There has been no reputational harm to us so far, but there is concern that what is happening may cause a delay to the project. If the Newfoundland government call in the licence for review because of the weight of public opinion then we lose a huge amount of revenue from our forward projections. You have to believe me when I tell you that that is utterly unacceptable to our shareholders," he noted, with undue emphasis on the 'utterly unacceptable' bit.

Pugin's sharcholder issues were of little concern to Molyneux. Bell still had 85% of the shares in the project and had already begun frustrating drilling activity to push things into the long grass whilst they played this out. If the Russians were going to be problematic then there was little point in helping them towards parity, now was there?

"I agree," offered Molyneux, "this is far from ideal but you'll see today that we still have plenty of firepower and that our way of dealing with issues can deliver the killer blow without, well, killing anyone." He held Pugin's gaze to signal that muck, blood and bullets were way off the agenda. Or radioactive poisoning, or whatever the Russians' preferred method of disposing of enemies was these days.

"But every day that you play out your gentle dance is a day that harms our shareholders' interests. We need to deal with this decisively. If you will not help us, then we will help ourselves," said Pugin, grimly.

Molyneux was in no doubt what he meant but piling up the bodies of the antagonists was not going to see things smoothed through the Newfoundland government, never mind what the media would make of it.

"That would not be wise or helpful in any way. The Canadians and our media would see that as highly provocative and any hope you'd have of your licence coming to fruition would be gone after that," said Molyneux, appealing to Pugin's pragmatism. Although it's probably not Pugin's temperament he needs to worry about, he admitted, but his boss's.

"I cannot allow that to happen," Molyneux added. "We will not and you must trust me on that," he concluded, letting the implied threat hang in the air.

Opposite, through a rather elegant, horizontal mirror, Nikolas Adaksin stood watching the conversation unfold. He was impressed with Molyneux's calm certainty but there was something in his last statement that made his instinct jangle. Pugin heard a gentle whisper in his tiny earpiece and excused himself, allowing Molyneux to stretch his legs and take in the 150 degree view of the central Moscow skyline. More than enough for your average megalomaniac, he estimated.

Pugin entered Adaksin's small and cosy study. "Yes boss, what is it? You sounded concerned."

"Did you scan him?"

"What?" Pugin knew something was up but the penny hadn't dropped.

"Did you scan him and his briefcase before you brought him up here?" The mix of irritation and contempt caught Pugin off guard and he knew that he was finished.

"No, sir. He is a partner of the business and so I afforded him the professional courtesy of bringing him straight up here."

Adaksin's snort was final and Pugin watched through the mirror as Nikolas strode purposefully into the lounge and greeted Molyneux like a long-lost friend.

"Sir Meredith has mentioned much about you," he offered, with a warm embrace that Molyneux took as normal hereabouts. The Russian bear, and all that.

The sophistry didn't work, it never did, but Molyneux feigned flattery whilst wondering what the fellow was up to.

"Come with me, I want to show you what else we do outside of our Newfoundland interests," and he swept Molyneux forward by the elbow and out of the office.

The tour lasted fifty minutes and was a canter through their research, exploration and extraction divisions. Interesting, to be fair, thought Molyneux, who had grace enough to nod in the right places and ask the odd question. He was returned to the lounge, where Pugin was waiting for them.

Molyneux insisted on more time to let this play out according to the British and American models and provided cast-iron reassurances that their take on dirty tricks – reputational destruction, bunging friendly journalists a few grand

and the careful burying of incriminating evidence in the archive - was the way to do it.

Pugin proved pliant enough in the end and Molyneux rose to his feet feeling that his job was done for now, though he didn't doubt he'd be back here again. Pugin escorted him down to the waiting E-class and made a point of instructing the driver in English to take their valued guest at all haste to his hotel, the Ritz-Carlton, before suggesting that they would pick him up at five for a few beers and vodkas before dinner. Molyneux nodded his assent, having reflected on how things had gone and got into the car.

He awoke stripped to his vest and underpants and tied to an old wicker chair, the broken lattice work scratching and irritating his legs and back. Waves of panic swept over him because he knew this would not be a happy ending. In Russia, in these circumstances, it could only spell one thing. The gag was tight and his initial screams and exhortations were as much for release as any practical purpose. Even if the gag was removed screaming would be pointless, of that he had no doubt. So best to sit still, stay calm and take stock he thought, trying to relax.

Wherever he was it was dank, cold and dark, with only the dimmest of 25 watt bulbs to light the gloom of this vast interior space. His head throbbed and his throat was coarse and he assumed it must have been a gas or chloroform that had taken him out.

His captor smiled acknowledgement before landing a thundering kick to his mid-riff with a practiced aim that spoke of some form of military training. The chair skitted backwards a short distance before gravity and physics combined to flip it over with a thump. Had he not had the presence to hold his head up then the smack on the rough concrete floor would probably have taken him out again. Boris, as Molyneux decided to call him for amusement and morale, came and picked him up and left him alone whilst he finished his cigarette.

So this is how it's going to play out is it? You torture me for information, I give in and you use whatever you find out to aid your negotiations with my boss. Whether I survive is probably incidental to these boys, he thought. There's no value in someone able to talk about what happened.

The questions never came though – just a steady stream of burns, electric shocks and a particularly sadistic line with pliers on any protruding body part this psychopath could find. Molyneux roared and fought hard against his restraints but the terror and the pain were getting too much for him and he prayed for a quick end. When his torturer produced a small blow torch and tugged at his underpants he felt a release and soiled himself before fainting. It saved him that particular agony as his captor thought better of going anywhere near his shit-covered genitals. Too unpleasant by half.

~~~~

The reels and jigs went around in his head and he thanked Christ he'd made Paddy's Day after all. He could hear voices and craic and wondered why he'd got so pissed that he'd passed out in a pub, before drifting off again. He'd been having a bad dream and just wanted his hotel bedroom, Egyptian cotton sheets and all.

They let him wake up and he blinked, even in the gloom, although his swollen eyes weren't helping any. The music stopped, abruptly, and a rough hand grabbed him by the chin and its owner spoke. It was then that his past life caught up with him and he learned the identity of his adversary. It was no bloke called Boris.

"Molyneux, ye fuckin' gobshite, I have waited so long for this moment ye cannot imagine. I do not intend to hurry. Ye never did wi' me, remember? Liverpool central bridewell, July 1979, me just off the boat. Comin' back to ye?" he asked rhetorically, dripping with bitterness.

Tommy Sinnott, he thought, I'd recognize that miserable, murdering fucker's voice anywhere. The Belfast Butcher. And he knew what this was: payback for a fit-up and he had to admire the Russians for doing their homework. How had they found him? And how must he have reacted when he was given news that he could sate all that bitterness over a pleasant weekend as someone's guest in Moscow? Happy as fucking Larry, he didn't doubt. And it was a fit-up, but everyone knew he was IRA and that he commanded their south Belfast unit. They even had moles inside the Provos that told them as much, but catching the bastard at it was another thing. He was clever, that was for sure, exploiting their cell structure and deploying Ruthless brutality to stay clean. So they planted evidence and roughed him up to get a signed confession. The man who appeared before the committal magistrates and then the High Court two days later was defeated and there was a confession so it was twenty two years without remission. The Good Friday Agreement had foreshortened his term but it was still a long time in clink and he had reflected every day on how he might exact revenge. This was better, much better, than even his wildest imaginings.

Molyneux died slowly and in awful pain, his screams a symphony to

Sinnott's ponderous drum beat of fist, of blade and of tool-kit. It was a mistake by Sinnott that eventually brought the hoped-for end, a slip as he sliced Molyneux's right ear off, struggling with the gristle, leading him to gauge across the jugular. Sinnott's ageing bones couldn't take him quickly enough out of the blood's crimson arc but he took the warm splatter across his face as proof of his final pay-back. An old wrong had just been put right.

~~~~

The tour of HQ had allowed the team to scan and then search Molyneux's luggage and the recording equipment had been found immediately. They were particularly impressed with the technology hidden within the Mont Blanc pen in the breast pocket of his suit – very clever indeed. It did not transmit, which was a relief, but it was proof to Adaksin that he was dealing with adversaries, not partners. If they wanted to play those games then he could too and he would be ruthless in his methods and choice of targets. Not enough to tip the deal over the edge but more than enough to bring them to heel. He wanted that additional 35%. Had banked on it already, in fact. And once he got it he'd have a hold on them that made it a very unequal partnership.

The pen had given the game away to Adaksin. He'd met many men like Molyneux and they were instinctively conservative and certainly not given to bouts of extravagance like a Mont Blanc and the little aesthetic flourishes that one in a jacket breast pocket might offer. A silly mistake that only a person who lacked the class and sensitivity to recognize their own limitations would make, he thought.

It was Molyneux's conceit that was his undoing, not that the Moscow Police knew any of that when his decomposed body was found thirty miles outside the city six weeks later. Their investigations led them nowhere. There was a video of Molyneux being dropped off at the hotel and plenty of CCTV, email and phone activity as evidence to prove that Adaksin's security personnel had been gainfully employed in their normal line of business when Molyneux was thought to have disappeared. His removal via the hotel's service stairs didn't make it on to the security video, courtesy of a $300 bribe, and no one was any the wiser as to his disappearance.

It was time to take control, thought Adaksin, and his next volley would shake a few players out of the tree, he reckoned.

CHAPTER THIRTEEN

The media interest in The Madden Files, as they had termed it, remained intense. Journalists revelled in the hint of corporate skullduggery and the Bond-like overtones. Bell had been as good as his word and sent his private jet from John Lennon Airport to JFK and there was a welter of TV crews and photographers to film its departure and subsequent arrival, with breathless descriptions of what was unfolding from eager young journalists sent to report on this more prosaic element of the story. Still, it would blood them in, their directors had thought.

Bell Group issued a statement confirming that no-one called Molyneux was in the firm's employ, a sleight of hand based on the legal structure they had put in place for just such an eventuality. He was a self-employed computer consultant under the terms of the service contract they had agreed, which also helped them avoid the issue about the work in which he was involved. They'd told no lies, key to Godber and Middlewood's entire relationship with the media and to their professional standing. It's just that they'd not told the truth, either.

So the focus returned to Team Fabrini's next move. The flight was scheduled to depart JFK at 11pm on St. Patrick's Day and a press conference had been arranged at the airport's private terminal so that Heuston could remind the media what was at stake and keep the story firmly in the public eye. The heat of publicity, with its continued implication of historical impropriety and the moral obligation that placed upon Sir Meredith to ensure justice was served would, it was hoped, bring him to the table to negotiate an early settlement. They figured he'd want to avoid the risk, cost and time-delay of seeking recourse to the law.

Kathleen had agreed with Joe that a pint or two of Guinness at Pearl River's famous Paddy's Day parade would be good preparation for a long flight. They needed to take their minds off things and being amongst their own on the most important day of their year counted as therapy right now. He picked her up in a cab and they made their way through the Pallisades feeling altogether better.

The roads into Pearl River were jammed and the cabbie, fearful of being stuck and losing fares, suggested they walk the last mile. They hopped out, pleased with the unseasonally mild weather, and Kathleen linked arms with Joe as they joined the crowds heading towards the action on East Central

Avenue. It was a riot of false ginger beards, bunting, Irish rugby shirts and b'Jaysus – Paddywhackery at its finest and best-humoured. In the distance, the sound of pipe bands told him that the first leg of the parade – the police, fire department and social institutions' marching bands - were on the go. The floats would follow later.

Joe spotted the short-cut to South Main Street where the best vantage was to be had. It was a tip from Ted and sharing his knowledge made him feel like an insider. Christ, I've gone native already, he thought. They had forgotten, for now, the hammer-blow of yesterday's press conference and were ready for a pint. We've earned one, Joe had said.

~~~~

The couple were spotted on the van's second slow crawl around Pearl River. The team lacked a plan about how they would get the Irish into the van and it made the older of the two, Gregari, nervous. He didn't like fluid situations like this and he liked his volatile side-kick, Mikhail, even less. The kid needed to calm down and learn that brains beat brawn all ways up. Gregari had seen his share of extreme violence in Grozny and preferred using the threat of it to the real thing. It worked just as effectively in most cases and was a lot less messy. His job as an enforcer for one of Brighton Beach's largest Russian mobs beat the army hands down – better pay, better conditions and remarkably, given his job description, much less violence. Menace was his tool of choice these days and he knew he could out-menace anyone. Bulk, cold eyes and some rather disturbing facial scars saw to that but it hadn't stopped him landing Lara, a rather curvy little barmaid twenty years his junior. He lived for returning home to her embrace and her fish stew and his plans were turning to his retirement in ten years' time.

Whatever the risks, they had their instructions and the boss wouldn't broach anything other than complete success. If that meant winging it, wing it they would.

Their instructions had been simple: to find Delahunty and Fabrini and bring them back to Brighton Beach where they were to await further orders. The warehouse on West 5th Street was owned by his boss's import/export business and they'd used it plenty of times for 'interviews' and more besides. They'd watched the TV coverage of the press conference and seen their targets' pictures in the newspapers and there would be no mistaking them when they saw them.

So when the pair took a turn down a quiet side street Gregari knew that his luck was in. They looked absorbed in one another's company and would think nothing of a van pulling up ahead of them. He briefed Mikhail and the two grabbed a hood each before parking, putting the van into neutral and walking towards the rear double doors, which they opened before proceeding to help each other carry a large packing box towards the sidewalk.

It was easy to feign weight and Joe smiled as the two removal men struggled with their load. He stepped to one side to allow them past and then they struck with practised ease, dropping the box and pushing the canvas hoods over their targets before pulling the draw strings tight and putting each of them in an arm lock. It took no more than a second or two and the element of surprise worked as it always did.

They were bundled into the van, grazing shins and elbows and Joe yelped in pain, hearing his trousers rip and feeling the warm trickle of blood down his shin. Mikhail kept his foot on Kathleen's back whilst pulling the doors to behind him and Gregari growled an instruction to them both to remain still and silent. The handcuffs were administered without ceremony and the two lay terrified and in shock as their kidnappers closed the rear doors and drove off.

The chord around Kathleen's neck chaffed and meant an economy of movement was vital if she wasn't to find her airflow restricted further. Her head was pressed against the internal wheel arch and every bump in the road brought a bruise and contributed to the throbbing pain behind her eyes. She knew she had to remain focused and calm. Panic and the terror that followed would damage her forever and she'd repaired enough damage in her life to know she didn't want any more. So she focused on Joe and attempted to adopt a role that came easy to her, given her vocation – leader and carer.

"You okay, honey?" she asked, softly.

"I've paid for worse sado-masochism than this," Joe offered. "Next time, I'll know where to go looking."

He was fine then.

"What should we do? What's gonna happen?" asked Kathleen, with a strain in her voice suggesting that this staying calm shit wasn't the easiest of gigs. Joe sensed her fear and knew that if they had any chance of survival, then calm co-operation was their only option. Assuming of course that they didn't pull out the pliers, in which case he'd probably shit himself and scream, he confessed.

Ah, Confession. That brought a wry smile. It seemed an age since he was last on his knees at Our Lady's in Salford. What he'd give for that now.

"Let's keep talking and stay calm. We'll co-operate with them and not do anything rash. Let's see what happens but I'm right beside you, sweetheart." With that he wriggled over towards her voice and found her hands and took them in his as best as his constraints allowed. She needed that tenderness and reassurance.

Joe tried to work out who they were. They were obviously eastern European but what had they to do with the Bell Group issue? Kidnapping like this wasn't the English way. For all Bell Group's moral flexibility he was fairly sure that gangsterism wasn't part of their modus operandi. Something didn't stack up. But that was secondary, he realized, to keeping Kathleen calm and focused so they talked. He was good at getting women to open up and even in these circumstances he knew he could perform.

It wasn't long before the subject of her husband came up. Joe was curious to know how such a well-bred lady had ended up with a Mafia boss's son.

"Tony wasn't Mafiosi," she explained. "He was a sweet and thoughtful man, quite bookish really. Like many mobsters his father was a social climber and he'd sent Tony to St Philhomena's, a top private school in the Upper East Side. He wanted his kids to be smart and well-rounded. That made for better mobsters in a changing world, he thought.

"But Tony wasn't cut out for thuggery or even white collar crime. He wanted to read, to learn music and to play the clarinet and his father saw that. Give him credit, he knew that it would only spell trouble if he tried to bring him into the mafia fold so he let him be and took pride in his academic achievements. It was odd, really. Here was a sophisticated and urbane man who knew all about his father's business and who rejected it absolutely, but without judgment. He loved his father and his father loved me, too, when I became part of the family. Tony only let me in on his background when he was sure that I was in love with him as much as he was with me."

"How did you react?" asked Joe kicking himself for interrupting her flow with such a bloody obvious question.

"I loved the man completely and it was clear that he was divorced from the family business and family ethics. I saw, too, in his father a pride and a love at a son's achievements and it was an easy accommodation really. We never talked about it, ever. And then they shot him."

Kathleen sobbed uncontrollably, the pain of the memory and the fear of what lay ahead convulsing her body as she lay cramped up against the wheel arch. Joe stroked her hand and shushed her gently until she was able to compose herself.

"He was a good man. He didn't deserve a death like that." She let the observation hang, composing herself again for the story ahead.

"His father had been in dispute over a protection racket targeting trucking businesses servicing the container port near Newark airport and it got out of hand. One of his men had shot a young member of the Bonino clan, a favourite of the capo and so he took out Tony on the basis of an eye for an eye. It nearly broke his father and it took me years to recover. It was the school that saved me, really," she added. "I realised that whatever shit I went through I still had options, advantages, a future. Those kids had nothing, but I could give them something if they'd work with me. Their achievements in the face of incredible disadvantage is my greatest source of pride."

Joe heard her voice firm up as she talked about the kids and her plans to take her teaching and management model to other inner city communities. It was only money that was stopping her and if she could get the federal government as well as local authorities to realize what she was saving them by keeping those kids out of jail and making them productive members of the community then maybe they'd give her the funds. That was her dream and it was keeping her alive right now so Joe let her talk, asking her questions that allowed her to explore the minutiac of her methods and programme. He knew a bit about schools from his work in the Dingle in Liverpool's south end and it gave him enough to oil the wheels of the conversation.

It took them more than two hours to drive to South Beach and when the engine stopped, Joe and Kathleen froze with the realization that whatever was to happen was likely to happen here.

"Stay with me, sweetheart," he urged as he stroked her hand one last time. "We'll be okay. They're looking for us now," and with that they were unceremoniously yanked apart and dragged out of the van.

Their hoods were removed and they were allowed to stand, adjusting to the gloom. They were in a large warehouse with shelves stacked with goods and packing boxes – toys, it looked like. They were taken by their arms into a side office with a glass screen overlooking the picking and packing floor. Probably where the boss sat, thought Joe, barking out his orders from the doorway. He was wrong. There was no desk, just two chairs and a credenza, on top of which was a metal tray with a series of scalpels, pliers and other instruments and Joe's eyes went wide with fear. Kathleen hadn't seen them, he was sure, for she made no noise and they were placed on wooden chairs, with their backs to the credenza and tied by their ankles to the chair legs. Their arms remained handcuffed behind their backs and it was a blessing that the chairs were low as they had to loop their arms over the backs in order to gain some semblance of comfort.

Joe could see a slight ligature mark around Kathleen's neck and he hoped it would heal. She was elegant and beautiful and there was love left in her to give. She'd make a fine prize for any man willing to treasure her, he thought.

Gregori had seen Joe's reaction to his torture kit and he knew that would deflate any bravado he felt. The power of suggestion. Worked every time. Still, he wanted to ladle on a little more just to be sure and he pulled Kathleen's hair back sharply, bringing his cheek to hers.

"I do not want to hurt you unless my boss tells me to. But if either of you make one move then you will experience pain and terror that nothing could ever prepare you for. Do I make myself clear?"

Kathleen offered a defiant 'yes' and Joe just nodded. He was thinking coolly still, in spite of the fear induced by the hardware on the credenza. So these guys were just hired muscle and there wasn't a clear plan for their detention yet. That was promising. He knew that it would be a few hours yet before they were missed, but any hint that they were on an indefinite timetable was good for morale. If they were to get out of there alive then keeping Kathleen's spirits up would be key.

Mikhail framed the office doorway, his arms folded with a look of utter contempt. Was it for us or for his colleague, thought Joe? Probably for the other bloke. We were just passing through and part of the job. He looked much younger and was probably impatient for some action – a hot-head, where as the other chap was clearly more measured. He thought about how this dynamic could be exploited, although nothing came to him immediately so he sat and waited, giving Kathleen smiles and winks when he thought he wasn't being watched.

~~~~

Anna was worried. She rang Roz and asked if she'd heard from Joe and Kathleen and, of course, she hadn't. Their cells were off and Roz knew that that was something her friend would not do in circumstances like this. They'd only gone to the parade and they weren't lovers, so it wasn't like they were holed up in some boutique hotel getting all hot under the sheets. Her instinct was screaming 'help' but neither she nor Anna could figure any plausible reason why they'd go off the radar like this.

There was only one logical conclusion: they were in trouble. The police would do nothing, of that they were sure. Someone had to be missing for more than twenty four hours before they stepped in and given the very public nature of the pair's recent travails the police would probably think they'd done a bunk, fearful of further bad publicity and just wanting to put the whole charade behind them.

"There's only one thing to do," said Roz. Anna was up for any sensible suggestion but not this one. "We need to get the mafia looking for them."

"What?" she exclaimed. "Are you nuts? We're trying to win a PR battle here, not reinforce to the press that we're a bunch of misfits with no regard for due process. And why the hell would the mafia help us?" she said, dismissively.

"Listen, honey," said Roz, trying to sooth things, "Anna's family to them. There's a tie between them cast in blood and these things count. She's told me all about Tony's upbringing and his family's business and how they let them both be, content for them to find their own way in life. But she told me once that if she was ever in deep trouble, that she would probably turn to them."

"Why would she say that?" asked Anna, incredulous.

"I think it was to do with the school. It's in a pretty rough neighbourhood and some of the folk down there didn't like a smart Irish girl coming in and disrupting their supply chain of willing young thugs. She'd turned some kids' heads and that meant fewer foot soldiers for some pretty nasty guys. I think she saw Tony's family as a form of insurance or protection should things get ugly."

Anna sat open-mouthed, wondering what she'd gotten herself into and trying, at the same time, to figure the next move. It was always about the next two moves for her, in fact, but she was out of her depth and couldn't even see what the next one might be.

"Let me make a call," said Roz.

"What? You know these people? You've met them?" Each revelation left Anna stunned. There is so much beneath the surface that you never see, she thought.

"Kathleen gave me their contact details. She'd figured that if she found herself in a situation where she genuinely needed them she might not be able to contact them directly. She's good at weighing the options. 'If I'm tied to a chair, you're gonna need to make the call,' she said to me, laughing. So now it may be time to hit the phone." She would only discover later how prescient a call that was.

~~~~

Big Johnny Fabrini was enjoying a cappuccino in Mario's deli and café on the corner of 18th and 79th in Bensonhurst when his cell buzzed. He sat and listened without a word as the story unfolded and then asked some confirmatory questions.

"You sure they were at the Paddy's parade? Certain? Definitely Pearl River, not the Manhattan job? I'll send someone over to turn over a few stones. Keep your phone by you," he said before flipping the lid unceremoniously and thinking for a moment about the best way forward. Kathleen Fabrini was family – the clue was in the name. She may be a Mick but hadn't the mafia enjoyed some good dealings with Irish gangsters over the years? Yeah, the odd dispute, but plenty of respect too. There weren't any around these days but back in the fifties and sixties there'd been some fun. What did the Paddies call it? Craic, that's it. Shared turf, clear demarcation, good, business-like dealings. He had time for the Irish – they generally made good criminals. And they'd made a good wife for his brother too.

Marco and Bobby were reliable guys. They used their nous as much as their muscle and they left few trails. He called them up and described the problem, telling them to get up to Pearl River, blend in with the crowds and see what they could unearth.

Bobby thought Marco looked ridiculous in his tall black hat with its white top, designed to look like a pint of Guinness, but then Bobby's red beard and leprechaun's hat was no prize-winner either. How two olive-skinned blokes with brown eyes could pass themselves off as Irish was anyone's guess, though they reminded themselves that on Paddy's Day in New York everyone was a Mick. So no-one batted an eye-lid as they climbed out of their Toyota sedan and made for what was left of the parade.

They'd reasoned that if the pair had been kidnapped then it wouldn't have been on any main street. Way, way too busy for that. So it had to be in their guest house or hotel or down a side street, perhaps. Whilst Marco drove, Bobby had scoured the web on his iPhone to find the names and addresses of local guest houses when he remembered that these guys had been staying with relatives – heard it mentioned in some TV coverage when that priest had been found out for rutting with his parishioners. It didn't take long to find the Courtney's home number and he gave it a call. No answer. Of course, with a name like that they'd be out at the parade all day. And so they started with the guest houses, ringing and asking to speak with one of their guests, Mr Joseph Delahunty.

It was the same story every time: no-one of that name booked in with us, sir. You must be mistaken. And no, there was no-one called Fabrini either. So it was either false names and the two were hard at it on the bed springs or they had been grabbed somewhere quiet. She was an older broad – fifties, maybe – and he didn't figure a bloke in his thirties would be chasing skirt like that. Disgusting. So Bobby looked up the parade route and the ways into the town and figured that if they'd come up from the city it would to have been via Veteran Memorials Drive and on to Gilbert Avenue. They'd likely have had to abandon their car early or jump out of their cab to walk the last leg and so he reckoned that's what they'd do, too, even though the traffic had calmed a lot since Joe and Kathleen's arrival earlier. It proved to be a solid move.

They spotted the short-cut off Ridge Street and figured it would be a great place to grab someone. Not over-looked too much as the houses on one side and commercial plots on the other were well set back and it was long enough for people not to really hear or notice what was going on as they walked past the top at right angles. So down it they went, looking for clues, although not entirely sure what they might find.

The groaning noise stopped them in their tracks. It was coming from underneath some cardboard boxes. They grabbed the garbage, flinging it to one side, to find a vagrant lying asleep, half a bottle of cheap bourbon clutched in his right hand. They shook him awake, propping him up against the wall before recoiling at the smell of stale piss and alcohol.

"Hey, old man, wake up," chided Bobby, giving him a slap around his chops for good measure.

The man opened his bleary eyes and focused on the two hulks in front of him.

"Good morning offishers," he offered, grinning inanely. This was going to be difficult.

"You seen anyone or anything down this alleyway, old man? Anything at all today? It's important."

"Twenty bucks and I may have," he slurred. Christ, he may be pissed but he's not daft, thought Bobby. He waved a five dollar bill quickly in front of his eyes then stuffed it in the old man's breast pocket.

"There, that's twenty to jog your memory. Tell us anything useful and there's a twenty to follow." Marco grinned to himself at Bobby's game. Gotta bring humour into things if you can, he always said. Life's too short.

"I heard a van," said the drunk.

"Go on," Bobby encouraged him. "What else did you see?"

"I didn't say see. I said heard," he corrected them.

"So what else did you hear, then, smart-ass?" Bobby was getting irritated but he could be on to something so he kept his temper in check.

"Just voices, but not Paddies. Sounded odd for this part of town. Sounded angry, too. Something about keeping quiet and not getting hurt."

"What was the accent? Hispanic? Asian? Nigger?" Bobby wanted that clue if they were to kick over the right stones.

"Sounded Russian or eastern European to me. I may be sleepy these days," he grinned, "but I ain't too far gone."

"You done good, old man," said Bobby, stuffing another five dollar bill in his top pocket. "Thanks," and with that the pair headed back to their car for a conference call with the boss.

"Hey! Hey!," came the shout. The old man had done the math and there'd be no fine Scotch for him today. Bobby grinned again and they climbed in the car.

~~~~

Mikhail was bored with the hanging around. They were awaiting instruction and he was hoping for some action. A little torture, perhaps, or at the very least the chance to rough up the good looking fella. Maybe even permission to have a dabble with the pretty looking lady. He'd served his mandatory military service in the Russian forces and it had shaped his world forever. Hit people hard and take whatever pussy you can find.

He'd never been a fighter really, more an observer, but the Russian army needed hard men who killed first and asked questions later. He only questioned his drill sergeant the once. The team beating from his fellow squaddies on sarge's instruction had been merciless and he knew that he must embrace thuggery or be consumed by it. So he chose survival and learned to revel in the skills and strength his training gave him. I'll get through this with my fists as well as my brain, he thought, but he knew it wasn't a great choice. There was better money and less risk using his muscle on civvy street so, like countless Russians before him, he made his way to Brighton Beach and enrolled with the mob.

Gregori took a call, which put the entire group on edge. What was the instruction? Was this the end? Joe strained his ears for any sign or clue.

"I have to go. Just half an hour. You look after these," barked Gregori. "And nothing stupid. Just stand and watch," he ordered. He did not trust Mikhail at all – no judgement, no finesse – but what choice did he have?

The door clanged shut and Mikhail seized his opportunity, slowly unbuttoning Kathleen's blouse to reveal a white bra with simple lace edging. So, not new lovers then, he thought – she'd have put on something much flashier than that.

"Leave her alone, you fucking sick twat," growled Joe, his guttural Scouse accent dripping with hatred. Mikhail just grinned, grabbed an old rag from the floor and stuffed it into Joe's mouth, yanking his head back by his hair and forcing his jaws open with a practiced grip.

Kathleen spat in his face as he bent down to inspect her breasts and he slapped her hard, sending her head jerking backwards and leaving a huge red welt across her left cheek. The sharp pain and the terror at what lay ahead brought her to tears, but she choked them back. She was not about to give him the satisfaction.

He released her small breasts from their casing and fondled them idly, before placing the right one in his mouth and toying with the left nipple. Kathleen looked skywards and took her mind to another place. She wanted as much detachment from this as she could muster. Joe was struggling against his restraints, but it was to no avail. He implored Mikhail to leave her alone, but all that came out were garbled and muffled sounds. It was useless, and he turned away. I will kill you with my bare hands if I get the chance, he thought.

Mikhail's pleasure had made him hard and he unzipped his pants, stroking himself rhythmically in front of Kathleen. Her eyes went wide with horror as he yanked her dress up to reveal her panties, his hands grubbing for purchase on the cloth so that he could yank them to one side. Kathleen rooted herself in her seat with all her strength to deny him, so he grabbed her sharply by the hair with his left hand whilst running the other up her inner thigh.

"You ready for me, lady? Make me happy and you be okay," he purred, before rubbing his member around her mouth. Kathleen gagged at the smell of his sweaty piece and she struggled to turn her head away. Hadn't the disgusting little bastard bathed recently, she thought.

She suddenly gave up the struggle, relaxing her body weight and no longer resisting his grip on her head. She turned and smiled, a weak, submissive gesture but a smile nonetheless. Mikhail grinned. He loved that point of submission.

"You ready to play, yes? That's better. I'll be gentle. I'm not wild beast," he assured her.

The blow to the back of his knees was brutal and he collapsed to the floor in a heap, clasping his legs in agony as he shrieked in pain. Gregori followed up with a crack on the head, designed to hurt like hell but not to concuss, then he grabbed him by the hair and brought his angry face to his young charge's ear.

"I forgot my keys. You forgot your manners. Do anything like that again and you will be back to some shithole in Russia before you can beg forgiveness. Do you hear me?"

Mikhail nodded his understanding, his face a contorted picture of pain and confusion, his pants down by his knees and his member deflated to compound his loss of dignity and authority. Gregori gently and quickly cupped Kathleen's breasts back into her bra and buttoned her up, pulling her dress back below her knees to complete her modesty.

"I am sorry madam. That will not happen again," he offered, before removing Joe's gag and bringing a bottle of water to his mouth to relieve the dryness. "Sit here quietly and you will be fine," the bigger man said, before returning his attention to his side-kick, whom he dragged out of the office and stationed on the other side of the window, presumably before completing the errand the call had demanded.

Gregori was no monster, he reminded himself. If he had to kill these people then it would be with a measure of dignity. Put a bag over their head again for a while so that they relaxed a little then walk up behind them quietly and put a 9mm in the back of their head. A good calibre – there'd be no messy exit wound, which meant less evidence and less stuff to clean up afterwards. It was the same with torture. It just gave you more work to do later and the victims often soiled themselves, which meant picking up their bodies for disposal was a particularly disgusting affair. Who wants other people's shit on their hands as part of their day job? Your own was bad enough.

Joe assessed the situation and wondered what he could do to exploit the very clear division between the two men. If he could get to talk to the older fella that might help; he doubted he'd win a physical contest with either, though, fit enough as he was. He'd wait for his return and see what he could engineer. If he could only free his hands.

~~~~

Marco and Bobby reported back to Johnny Fabrini what they'd learned and got permission to go and speak with a few scumbags in the Russian mob's lower orders to see who might squeal. They needed to know who'd ordered the kidnapping and where they were being held, as well as letting it be known that this was something they wanted resolving, quickly. The Russians, like all mobsters, did not want any disruption to their activities and angry Italians, nosy policemen and even TV cameras fell firmly into that category.

And so it was that Vasily Gorchenko found himself pinned to the floor at the back of a parade of shops on Brighton Beach with a boot in his face. That can be highly persuasive when you're a snivelling little low-life, Bobby knew, and he wanted to max on the persuasiveness, as going into open battle with his Russian counterparts would just be messy and potentially painful. The quicker he got what he wanted, the quicker he could be out of there in one piece.

It was clear that Gorchenko knew nothing. No-one could cope with that amount of sustained pain without singing if he knew something. He was too low down the food chain, they realized, so they squeezed him hard for a name further up. And that is when things got interesting and dangerous.

"Speak with Gregori Markovic," he'd spluttered through what few teeth he had left. "He'd manage something like this around here. You'll find him at The Russian Doll on Coney Island Avenue if he's not working."

Bobby and Marco retreated to assess their options. Ordinarily they wouldn't call the boss each step of the way. He left them to their initiative as a rule. But this was a family matter and it was getting late in the day. They didn't know Markovic but the boss might and he'd want to assess what they were up against before anything substantive was sanctioned. So they made the call.

"Find him and if he's the man, reason with him. His boss will not want the disruption we can unleash on them and tell him if he co-operates, then we'll be minded to help if they have a similar issue. We don't want bloodshed, but he needs to know that this is family and that he's messing with the most sacred thing there is. If his boss wants a war then he will get one."

The boys turned to each other. They knew the boss did not make idle threats and that this was therefore as serious as it looked. Warfare should be avoided but if it couldn't, then they'd bring it to the Russians in a practiced and professional way. It was 7pm and off they went in search of Markovic.

~~~~

Roz and Anna sat on the edge of the sofa waiting impatiently for the call from Johnny Fabrini. When it came they leapt up to the table in unison to grab the cell and Roz switched it to loudspeaker, introducing Anna and explaining her role in proceedings thus far.

"She's trustworthy, Johnny. You're amongst friends," Roz offered, in return for a grunt of acknowledgement.

He told them what he knew, that it looked like the Russian mob had kidnapped Kathleen and Joe and that he had a team turning over stones in Brighton Beach looking for them. He was sure they'd be effective at some point because he was banking on the Russians not wanting the intrusion, but he couldn't give them a time. Time is what we don't have, thought Anna. There's a press conference at 8:15pm, designed to help make the late evening news. Then she had an idea and shared it with Johnny, figuring that to do it without his permission would be folly. He liked it, he said, smart. It'll turn the heat up a little and maybe flush them out.

~~~~

It was another packed press conference, this time in the media centre at JFK's private air terminal, more accustomed to handling the arrival or departure of film stars or leading politicians than private individuals in the eye of a very public storm.

There were just two chairs at the table instead of the expected four, which caused speculation amongst the press scrum. They could understand Joe Delahunty being kept out of the picture, but who else? Maybe Fabrini had flipped after news of her husband's death had been dredged up again after so long. Others thought the alcoholic lawyer would step out of the limelight after being humiliated so publicly. Either way, it wouldn't be long before they found out. They arranged their microphones, smallest to the fore, largest to the rear, in their time-honoured spirit of co-operation and waited to see who would come through the door to the rear.

Wrong on a few counts, they admitted, as first Heuston and then Goldstein walked to the small stage. Fifteen minutes later the press conference was to break up with another sensational revelation, only for one more to follow within the hour, courtesy of the time difference between the publishing of the first editions of British tabloids, five hours ahead of New York time.

~~~~

Adaksin received the call that he'd hoped for. Delahunty and Fabrini were in the care of his contacts in Brighton Beach and out of the picture. They could no longer press home their case and the drunken lawyer and that silly little attention seeker who ran the press conferences would doubtless pack up and go home. But he needed to give Bell definitive proof that he was now in charge and guiding the direction and pace of this issue. The Englishman had proven that he was unreliable and indecisive and it was now to be a partnership of convenience, not spirit. It was Bell's fault. He'd engineered it that way and he couldn't be surprised at the outcome.

His press officer in England, there to represent NovKos's interests to the London money markets, had a very different brief on her hands when the material from Adaksin landed on her desk, complete with instructions. Pippa Godwin-Jones was much more used to the dull but necessary release of formulaic financial announcements to analysts and City correspondents, not grubbing around with the tabloids, but she conceded it might be fun to see how the other half of the PR world earned their living and she got stuck in, as instructed. The results were to prove both highly effective and the low point for Sir Meredith Bell in this whole tawdry affair.

~~~~

"Ladies and gentlemen," began Anna Heuston , "you know why we are here. It is to put right a terrible injustice committed one hundred and twenty two years ago. An injustice that denied Theresa Brophy a substantial fortune and which changed the course of her life in a most terrible fashion. We have evidence to back up our case and are seeking the help of Bell Group to ensure that justice is served and a fair and equitable solution found."

Here we go again, thought the Bell Group team, gathered in their mahogany panelled boardroom in the Cunard Building. Middlewood and two lawyers from Barlow Hayes were scrutinizing every word and phrase for slander and libel. Godber was weighing up the claims with a view to her forthcoming rebuttals whilst Sir Meredith, still troubled by the lack of any word from Molyneux, stood silent and apart, weighing up the threat to the family reputation and the dynasty they had so assiduously built over two hundred odd years and innumerable wars and revolutions.

"We do not want to bring the company down, nor do we hold the current owners and management of the business responsible for those terrible events all those years ago. But we do believe that a responsible company should seek to make good their forebears' mistakes and it is to Sir Meredith Bell's credit that he has agreed to see us and sent us his jet.

"But he has been brought to this position by our campaigning and your support and we would like to thank you for that." Always a good move, they all admitted to themselves, giving the press the glory and reinforcing their sense of ownership of the issue. Smart kid.

"But we have been threatened with violence and now you will see that two of our number are missing. Today we heard through our grapevine that Joe Delahunty and Kathleen Fabrini have been kidnapped and are being held against their will somewhere in New York."

Chaos erupted as journalists shouted questions and hit their phones, seeking live links rather than the pre-record job they had been sent on. This was red hot and the viewers and listeners would want to get in on the action, right now. Anna understood this and let the chaos subside of its own volition, rather than seeking to bring it to order. Give them time to get those live links up, she had told herself.

When hush descended, she continued.

"We have discovered that Joe and Kathleen were kidnapped by members of the Russian mob in Brighton Beach. We do not know where they are or whether they are safe. But their disappearance is another step up from the threats we have already received and I want to know who is behind this.

"Sir Meredith, is this your doing?" she asked, looking straight into the BBC's camera, figuring he'd be watching it on their World Service. "I can't believe that you would extend the hand of conciliation to us and then place our friends in such danger. So who else would have an interest in halting our campaign, if it is not you?"

She let the question hang for a moment, scanning the journalists with an imploring look. And then she unclipped her final hand grenade and let it go boom.

"The only Russian connection we can see in all of this is the fact that Bell Group's junior partner in Newfoundland is NovKos, a Moscow-based energy business. They stand to lose a huge share of the profits from this deal once we have pressed our claim," and with that she let the implication sink in.

The room erupted once again as questions were hurled at Anna and Roz and journalists barked instructions down the phone to colleagues to get on to the Muscovites' press office or to Bell Group for an immediate response.

In Liverpool Sir Meredith Bell was pale. He had no doubt whatsoever that Adaksin's team were behind this and knew instinctively what was to be done. Middlewood was huddled with his legal advisors discussing their most immediate options whilst Godber was shouting a series of rushed instructions to each of her team members so that they could gather what they needed to produce a coherent and timely response.

In Moscow, Adaksin was quietly seething. This had not gone as planned. How on earth had these amateurs got so close? Of course, the trail to him would go no further than Brighton Beach and he could claim innocence. He wasn't naïve, however, and he knew that the connection was so obvious as to be fact in the minds of the public. Worse, the politicians, too. They were the ones that could cause him greatest difficulty. He ordered Pugin, on probation for his earlier stupidity with Molyneux, to contact their friends in Brighton Beach for a report. Then he remembered his own little surprise with the British press and smiled quietly. He was still in control – just – and they were going to find out soon enough.

~~~~

Bobby and Marco had been busy, tapping up contacts in the NYPD to get the low-down on Gregori Markovic. He wasn't in the Russian Doll but they'd secured a photograph of him and his home address, a small two bed apartment which he shared with his girlfriend Lara who was pregnant, their informant told them. They figured they'd go knocking. If Markovic had the boss's family, then they'd go and talk to his. Nothing heavy, just some gentle persuasion. They weren't monsters and they didn't hurt pregnant women. Not if they could help it.

They found the apartment without too much trouble, two blocks back from the front on 7th Street. It was on the second floor of a co-op development built in an oblong U-shape around a dirty and unloved swimming pool drained for the winter period. Theirs was the third door along from the top of the stairs.

Bobby's knock was firm but not intimidating. "NYPD, ma'am," he announced, holding a false badge to the peep-hole, "would you open up for me, please?"

A petite woman in her late twenties with jet black hair, a wide face and pale white skin opened up, a look of weary resignation on her countenance. It was late, Gregori was still at work and she was being troubled by these meatheads. What did they want, she wondered. Gregori was usually far too discreet to get on their radar so she was worried.

She signalled them in and offered them the sofa. Bobby accepted, but Marco leant against the door post with his arms folded. So that's how' it's going to be, is it, she thought to herself. Good cop and arsey prick. Fire right away, fellas and see how far you get.

Bobby sized her up. A sullen little madam, he thought, but pleasant enough on the eye. A lot younger than Markovic, who was probably prepared to put up with some shit to get into the pants of a firm young broad like that. And he clearly had, as the bump showed. Twenty weeks he reckoned, with a seasoned eye. There were three bambini back in Bensonhurst.

"Lady, we gotta know where Gregori is and we gotta know now. We think he's in danger, see, and we wanna get to him before some very bad people do." Bobby was good at this, Marco conceded – a voice that said 'no messing', but concern too.

To Lara's ear that voice said Italian knucklehead. These guys were never cops, that was blindingly obvious, but her face gave her away and Marco moved in from the door, slowly. She looked from one to the other, smiled, then lunged for the heavy glass ashtray on the sideboard, but Bobby had anticipated the move and sprung from the sofa to grab her. She was trussed up and gagged with practised efficiency and her cell phone yanked from her back pocket.

The call to Gregori was perfunctory and yielded the desired result.

"Markovic, we got your broad and your little baby. We ain't gonna do them no harm, so listen up." He did just that and a deal was agreed inside two minutes. Honour amongst thieves. No need for a war. He could sell this to the men in Moscow. The Italians would be over in thirty minutes and the merchandise better be unharmed and ready to go.

~~~~

Sir Meredith had excused himself and retired to his private office for what was a long and difficult conversation with Sir Quentin Fanshaugh. He would need all his political and diplomatic goodwill to help steer the company through this mess and he let his irritation show when he was interrupted by Godber, who looked uncharacteristically flustered and asked him to return to the board room.

He'd dealt with the business at hand anyhow and was bringing the conversation to a conclusion when the line went quiet.

"Quentin, are you still there?" Bell asked, perturbed at the second steady person in a minute to go turtle on him.

"You'd better get back to your team," said Fanshaugh, with a mild urgency in his tone as he gawped at the TV screen in front of him, "there's no diplomat in the world's going to get you out of this pickle, old chap."

Bell put the phone down and strode to the boardroom, turning ashen for the second time that night as he saw what was before him. At the end of their forty foot board table made from teak his ships had brought back from Indonesia was a huge screen fed with TV pictures via a projector suspended from the ceiling. It was purposefully dramatic, offering crisp images across eight feet by ten feet to aid them when making presentations to institutions, politicians and other key stakeholders. Always room for a little bit of showbiz, they'd thought.

An almost life-size image of Bell showed him tied to a bedstead with silk scarves and wearing nothing but stockings and high heels. Astride him, in full coitus, was the leggy and beautiful form of Anatalia Kolliakov with her nipples blacked out for decency and a TV caption which read: 'British shipping magnate exposed for part in Russian porn ring'.

The story then moved on to the reaction of the British media. First up was the house bible of the business community, the FT, with a front page story headed 'Sir Meredith Bell caught inflagrante with Russian prostitute.' She wasn't a prostitute he protested silently, she was my girlfriend, and almost before he finished his lament the realization that he had been stitched up royally by NovKos hit him like a sledgehammer. Of course, she worked in their office reception. They'd planned this from the very start to have some leverage in their top drawer should they ever need it. And he'd fallen for the oldest sucker punch in the book. How could he be so damned stupid?

He grabbed one of the leather sofas at the end of the room for support and collapsed into the seat. Caroline would never forgive him. Could never forgive. The girls would be distraught. Those stockings were just for a laugh, not a fetish thing. Anatalia had suggested them, of course, doubtless part of the plan to cause maximum embarrassment. It couldn't just be a fling. Plenty of industrialists had been caught doing that and it hadn't ruined their careers. It had to smack of perversion and dark secrets to do maximum damage. That was him on his way out of Royal Liverpool Golf Club, no doubt.

Next on the screen was that morning's Sun newspaper, predictably irreverent as well as inventive: 'Big cheese caught up to his spuds in Kolli', in a culinary play on words that would win headline of the year if there was a poll of the average British punter that week. And there he was again, a different picture this time, enjoying the delights of Anatalia but wearing a feather boa.

He sat and pondered the chain of events that had led him to this pretty pass, and the role of happenstance in a man's downfall. But there was still the issue of the Madden Files to be concluded, which brought him back to the hear and now. What the bloody hell was Adaksin thinking, having those idiots kidnapped? How was that calculated to help things? He sensed a power-grab here and he wasn't sure if the diplomatic manouevrings he'd agreed with Sir Quentin Fanshaugh would be enough. Ostensibly, it was a straight forward plan. The Foreign & Commonwealth Office would prevail upon the Newfoundland & Labrador provincial government to invoke a clause in their license agreement which allowed them to order the cessation of drilling and exploration activity whilst they assessed whether their partners in the process were fit and proper. That would buy Sir Meredith time to negotiate the buy-out of the Russians' 15% stake, having failed to pass the necessary tipping point to give them their remaining 35%.

They would be bloody negotiations and it wouldn't be a cheap affair. If the Ruskis chose to litigate then it would be a long and complex process though, thankfully, in the British jurisdiction. But it all hinged on how quickly the Canadians acted. The Russians were in the thick of the drilling activity and doubtless would seek to push it through at break-neck speed so that they reached the discovery threshold of 1bn cubic metres and with it the tipping point to 50% of the shares in the enterprise. If they reached 50% shareholding then the game was up. It would be a deeply unpleasant and frustrating partnership. Not a partnership at all, really, but a slog.

They could ask the Canadians to escalate matters, ruling that NovKos were not fit and proper license holders, which would invoke a 'put' option in their agreement, meaning that they had to offer their shares up for sale to Bell Group for the figure they had invested thus far in the project, or £200m, whichever was the lower. But they couldn't count on the Canadians pulling that stroke because they had their own diplomatic issues with Russia and he knew that Adaksin was well connected with the Putin government. Probably a regular donor and supporter, if you got his drift.

So it all hinged on the speed with which they could get drilling suspended. He ordered Middlewood to find someone who could get his chief engineer over in Canada, Marley Clitheroe, on the line and took a large slug of whisky from the boardroom drinks tray before heading back to his office and letting the heavy mahogany doors thud shut. He needed to ring Lady Caroline, and in peace.

~~~~

The report back to Adaksin was as expected. His 'guests' were still sitting comfortably in their chairs, their captors awaiting instruction. Adaksin had to weigh up a number of issues, none of which was necessarily helpful. He should have thought this through better, he chided himself, but the bloody British being so damned nice about things had forced his hand. When your back is against the wall it is absolute force or nothing, he always felt.

And that was the trouble with working in democratic jurisdictions with their nosy journalists. You had to be more measured and refined. The good old days were gone, increasingly even in Russia: bribe, kill, maim, terrorise or ply with prostitutes and drugs. Simple, really. Try doing any of that in modern Britain, apart from the prostitutes bit perhaps. Impossible.

If he let his captives go they lived to pursue their vendetta, as well as talk about their experiences. It would not come back to his door – the chain of command was too opaque for that – but the inference was clear and the western media would make celebrities out of these low-lives. It would be a recurring stain on NovKos's reputation, every Google search going forward leading to pages and pages on the fuck-happy priest and his collection of misfit friends.

If he killed them and ensured they disappeared forever the media speculation would run for a while, but the core problem – this ridiculous claim against the title to the shale gas reserves – would disappear. NovKos could deny all involvement, pointing to how these people must clearly have gone through life making enemies and even claiming another mafia hit for misdeeds by the Fabrini family.

He made the call to Pugin, satisfied that his decision was the more sensible of the two.

~~~~

Bobby and Marco found the warehouse with little trouble and sat outside weighing up their options one more time. They'd agreed with Markovic a sensible solution and he'd been pragmatic and thoughtful, adding a few details himself they hadn't considered. He'd make a good Mafioso, they thought. Their job was about flying under the radar, not running around waving guns and engaging in drive-by shootings. That was for the clowns in the South Bronx.

They checked their weapons, a Colt XSE each, holstered under their left arms for ease of access and a necessary precaution in their line of business. They weren't expecting any trouble but there were other risks – New York State didn't allow concealed carry and they were looking at a stretch inside if stopped by the police. Nevertheless, they had to pack on a job like this. If it was pure muscle – squeezing money out of a local trader, say – then muscle was all that was needed. But it would be folly to go unarmed against this lot, even when they'd struck a deal for a hand-over.

Markovic had given them instructions to come to the blue sliding door at the front of the building and knock only twice. The door would slide from left to right and they would come into a small open area of warehouse, facing rows of shelving and products. To their right would be an office in which their merchandise would be waiting.

It was standard procedure in such instances to let the other side know about the environment in which they were entering to avoid jitteriness, which tended to have a dilatory impact on itchy trigger fingers. No surprises, that was the rule and Markovic played by the rules. It had got him to 48 years old with only one bullet hole in his body and he wasn't about to change a tried and trusted method when his beautiful Lara and future child were in the mix.

He'd not got angry at the news. It was always a risk in this business and when the Italian had explained to him that one of his captives was family he respected their need for collateral. Good job he'd managed to stop that fucking idiot Mikhail from raping the red head. That sort of thing would only end one way in circumstances like this.

The knock came just as the phone rang. Mikhail looked to Markovic for instruction: door or phone, his face asked. The call may well be another instruction and Mikhail could whisper that to him if need be; Markovic wanted to see Lara and to put her to one side and to safety. So he nodded towards the phone whilst making for the door himself. It was a huge aluminium composite affair on a track and rolled easily enough once you'd put some shoulder into it. The space allowed small trucks to reverse into the warehouse – all the better for unloading merchandise, human or otherwise, away from prying eyes.

He opened a small gap to check what was awaiting him and, seeing no surprises, created enough space for the two Italians and Lara to squeeze through. He stood back, showing both his hands to reassure the Italians that he wasn't holding a weapon and they allowed Lara through first. Markovic gave her a quick, gentle hug and led her to one side, down one of the packing aisles, just in case.

He thanked the Italians and led them to the small office, where they reeled at what they saw.

"What the fuck?" exclaimed Bobby. "This ain't no part of the deal. Wassup?" he asked, looking at Markovic as both he and Marco instinctively went for their weapons.

Joe and Kathleen, counter to their agreement, remained tied to their chairs, but with hoods over their heads now. Mikhail stood over them with his 9mm pointing at Kathleen's head and a determined look on his face. He was taking charge now, not Gregori. He was still smarting from that humiliation earlier and the call had changed everything. This was his chance to climb the ranks.

"Our instructions change," he explained. "I am sorry gentlemen, but deal is off. You back off now and live, or you die with these two."

Markovic stepped forward, holding his right hand up to the Italians behind him as a conciliatory gesture. Leave this to me, fellas, it said. Joe was fidgeting in his seat and Markovic knew the man feared his imminent demise.

"Mikhail, you do not get to make those decisions," said Gregori. "Now stand down. We have an agreement with the Italians and failing to keep to it will cause our employers far greater distress and disruption than if we comply. You are not aware of the special circumstances at play."

"What 'special circumstances'?" Mikhail asked with a sneer. "You never told me such thing."

"You dumb fuck. Have you not learned that you only get to see the big picture when you have earned the right? And right now you couldn't be trusted with opening a carton of milk. She is family, Mafiosa. You kill her and we have a war on Brighton Beach and as the man who caused it one of the only certainties is that you will be amongst the first to die."

Marco and Bobby looked at each other, uncertain about how this would play out. Bobby kept his gun firmly pointed at the young buck, Marco at the older man. Mikhail was clearly weighing the odds, which troubled Gregori no end. He knew he lacked the judgement or experience to pick the right suit for church, never mind something as nuanced as this. Joe, meanwhile, had stopped wriggling and was just gently rocking backwards and forwards. He's lost it, thought Gregori, who'd seen it all before. He'll piss his pants in a minute.

"Mikhail, lower your gun and untie our guests," said Gregori gently. It was intended to take some heat out of the situation and reassure the Italians that he was still very much party to the bargain they'd struck.

Mikhail smiled ruefully, shrugged his shoulders and moved a step closer to Kathleen. "Sorry boss," he said, before calmly raising his gun and shooting his mentor through the chest. Bobby and Marco ducked instinctively onto their haunches, guns trained on the younger man but unsure of their next move. He was fully behind Kathleen and from their angle it was a head shot or nothing.

Mikhail put the gun against Kathleen's head and Joe heard her whimper. So she was still alive. Still time. He heard the hammer on the gun pull back and click and triangulated the sound before launching himself, chair and all, sideways. He'd found a sharp edge against the back of the cheap metal chair and his fidgeting had been his clumsy attempt to cut through the tape that was holding his hands behind his back. That much had worked whilst the younger man was distracted by his boss's challenge so his hands were free now and he aimed them in the direction of the sound to push the gun away from Kathleen's head.

The element of surprise worked and as his muscular bulk crashed in to Mikhail, the Russian's arms were knocked off target and a bullet was let off a good three inches over Kathleen's head. She screamed and ducked as Joe knocked the Russian to the ground and landed across his legs. Sensing his body position correctly, he was able to land a winding blow in to the man's tackle, using his other free hand to remove his hood. He'd stand no chance fighting blind.

Mikhail was trained in hand-to-hand combat, however, whereas, for all Joe's street brawls in Bootle as a kid he'd been trained in dispensing communion wafers. Plus, his legs were still tied to a chair. He was in for the hiding of his life or a bullet and neither was ideal, but at least Kathleen was still alive. The Russian brought his knee crashing in to Joe's face, knocking him backwards as Mikhail's hand quartered the floor around him in search of his weapon.

Marco dashed forward, kicking the gun to one side and distracting the Russian sufficiently to allow Joe to reach to his right and grab the baseball bat that Gregori had used so effectively a few hours earlier. He could only move from his waist upwards, but with his upper body strength that was enough and he pivoted from right to left, using the arc of his arm to full effect to bring the bat crashing down on to the Russian's right hand collar bone. Mikhail screamed in agony as it snapped and instinctively clutched his shoulder, allowing Joe time for one more crushing blow. He judged the angle better this time and the bat smashed in to his assailant's head, knocking him unconscious.

Joe lay back, panting at the exertion and he felt the pain in his cheek bone for the first time. He rubbed his face then hauled himself up on to his hands to survey the room. Marco was cradling his buddy in his arms and Joe realised with horror the result of his intervention to save Kathleen. He ripped at the masking tape constraining his ankles as he sought to free himself and help.

In the quiet they could hear Lara's anguished sobs in the distance. She couldn't have seen anything but she'd be working the odds and chances were her man was one of those down.

Bobby groaned gently, clutching his stomach wound as a large pool of dark red blood gathered at his side. Marco knew he'd need to get him to hospital soon or that would be another three children without a father.

First he needed to get what they came for, which was the Irish broad and her pal and he pulled a penknife from his pocket and threw it to Joe to cut himself and Kathleen free. Joe lifted Kathleen up from her seat and led her gently outside, whispering in her ear. He kept her hood on to save her from seeing the bloodshed, removing it as they approached the warehouse door. Outside, she flung herself at him, sobbing, and Joe allowed the release to abate before unwrapping her arms from around his neck. She grabbed him by the wrist as he made to return to the office, a look of fear and relief in her eyes.

"Joe, thank you," she said, simply. He nodded then ducked back inside.

"Help me here," Marco said, pointing at Bobby. "We gotta stop that blood flow. You see anything we can use around here?"

Joe remembered the large cuddly teddies and rushed to grab a big white one, thinking it would make a fine present for Paula Kelly's twins. He retrieved Marco's knife from his pocket and sliced one of the arms off, lifting Bobby's hands so that he could press it himself into his wound. If he was conscious enough, he'd know what pressure worked best, but the hands flopped away and Joe did it himself.

"We've got to lift him into your car, now. Drive it up to the door so that we don't have to carry him too far," and with that Joe weighed down the teddy's limb with Bobby's arm and ran for the sliding door, putting his shoulder into it so that the big Italian could reverse right into the warehouse.

Lara had emerged from her hiding place and was cradling her dead man in her arms, his head resting on her bump as she sobbed uncontrollably. Doubtless he'd rested it there many a night as they sat on the sofa, listening for a heart beat and waiting for that magical kick that signifies energy, life, vitality. The child had been his sign that he was settled, and heading for a more cautious existence, using younger muscle more and taking a cut of their pay. It was working out and he had savings – Lara's now, of course, and she'd need them, with a little one to raise on her own. She doubted that the mob would look after her. They lacked that code that the Italians had, she thought, and she wept all the harder at the hopelessness of her prospects.

The Toyota reversed at speed into the space and Marco leapt out, ready to haul Bobby into the car with the Irishman's help. But the Mick was kneeling over his friend now, praying, before administering the sign of the cross on his forehead and muttering a gentle incantation.

He knew what that was – you couldn't avoid the last rites in this line of business. "You a priest, or something?" he asked, his words catching in his throat. Bobby was his only buddy and they were tight. This was a bad day. A bad day.

"Yes, I still am, but I'm without a parish," said Joe, softly. "Your friend has gone, but with the Lord's blessing."

Marco hung his head as though in prayer and Joe's guilt left him feeling miserable. But if he was honest, he'd swap a gangster for Kathleen and then let the Lord be their judge.

Marco raised his head and gave Joe what he could only describe as a look of pure hatred. It was his turn to close his eyes and pray as the Italian raised his gun. He let off two bullets in quick succession then holstered his weapon calmly. Kathleen rushed back inside and Lara clutched her man to her tighter, wimpering quietly.

"You're dead now, you dumb Russian motherfucker," said Marco, and with that he hauled Joe up by his elbow. He assessed the two bullet holes in Mikhail's chest and never felt happier at seeing someone murdered.

"C'mon. Let's get Bobby some place better."

CHAPTER FOURTEEN

Sir Meredith Bell was not at John Lennon Airport to greet his guests, as had been his plan. It would have been impossible to control the media scrum and Godber had weighed that now was the time to conclude these discussions behind closed doors. There had been enough megaphone diplomacy already, driven by the little PR girl and her legal sidekick and they needed to close this story off. Deny them the oxygen of publicity, as Margaret Thatcher had once said of Sinn Fein, the IRA's political mouthpiece.

Two blacked out Range Rovers taxied carefully to the company jet as it parked on the apron to the south of the airport's main terminal building, a gleaming glass affair built during the boom years when European money was sloshing around Liverpool to help drive its transformation from basket case to functioning metropolis.

The camera crews and reporters were held back, thirty yards away, behind a chain-link fence in a rubble car park used by plane spotters, delighted to be able to get so close to the runway of a major airport. There was a soft drizzle and the puddles and mud affected their mood. Worse, the Range Rovers blocked their view and they could only film fleeting images of Goldstein and Heuston emerging down the short flight of steps before being swallowed up into the cars' cavernous interiors. Their shouted questions and pleas for a pose for the cameras were ignored and it proved a less than satisfactory morning's work for them.

It was an eight mile drive from the city's southern fringe to the Pier Head, largely through pleasant leafy suburbs before hitting the inevitable pocket of inner city shabbiness. It wasn't long before they were on the famous Dock Road and Liverpool's showpiece architecture hoved into view. No New York, but muscular and handsome, Goldstein thought. So this was the Beatles' stomping ground, then? She'd have to come back one day without cameras in tow and see for herself what gave them their inspiration.

They drew up on the pavement to the very front steps of a magnificent white stone palace, where a phalanx of security guards and barriers held back the media. So this is what Theresa's legacy helped fund, thought Goldstein, as she thought ahead to the hard ball she was going to play during her negotiations for recompense. The subpoena allowing her to assess the company's archive had come through and she had the first of her two big negotiating chips – the other being Sir Meredith's DNA. Whether Kathleen was alive to benefit from her work remained to be seen but she knew who would, if not.

Godber's plan was to rush them up the steps through the front door then wrap them in the quiet, luxurious cocoon that was life in Bell Group's inner sanctum and not let them out until a deal had been struck. Anna Heuston had other ideas, of course, and had briefed Roz on how it was likely to play out.

They wriggled free of their guards in unison and walked straight to the line of waiting media. Four of them were holding out newspapers, which seemed odd. They instinctively grabbed one each, a Daily Star and a Daily Mail, the former an avowed red top and the latter fancying itself as the voice of Britain's hard-working, silent majority. There was nothing silent about its headline though: 'Merry hell for Merry Bell as wife vows to take him to the cleaners', with a claim that 'sources close to the family had revealed plans for Britain's most expensive divorce'. The Daily Star had taken a different tack: 'Bell's brass is bikini babe' beneath the sub-head 'We grab first posed pics of shipping magnate's ice maiden. See pages 4,5,6 and 7.' Quick work and doubtless set up in advance by Adaksin, thought Godber. When the Russians played dirty they did so with a good deal of lateral thought, she had to give them that.

Roz and Anna were quick to the issue and it was the lawyer who stepped forward this time to make a statement. Godber stood back, trying hard to hide her look of irritation, whilst up in the boardroom a dishevelled looking Bell stood with just Middlewood and a trusted PA at his side, watching a live feed on an elegant flat-screen TV sitting flush within a fitted cupboard system.

"Ladies and gentlemen, once again we're happy to acknowledge Sir Meredith Bell's conciliatory gesture in bringing us here today. We are sure that he wishes to continue to conduct discussions in a spirit of openness and we shall reciprocate. He has clearly had a difficult day of it and we do not wish to add further to his troubles."

"But let us remember that we have been threatened, that innocent American school children have been threatened and that two of our party have been kidnapped and are doubtless in grave danger – all, we suspect, to stop us pressing our case and seeking justice for Theresa." The truncation to just her first name personalized the issue neatly, reminding people that at its heart was an innocent young Irish girl who had been tricked out of her land and the fortune that went with it.

"We will be resolute in our negotiations and we expect full compliance with the court order we received last night instructing Bell Group to give us full access to their archives. If we get the faintest whiff that they are hiding something from us then they will feel the full weight of the American legal system. We will say no more at this point and will update you as our agreement allows" and with that the pair turned on their heels and up the steps, followed by Godber and a retinue of advisors and security staff.

~~~~

Nikolas Adaksin sat alone and in silence in his vast personal suite on the 48th floor of his Moscow headquarters. His calculations had gone seriously awry and he had only discovered the disastrous outcome in Brighton Beach later from sources dispatched to investigate the reason for radio silence. The picture was sketchy but the key facts were known. The two men hired to guard his assets were dead and his collateral had disappeared. Evidence pointed to a third injured person and word was that the mafia had been involved, a fact squeezed out of a low level bag-carrier who had been beaten by some Italian thugs the day before. He'd not told them anything, of course: look at my face and tell me it is from someone who squealed. I took this pain for the team he had said, defiantly. It was a lie and he was a weak link that could no longer be trusted, so they tortured him a little before shooting him in the eye and leaving him in the car park of the Russian Doll in clear sight as a warning.

Worse, Adaksin's people in Newfoundland were reporting that technical problems and a souring of relations with the British team had delayed exploration. He needed to get across the line on the discovery of recoverable reserves and one last drilling, in a highly encouraging spot, would seal it for him. They'd already got past seventy per cent. When the call came that the Newfoundland government had temporarily suspended their license he saw the hand of British diplomacy and flew into a rage that staff in the hushed lobby outside heard, but no-one else. When he had calmed down, Adaksin sat once more to ponder his options. He'd played dirty and it hadn't worked, so clearly it had not been dirty enough.

~~~~

Roz and Anna were welcomed with all the felicitousness they had expected from blue-blooded Brits on home turf. The offices were magnificent, panelled, gilded testimony to Britain's maritime hegemony over so many hundreds of years. What was the song? Britannia rules the waves. They must have done to build places like this, thought Roz. The Borgias didn't manage anything this grand and they ran a city state.

Bell greeted them at the door of his sanctum. He looked tired and slightly distracted and Goldstein sensed an opportunity to drive home some advantage. She was looking forward to putting herself in the box seat and staying there.

"Welcome Roz. I've been looking forward to meeting you," said Sir Meredith, suddenly animated. "And you will be Anna," he said, extending his hand to her and guiding her into the lounge area of the boardroom. They sat around a large glass coffee table in a U-shape of modern sofas straight out of the Heal's catalogue. Copies of Country Life and The Field were scattered about and there was a smart glass-fronted wine fridge with a very fine selection, by the looks of things. Memo to myself, thought Roz: must work harder.

And then the mood changed.

"Ladies, you have come over here on a wild goose chase, I am afraid," Sir Meredith Bell opened. He looked stern and purposeful now; even his hair look somehow less tousled than it had earlier. He was getting down to business and business was what he did best.

"We have anticipated your subpoena and the company librarian has searched our archives from top to bottom, carefully and methodically, looking for any reference to Theresa Brophy or Madden and her alleged land deal with my great-grandfather. We have gone through his personal diaries and correspondence. We have examined company accounts, asset registers and share certificates. Even ordered a search of the Newfoundland provincial land registry. And we have not found a single shred of evidence to substantiate your claims."

"You are welcome to stay in my hotel for as long as you need in order to undertake your own trawl of those same archives, but I can guarantee that you will find nothing," said Sir Meredith, his tone suggesting that he wasn't finished yet.

"If there was merit in your claim I would happily entertain it, ladies. If my business is responsible for something then it is right that it faces up to that. But I see no evidence at all to suggest that it is. My only conclusion is that you are behind a falsehood. This adventure is nothing but a scam and you are seeking to defraud my business, and in such circumstances I will defend our interests with a will and a force that will take your breath away."

Roz went to interrupt, but Bell was warming to his theme and held his hand out. "You will get your opportunity to speak, Miss Goldstein. Indeed, I am very much looking forward to your explanation for how you got embroiled in this fraud and if you persist with it then I shall see to it that your professional reputation is thoroughly traduced, if it isn't already. Now would you like a whisky?"

It was a low blow indeed, referring to her alcoholism, a fact he'd already had brought to the world's attention during an earlier press conference.

"I never drink before ten am, thank you," Roz shot back. "Do you sleep with whores in the morning? Is she a prostitute?" she said, tilting her head towards Godber and trying hard to imagine someone so prim in Miss Whiplash gear.

Godber jumped in. She could see where this was headed as she thought how out of character it was for Sir Meredith to stoop so low. He could be as tough as the next man, but she'd never seen him get personal.

"People, this will be a much more productive meeting if we keep it civilized please," she pleaded.

"You growl at me, I growl back. You smile at me, I smile back. The choice is yours, lady," Roz said, deadpan.

"Fine, we get that," offered Middlewood, "but you have to see it from our side. A manuscript is discovered in an empty house which purports to reveal the secret of a grand fraud we committed one hundred and twenty two years ago but we can find no evidence of the transaction to which it refers – and when you see the extent and orderliness of our archives you will see why we are so skeptical. Moreover, the people who present us with this evidence turn out to be a group of what I shall kindly describe as misfits, giving the firm impression of a band of losers who have come together for a roll of the dice that one of them – Delahunty, was it? – convinced you all was going to be a winner. You cannot blame us for being both cynical and determined to defend our reputation." He paused, scanning their faces with his usual scowl.

"You have indulged in megaphone diplomacy of the worst kind, throwing accusations around willy-nilly, the latest of which is that your friends have been kidnapped and that somehow our business partners were involved. And yet, once again, you fail to present a single shred of evidence to support your case. All the while, our reputation is being taken to the cleaners whilst you play out your sinister game and the weight of media attention is forcing us to tip-toe around you. It's a disgrace, frankly," he spat.

"This ends here," he said, emphatically. "You will be allowed unfettered access to our records; we will even give you support staff to fetch, carry and interrogate, but you will not find anything, and after that you will go home to America and we will not expect to hear from you again. Ever."

It was Anna who spoke first and she did so quietly, forcing them to lean in and listen. It was an old trick that she'd picked up from her first boss and it had the effect of both calming the mood and making them concentrate.

"Who was George Molyneux, Sir Meredith?"

The question hung in the air and she watched as the home team shot one another glances.

"Your reaction is as big a give-away as the threats he made to us. You have lied consistently through this process and we have been presented with evidence to prove that." She was almost whispering now.

"It was precisely because of the utter absence of any evidence that Theresa Brophy's claim existed that we were about to walk away from all this. To consider it some historical curio or even, as you contend, some sort of falsehood. But George Molyneux got intouch and told us in no uncertain terms to stay away, as big an indicator that we were on to something as if you'd fired it up in neon. People with nothing to hide, as you contend, don't issue threats. What did you have? Some sort of search term watch on Google? I'll bet you did," she said, looking pointedly at Sir Meredith. He dropped his eyes.

"So you are all lying. We will prove it and some of your people are already passing us information to help us prove it. I don't doubt you've combed those archives and burned anything relevant, but you'll leave a trail doing that, unexplained gaps. There'll be links in other, later, documents referring to the contents in those gaps and that'll suggest that the information was, indeed, there at some point. And the web of deceit will unravel, bit by bit, with the American court system testing your resolve every step of the way.

"You'll be under oath and, in cases such as this, if any of you are proven to have perjured yourselves then you will spend five or six years minimum in an American jail." She scanned the room as she said this, her quiet voice and measured logic starting to unnerve them now.

"How often will your three children be able to visit you in jail, Mrs Godber? Will you become a lesbian for comfort whilst you're there? I think you call it 'prison bent' over here. Will your husband hang around if that happens?"

Godber was stony-faced, but inside there was turmoil. She had a great affection for her boss and for the company and all its achievements but the logic of Heuston's argument was disturbing, as were the images she'd planted in her mind.

"Sir Meredith, we have testimony from our friends in New York that it was your partners in Russia who ordered Joe and Kathleen's kidnapping." It was a lie, but on top of the other evidence she'd discovered she figured they'd think it was true. This was about turning the screw, because she was as aware as Roz that theirs was, indeed, the flimsiest of cases. In the absence of DNA evidence – and it would be hard to compel that at this stage – this was the only avenue open to them.

"If we can make any credible link between the Russians' actions and knowledge on your part, then the jail sentences and other sanctions will be punitive. So you see, Mr Bell," – a demotion in status calculated to wound – "we are not troubled at all by your bluster or that of Mr Middlewood. You can threaten us, dissemble, lie, cheat, hide evidence and bully, but we will not go away and we will not be cowed. So do you want to do a deal or don't you?"

The ultimatum hung in the air and not even Middlewood dared to jump into a space that Sir Meredith had been challenged to fill. The atmosphere was frosty, now. This had become too personal and Bell knew he needed to lift it.

"Miss Heuston, I am lost in admiration for your performance. When this is over I can guarantee you that there will be a senior position for you in my business should you ever wish to join us. I look at my team and, competent as they are, I find it difficult to imagine any of them having the gumption that you possess." Godber blanched. Was that a barb aimed at her, too?

"But I return to Mr Middlewood's point: evidence. Show it to me. Show me what you know about Mr Molyneux and reveal to me your source, as you will be compelled to do in court should we all be foolish enough to take this there. Show me this evidence from whom I assume to be Mrs Fabrini's mob family about the Russians. Mobsters make very credible witnesses in the eyes of juries, I always find. If we are to do a deal then it has to be business-like and you are not being business-like. Negotiations are a give and take based on shared facts and understanding, but I see only a one-way street here. You've put on a good show, but I don't see how you've moved even an inch in the process," and he held Anna's gaze, almost paternally.

"I am going back to work now and my team will do likewise. My drivers will take you to your hotel so that you may check in and refresh yourselves, then please return at your leisure and Mrs Taylor, our head librarian, will be at your disposal for as long as you need her. Good day."

And with that he rose and left his boardroom, with Godber and Middlewood in pursuit.

~~~~

The call from Nikolas Adaksin took Bell by surprise. He was hoping to postpone the necessary showdown with his partners whilst he boxed the Americans into a corner and then dealt with his wife and family. Caroline had thrown him out of the house and he'd taken the Skyline Suite in his Hahnemann Hotel on Hope Street indefinitely whilst he let things cool down at the marital home. He was sure they would, for the girls' sake, but he knew he had fractured his marriage beyond repair. It would be a miserable existence but children want both parents in their lives, no matter what, and he wasn't about to screw them up just as they were blossoming into such bright promise.

The Americans were in the Hahnemann too, but his was a private skylift up the side of the building on Hope Place and with a butler providing breakfast and his driver waiting outside, he didn't worry about bumping into them.

Adaksin dispensed with his usual bonhomie. This had gone way too far for that. He was coming over to Liverpool the following day to discuss their position and he told Bell that it would be a focused and business-like day. Bell took that as code for bloody unpleasant and wondered what cards Adaksin had in his pack. A man like that didn't come to Liverpool unless he was going to deliver the coup de grace and, given the dirty tricks he'd indulged in these last few days, that made Bell nervous.

He sat in his office, lost in thought, admiring some late snow on the Welsh mountains in the far distance and he realized that he had only one chance left open to him if Adaksin really did have some sort of poison pill he was about to drop into the deal. He picked up the phone and called Sir Quentin Fanshaugh.

~~~~

Marco had taken Bobby to the mob's safe house in south Brooklyn, not too far from Brighton Beach. He'd called ahead and a well-rehearsed plan swung into place. They've done this a few times, thought Kathleen, wondering sadly if this was where her husband had first been brought. They'd never told her. Bobby would be washed down, sewn up, dressed in new clothes and then put in cold storage. A friendly doctor would sign his death certificate identifying a massive heart attack and the mourning widow would publicly lament his poor diet and lack of exercise. The children would be none the wiser and his body would quickly be cremated – there could be nothing more distressing than the cops digging him up to gainsay the family's claims about how he died.

Bobby's wife Angelina knew the risks and that the mob provided a generous pension for widows and their children. But there was evidence aplenty back at the warehouse and Marco needed to deal with that. Charred bodies and buildings left little that was useful, in his view, whatever they said on CSI New York.

He turned into the small commercial lot's turning circle for visiting trucks and he could see activity in the Russians' corner unit. He carried on driving, figuring it would look suspicious if he did a quick u-turn, and parked two lots down. They didn't know who he was, after all. He'd just sit and watch, making out he was asleep in the front, and see what gave.

They were gone in fewer than thirty minutes, the great alloy doors opening to allow a Ford pick-up truck covered in a tarpaulin to pull away. The passenger jumped out, closed the doors and the Russian mob's two sweepers were gone. Marco knew to wait: either they'd done a clean-up job par excellence or that place was going to blow. His money was on the latter: far quicker, much less risky and there was even a good insurance payout at the back end. And then he saw the tell-tale signs of smoke emerging from under the alloy doors. That'll do me, he thought. Don't want to be here when the cops come looking for witnesses.

The place was full of cheap Chinese toys – doubtless a cover for something else. Heroin? Girls? Or both, probably. But what it meant was that the flames took quickly and by the time he'd executed his u-turn he could see them licking out of the building's skylight. Good on them, he thought. Thorough.

~~~~

Kathleen wanted to strip and wash after her ordeal. She could still smell the Russian's vileness in her nostrils and she wanted out of the clothes and underwear that he'd despoiled. The safe house had a stock of everything and she was impressed both with their foresight and the fact that they'd come good on her insurance policy. Which reminded her: Roz. She found a phone and dialled her cell number, committed to memory after thousands of calls these last number of years.

Roz picked up after the third ring – doubtless scrabbling about in that capacious purse of hers to find the thing. Joe listened as she gave Roz her news and heard the tears flow on both sides of the Atlantic. She recounted the story in detail, about how Joe had saved her life and stopping only to wipe her eyes and, in the case of her sexual assault, to catch herself from sobbing uncontrollably. But she held herself broadly together and Joe couldn't help but admire her bravery. He thought nothing of his own.

The call ended after twenty minutes and Kathleen turned to him, energized and optimistic.

"Come on," she said, "we're going to Liverpool."

CHAPTER FIFTEEN

Adaksin's jet taxied to the executive terminal at John Lennon and it was the biggest on the apron. There were no waiting members of the press to hijack him – this was to be a private visit. Bell had extended him the courtesy of two Range Rovers to accommodate the Russian's retinue of thugs, gangsters, pimps, hangers-on and scabby whores. Sir Meredith was still feeling sore, he admitted to himself, but good manners demanded he extend the courtesy, no matter what he thought of them.

It was Tuesday, three whole days after the St. Patrick's day kidnapping and still he had not heard whether Joe Delahunty or Kathleen Fabrini were safe. But here he was welcoming their likely captor who, unfortunately, was also his business partner.

He had reserved them rooms at the Hahnemann for two nights but hoped it wouldn't be that long. That all depended on how their negotiations played out. Middlewood would be present, of course, as well as a retinue of lawyers from Barlow Hayes. The negotiations would be filmed and recorded, too. Belt, braces and bloody baling string if that's what it took, thought Bell.

The convoy arrived at the Cunard Building at ten am and their guests were ushered upstairs to the executive suite adjacent to the boardroom where they were invited to make themselves at home. We'll have to count the cutlery, thought Middlewood, already underwhelmed by the tawdry display of wide suits, bling and peroxide he saw before him. Peasants with oil wells in their back gardens, he mused, scornfully.

Bell was waiting on a response from Sir Quentin and the radio silence did not bode well. He felt a dread that he was heading into whatever Adaksin would throw at him with defences down.

He entered the board room looking grim, accompanied by his team, with Middlewood to his left, loins girded for the scrap ahead. This was his métier and whatever happened he, personally, was bullet-proof so bring it on, he said to himself. The Russians had been shown in from the other side of the room and when everyone was settled there were fifteen of them around the table, six from Sir Meredith's side and the balance to the Russians, whose number included a blonde whose purpose Bell could only imagine.

It was Sir Meredith's parish so the Russians waited for him to open proceedings.

"Gentlemen, madam, we will not kid ourselves that this has been an easy week for our relationship. However, we are where we are and we must work together to achieve the original aims of our partnership, which is to enrich ourselves. If the partnership fractures, that objective suffers and so I would caution us all against heading down any road which veers away from our goal. You have called this meeting, Nikolas, so it is over to you."

Nikolas Adaksin rose from his seat at the far end of the table. He wanted to command the meeting because what he was about to deliver merited his grand-standing. It was to be one of his finest hours, in a career marked by many, and a little showmanship would go down well with his entourage, as well as grate with his hosts.

"Sir Meredith, we entered our relationship with Bell Resources at the behest of our two governments, assured that we were in the company of one of your nation's finest, most upstanding businesses. We now know that it is led by a weak, disloyal, dishonest and tawdry individual who dresses as a woman and consorts with whores. I am aghast at the scale of my mistake and how doing business with you has tarnished our good reputation."

Middlewood nearly choked on that bit and Bell let out a weak, nervous smile. What else lay ahead, he thought. Insults he could cope with, but it was the hint of looming disaster that made him nervous. And where the hell was Sir Quentin when he needed him?

"But we have an agreement," Adaksin continued, "and we must be guided by its terms. We both know that the Canadians will drop their investigation when things have calmed down and that drilling will commence again. We had almost reached the point where our expertise would have led to us discovering a billion cubic metres of gas until these lice emerged from under a tree in New York. But they have been dealt with and the point at which the remaining 35% of free shares vests in us is nearly there."

Bell dreaded to think what he meant by the phrase 'dealt with' but he let him press on.

"There can be no doubt that a word or two from your government will speed the Canadians' decision and this meeting is to ask you to request that," said Adaksin.

"You'll be asking me to marry Anatalia next," Bell snorted. "Why in God's name would I ask the Canadians to do that?"

"Because you have no choice," said Adaksin, before strolling over to Bell's own AV unit and inserting a dvd into the console.

The screen above flickered into life and Bell's Newfoundland consiglieri, the Texan, Marley Clitheroe, appeared, fixing the camera with a firm gaze. Bell's stomach flipped. This could only spell disaster.

Clitheroe was compelling and authoritative, taking the viewer through a structured file of evidence to demonstrate that Bell Resources had consistently sought to doctor the drill findings to defraud NovKos. By suggesting lower than expected reserves had been discovered they hoped to avoid reaching the tipping point at which NovKos would be entitled to the outstanding 35% of shares in the project and he had been instructed in this venture by none other than Sir Meredith Bell himself, providing diary entries as proof of their meeting to discuss the issue.

Middlewood was aghast and shot a glance at Bell, who had turned grey. It was all bollocks of course, but highly compelling, nonetheless – particularly for a jury, innocent to the ways of big business. Where on earth did they go from here?

Bell wondered how much money Clitheroe had been paid for this fantasy. Given his recent experience, he suspected that this whole enterprise had been entered into at the very start of the drill programme. A million dollar down-payment for Clitheroe from the Russians to show sincerity and intent, with another few mil on delivery. Something like that. There were lessons here for me, he thought, before reminding himself that he was probably best trying to fix his marriage first.

The dvd lasted eighteen minutes before Adaksin strolled over and removed it, throwing a copy like a frisbee to Middlewood, his contempt and triumph obvious.

"Sir Meredith, here's how it is going to be. You will sign over thirty six per cent of the project shares to me immediately, the additional one per cent in recompense for this fraud and for all the reputational damage you and your team of incompetents have caused my company."

"You will meet half our £200m exploration investment by way of an advance dividend to NovKos and you will hand operational control to my company. From now on, Bell Resources becomes a silent partner and we retain our majority stake in perpetuity. If you do not agree to these terms, then we release the video, pursue you through the British courts for exceptional damages and use our government's reach to ensure that your international business activities, whether in food, shipping or finance, are frustrated at every turn.

"Let me be clear what I mean. Whenever you apply for a license or operate under an existing regulatory agreement you will find that things suddenly get difficult. Unexpected rejections, license suspensions, extraordinary audits and bids you thought you'd win rejected on a number of grounds. We will grind your whole business into the ground, slowly and methodically. And if you try and sell any parts to frustrate us, we'll do the same to the new owners, assuming we haven't already warned them to walk away before the deal is done.

"Bell, you do not fuck over Adaksin. You have tried and you have failed and you now work for me."

That was final and his team looked smug and pleased with their boss's performance. Middlewood, by contrast, held his head in his hands. He could walk away from this personally, of course, but he still had a huge regard for all that Sir Meredith had achieved and all that the firm stood for. Granted, giving away the resources company – and allowing the Russians effective control was giving it away, knowing how they would manipulate the profit and loss account – meant he could run the rest of the Group as planned, but who could trust a Russian? They were bullies and once bullies had found a weakness they came back for more. It never ended there.

Bell himself looked defeated and it was almost a god-send when his PA, Mo, came into whisper in his ear. Anything to get out of this room. He was staring defeat in the face and his mind was racing, weighing up his options as he breathed quickly and shallowly. But the worst of it was that it was on his watch that Bell Group was facing annihilation. Eight generations of skilful, patient development undone by the greed of easy money in the energy market. If his great-grandfather hadn't defrauded Theresa Brophy then none of this would have been possible in the first place. No land, no wharfage, no in-shore drilling rights. Karma, wasn't that what they called it? Jolly bad luck, more like.

He excused himself and Adaksin waved him away with a flourish of his arm. I'm the boss now, it said.

~~~~

Joe and Kathleen arrived at JFK booked on a Continental flight to Manchester. It was a forty minute taxi ride to Liverpool city centre which, in English terms felt like an age but to a Yank, Joe had discovered, was a quick hop.

They had cleaned up at the mafia's safe house and helped themselves to a few changes of clothes finding, to their surprise, it was rather nice gear. What, they had a fashion consultant to stock their wardrobes? Stranger things had happened and, as Kathleen pointed out, it was hugely profitable being part of a global criminal enterprise. They looked after their employees as well as any international corporation, she said.

They returned to Kathleen's home to collect their passports and other effects. They had stayed there the night before St. Patrick's Day, Joe in the spare room. The cab was running outside and they had no intention of hanging around. They needed to wash New York out of their hair for a while and a few days in Liverpool would do just that.

The queue at JFK's Terminal 7 moved slowly and Joe and Kathleen stood close to each other but in silence. There was so much to reflect upon, not least of which was their luck. Kathleen shuddered when she thought about the Russian's shooting and how close those bullets had come. But they were alive and they had laughed since, even sharing a few jokes with their cab driver, the son of a Scottish émigré who swore they modeled Willie, the caretaker in The Simpsons, on his father. He was no impressionist and conceded defeat to Joe, who had the Glaswegian accent off pat. He had a good ear and three months in the bed of one of his parishioners who hailed from Kelvingrove had helped.

JFK's facial recognition technology was amongst the best in the world for reasons that no-one need entertain. It had identified Delahunty and Fabrini as they walked through the terminal doors and a dozen eyes followed their movements through the airport. They arrived at their check-in desk and handed over their passports, which were taken from the attendant by a stiff-looking gentleman with a buzz cut. He wasn't in the airline's uniform and the penny dropped immediately, at which point three agents appeared at their side and ushered them away.

Bobby had explained that they couldn't remain out of sight forever and that when they appeared back in the public view the police would want to talk to them. So he tutored them on how to cope with an interrogation, ran them through a crib-sheet of answers they should give and asked them to commit to memory all the salient facts about their kidnapping and rescue. It was a lot to take in but they were bright and their respective professional training had taught them to remember detail by rote. Not forgetting, of course, they had the golden get-out clause: they'd been chloroformed and spent most of their time with a hood on their heads. Hey, look at Kathleen's ligature marks, they'd say.

It was a day before they were released, The police kept telling them they were free to leave at any time, but that their co-operation would be noted and was welcome. They were well aware of Fabrini's mafia links and local intel in Brighton Beach was talking about a body count of four and something about an Italian/Russian war being avoided. One well known enforcer, a Gregori Markovic, had disappeared from view and there was the small matter of a Russian-owned warehouse going up in flames. But they were frustrated at every turn and there was a cohesion about the pair's story which made them doubt themselves a little. Still, it didn't smell right and to cops as seasoned as this if something was vaguely whiffy it meant there was a whole pile of shite beneath if they dug deep enough. But they couldn't find a chink, in spite of their suspicions, and so 24 hours later the dishevelled and shattered pair jumped a cab back to Kathleen's and to their separate beds, having booked themselves on the next flight.

Waiting for Sir Meredith in his private office was a tall, slim man in his early fifties and his bearing shouted military. Or spook, perhaps. What the hell did he want?

"Sir Meredith," he said, with the authority that comes with years of leadership, "Sir Quentin Fanshaugh has asked me to have a quiet word, if you don't mind? My name is Green."

Sure it is, thought Bell. And it'll be Black tomorrow, Brown the day after that and all the way along to Purple by Saturday.

"This will take at least fifteen minutes, sir," he continued, without waiting for Bell's response. "You may wish to ring through to your guests to put them at their ease," said Green.

"Ah, yes, right. Good idea," said Bell, suddenly energized by Fanshaugh's emissary. Adaksin had him on the ropes and the arrival of the government's corner man gave him encouragement. He headed for the board room.

"Sorry folks, awfully rude of me, I know. I don't mean to bugger you around but something has cropped up. I'm going to be another quarter of an hour then we're good to go. Help yourself to whatever you can find. Ah, you already have. Right then," and with that he backed awkwardly out of the room to the smirks of his guests, Adaksin in particular, who was tucking in to a very fine 45 year old single malt. Take all the time in the world, you bumbling fool, he thought. By his reckoning he was about a billion pounds up on the morning and that could buy him an awful lot of influence and reach.

Bell returned some twenty minutes later to the head of his table, a brown file under his arm. His cheeks looked flushed but otherwise his countenance was stern and thoughtful. Adaksin was happy to be patient now. He'd delivered a remarkable coup de grace that left his adversary with few places to go. Wherever he headed, it would profit NovKos and leave room for him to come back in and pick off prized assets at will. It reminded him of the siege of Sarajevo, when the snipers took their time and only shot the most prized targets. He would do the same, as the only company that could realistically acquire Bell Group assets. Who else would he sell to, when the might of the Russian government could spike their guns?

"Nikolas, thank you for that very considered presentation, which only served to reinforce my view that you are a corrupt and deeply unpleasant little man." Bell knew the word little would rankle. Russian culture placed huge store by the Big Man, either in stature or outlook and the barb worked, he noted, as Adaksin bristled.

"I shall admit that I have not been without error in my recent dealings, particularly in relation to my dear family, so it gives me less satisfaction than it might to also note that your conceit and vaulting ambition have been your undoing."

Adaksin growled. "Bell, you are sinking and petty insults will not keep you afloat. Tell me how you wish to resolve this or we go straight to the lawyers. Think at what cost that will be personally and to your business."

"You're right, I am sorry. It was rude of me so I shall cut to the chase," said Bell, clearly feigning humility. What is he up to, wondered Middlewood. What is in that file?

"You have been funding the Russian President's sworn enemy, Boris Mosavic, for the last six years. You have given him assistance on multiple levels, including using your security apparatus to amass evidence against the President, corrupt his aides, feed him misinformation as a trusted ally and feedback, from that same position, political information to Mosavic. I note you are going red. Should I continue?" Bell taunted. Adaksin twitched, but gave nothing further away.

"In this folder I have copies of bank statements, recordings of conversations, secretly filmed meetings, photographs showing clandestine liaisons with the President's staff, with corresponding bank transfers that lead back to his men and all manner of other clear evidence that you have sought to corrupt the office of the President whilst helping his most potent political threat. Here, you can have it," he said, sliding it violently down the table and forcing Adaksin's aides to scrabble after the contents as they slid around the polished surface.

Adaksin went from red to pale, as he turned page after page of evidence gathered over six years by Britain's secret service.

"Now, you won't need telling how the President views such treachery. There have been two or three cases these last five years of billionaire oligarchs who have found their assets confiscated whilst they play bitch to some lonely former soldier in a Siberian prison cell. Not a jolly experience, I should imagine." Adaksin gulped.

"This file goes straight to the President himself, via our ambassador, tomorrow tea time if you do not agree to what I am about to say. You can consider asylum here or elsewhere, but you yourself have already noted the long reach of the Russian bear's arm and I hardly think that spending the rest of your days looking over your shoulder will be much fun. Not that they'll leave it too long before they have you killed, I suspect."

Adaksin was slumped in his chair and his team utterly deflated. If the boss sank they went with him, and their gilded lifestyle too.

"You will withdraw from this project, citing differences in strategy over our resource extraction plans and saying you believe the reserves may have been over-stated. You will sell us your stake for £100m and we will conclude the deal within eight weeks. You will pay the wife and children of George Molyneux, whom I have no doubt that you have had killed, £2m within four weeks and will offer your best endeavours to have his body recovered and returned to this country. Failure to do so within eight weeks will incur a further penalty clause of £2m.

"Now, are Mr Delahunty and Mrs Fabrini safe? Can they be released?" asked Bell.

Adaksin nodded, reflecting on the irony of his previous thought that their bungled escape was the worst moment in this episode. Far from it.

"Good. I and our government have multiple copies of all of this evidence which we shall retain in perpetuity. Should I even remotely suspect that your organization or government is seeking to frustrate the legitimate interests of my business then I shall have it released immediately. Do I make myself clear?"

Adaksin offered the merest nod of acquiescence. He knew exactly what the President's team would do to him if any of this came to light and it would break even the hardest man. Never mind what they did to his family and closest allies.

"Good," said Bell, with an air of finality. "Now fuck off out of my office, there's a good fellow, and make sure you're back here for three pm when you will sign the heads of terms of our agreement before flying back to that shit-hole from whence you came," and with that he marched down to Adaksin's end of the table, gathered up the evidence file and called his security staff into the room to escort his guests off the premises.

Bell's Range Rovers were waiting to take them up to the Hahnemman and they slumped into the seats, sullen and bruised. Defeat, when it comes to a man like Adaksin, is absolute. There is no redemption, only shattered pride, a loss of authority and the awful realization of what lay within reach, but could never be grasped. His blonde companion shuddered at the beating she was sure was just minutes away.

CHAPTER SIXTEEN

The taxi ride to Woolton took twenty five minutes, heading up the hill from the Pier Head past the city's huge Anglican cathedral and down wide, elegant Georgian streets. Within minutes the prosperity of downtown ended and they were in altogether more pressing territory. Grand homes, boarded up, spoke of better times, whilst suspicious, pinched faces looked into each passing car or cab as though the passengers were likely to be bearers of more misery. But then, there clearly wasn't much upward mobility around here, thought Roz. It was like a tale of two cities, amplified further when, within ten minutes, they'd passed through the inner city ring and reached leafier suburbs, the tight terraced streets giving way to grand, tree-lined boulevards and large semi-detached and detached villas. You could make it in this town, clearly, but if you didn't?

Roz had a map spread over her lap. She liked to get her bearings and cities fascinated her, not that she'd been to many, fewer still abroad. She'd loved London on a visit in '08 – her sort of scale, but Liverpool felt provincial, for all the braggadocio of its downtown office blocks and its two cathedrals. Nice suburbs though, and plenty of parks, she conceded.

Anna was lost in thought and mildly pensive at the visit. The call had not gone well at first, but Caroline Bell was from proper breeding and Anna managed to mine a vein of empathy by discussing shared troubles, with Bell Group as the common denominator. She had sounded weary and maybe it was defeatism, too – not wanting another scrap, after the public humiliation she'd faced. But she'd conceded and invited them to her home.

The taxi driver whistled when he saw the house, called Moyville. They didn't have street numbers in this neck of the woods. He was familiar with Woolton, of course, its leafy, sandstone lanes amongst the most desirable in the city. He knew where all the footballers lived and pointed out a few of their homes as he went, not that Roz or Anna had the slightest clue about this side of British life. That made him smile, to find a pair of innocents in this, the most successful and soccer-obsessed city in all of Britain.

They paid the sixteen quid fare and pressed the intercom, the high dark sandstone walls looming over them, with no sight of the house through the heavy wooden gate.

"Hello?" came the suspicious enquiry. For the first two days of the tabloids' feeding frenzy they'd been camped outside Moyville House, hoping to snatch some photographs or force a comment from Lady Bell. Better still, they were hoping for one of those photo opportunities so beloved of fallen politicians, arm around wife as they explained that being caught in a rubber suit with an orange in their mouth in a cellar in Chelsea was a temporary aberration and that the good lady wife was standing by him. She would look solemn and smile weakly, then thrash the life out of the idiot once they'd got back behind closed doors. Which, of course, was what he was paying for in Chelsea in the first place.

"Oh, hi. It's Anna Heuston and Roz Goldstein from New York. We have an appointment with Mrs Bell," she said, expectantly.

"Ah yes, do come in" and with that the intercom went dead. After a three second delay there was a click and the huge wooden gate slid silently left to right, to reveal a long path up to the crown of the ridge and an elegant, white stuccoed house with a large portico and royal blue door.

Lady Caroline Bell was waiting for them at the door, a slight woman in her mid-forties in a twin-set, pearls and an Alice band. Altogether the complete young-fogey ensemble, Roz thought. Do rich women age prematurely around here or something? It was unkind, she knew, but for heaven's sake. This girl needed a style consultant as well as a new husband. God knows, she could afford one if the rumours about the divorce were true. She'd be on for more than a hundred million quid. How much was that in dollars? An awful lot more, Roz calculated.

She greeted them with as much charm as she could muster, but she was weary, they could tell. Fair enough. In her exalted circles it was probably expected that the husbands had some odd tastes. A legacy from boarding school days, no doubt. But they went unsaid and it was certainly poor form to put your wife through what Caroline had suffered. 'Big cheese up to his spuds in Kolli': that had made Anna chuckle, accustomed as she was to writing her own headlines for her clients' press releases. The sub-editor must have punched the air when that one emerged from the keyboard.

Caroline Bell led them across a wide, marble-floored hallway and down a narrow passageway with three steps at the end to a beautifully-grained walnut door. Behind it lay a huge, light and modern kitchen providing a wide panorama of the back garden through floor to ceiling glass curtain walling. Not such a fuddy-duddy after all, thought Roz.

The preliminaries with tea, coffee and biscuits involved minimal small talk from Lady Bell, leaving Roz and Anna to make some running, lest the atmosphere sink to frost-bite level before they'd even got down to the purpose of their visit. They cooed over the kitchen, just loved the English rose garden beyond and thought the portrait of the three girls a delight. They were sooo beautiful and even Caroline Bell, in the eye of an awful storm, saw fit to smile and loosen up a little. She talked about the children and their hopes and aspirations for them, as though the family unit was still intact. She'll have him back, thought Roz. Clear as day. These posh girls don't do divorce. British stiff upper lip and all that. That might make the conversation a bit harder, she thought.

They sat at an expensive white laminated table with a huge vase of white lilies as its centre-piece and the day's Daily Telegraph lying open on the business pages. Caroline folded it away and sat down, inviting her guests to do likewise. They cupped their mugs of coffee and Anna broke the silence.

"Lady Bell, it's kind of you to see us during such a difficult time. Thank you," she opened, with a hint of humility and understanding. "Our pursuit of the Madden Files, as I now know they are called within Bell Group, put in train all the events that we have witnessed and so we feel culpable, in some ways, for your distress. Please be assured of our sincerity in that regard. There's much about all this that I am beginning to regret." She paused, dropping her eyes a little. Roz, once again, found herself in rapt admiration for this young kid. And here she was playing a hugely wealthy woman like an old pro.

"I am going to level with you now. I suspect we don't have much of a leg to stand on, whatever our feelings on the matter." Caroline Bell looked up, allowing an eye brow to rise in surprise. Roz glared at her, her admiration diminishing rapidly. What you playin' at, m'lady, she asked herself. This better be good.

"We could carbon-date the ink and paper that Theresa Madden used and I'm sure that would authenticate its age. We have George Molyneux's threats on tape and people have told us he was a regular in your husband's employ, although as a contractor so that he could keep some distance between himself and Molyneux's dirty work. And we know that Bell Resources' Russian partner, NovKos, ordered the Russian mob in Brighton Beach to kidnap our friends, Joe and Kathleen. They have still not been found as far as we know and remain in grave danger. The warnings and the kidnappings tell anyone with eyes in their head that we must be on to something. If there was nothing in the firm's archives and if the alleged fraudulent transaction between Barrington Bell and Theresa Brophy never happened, then why would the heavy mob be brought in at the merest hint of interest in the issue? They wouldn't, now would they?

"So everything points to a conspiracy and to the truth of Theresa's claims. We've no doubt that a very professional job was done to vacuum the archives of any hint of a relationship between Theresa Brophy and Barrington Bell but we're sure, with time, we could find some gaps that would raise further interesting questions. But that's all they'd be. All we've really got is instinct, supposition and some strong circumstantial evidence – plus, of course, more than a whiff of skullduggery."

Caroline Bell nodded. She wanted to see where this was going. For all her own pain, she still had a huge vested interest in the success of Bell Group, whether she stayed in or got out via the divorce courts.

"But you know our biggest problem?" asked Anna. "We don't have the time or the money to pursue this legally. Put frankly, we haven't got a pot to piss in. Your husband will be able to walk all over us, of that I'm absolutely certain."

Lady Bell looked askance and Roz went red at the inference that her legal firepower would never be enough, even if, in a moment of reflection the day before, she'd admitted as much to herself. She'd been down in the archives for nine hours getting precisely nowhere and the hopelessness of their position had begun to hit home. And then Anna discovered something interesting, the possibilities of which pointed to Caroline Bell, and here they were.

"That would be a shame, because amidst all the victims that have emerged during the course of our investigation, one set seems to have been forgotten. Theresa Brophy and her family, who suffered terribly as a result of Barrington Bell's deceit and whose life-chances were dramatically curtailed over one hundred and twenty two years, whilst Bell Group kept its guilty secret buried and its owners' families thrived."

"Look at your beautiful daughters, Caroline." Lady Bell turned instinctively to the portrait in a frame on the kitchen counter. "Think of all the advantages you have given them: music lessons, ballet, horse riding, swimming, amazing holidays and the comfort that comes from the combination of material wealth and a loving home."

Caroline Bell nodded and her eyes welled up as she thought about the wreckage that was her marriage and how greed and ambition had thrust a jagged, bitter sword through the heart of her family.

"Now think about what the denial of those advantages would do to generations of a decent, hard-working family who knew they had been defrauded but lacked, as we do, the resources to put right that wrong. Think if it happened to you. What would you want to see happen?" Anna implored, with genuine emotion.

"There is a way to prove this beyond doubt, but before I explain how I want your help, let me assure you that our intention is not to bring down Bell Group. You will not see us press for the ridiculous and punitive penalties you see played out in the American courts. We have no interest in destroying such a fine business employing so many good, committed and innocent people. Where is the value in that? That was never our intention and give me five minutes with Sir Meredith and I'm sure I could convince him, too. But I won't need to, if you'll help me," and with that, she took a draught of her coffee and left the request – or was it a challenge? – to hang in the air.

Lady Bell gathered herself. "Young lady, that was most eloquent and I don't doubt your sincerity, but before I even begin to entertain helping you, I'd need a lot more certainty that the purity of your motives regarding recompense are true. You are right that Bell Group is a fine business and you cannot blame the sons for the sins of the father, so anything that might undermine the whole foundation of the business would be as unjust as the original fraud perpetrated against poor Theresa Brophy." Caroline Bell was no fool, but she clearly had a strong streak of decency in her, thought Anna.

"Lady Bell, I am happy to persuade my client to sign appropriate legal documentation that limits her claims upon Bell Group and I have no doubt that she will do so. We would seek to negotiate only fair recompense for the losses sustained, not punitive damages as any corporate lawyer we may hand this to on a commission basis would gladly seek. That option remains open to us, but your co-operation would close that off immediately." Anna knew she was close, now. If Lady Bell went with her then she'd kill or cure this whole goose chase.

"Miss Heuston, I believe there is still honour in the world. In fact, it continues to underpin democracy and civil society. Whatever the man in the street may read, it also underpins ninety nine percent of all business transactions and commercial relationships. Whatever Bell Group may have done in the past it is still, fundamentally, an honourable business." She held Anna's gaze to drive home the point.

"But I am prepared to take you at your word, Miss Heuston. Tell me what you think I can do to help resolve this issue and if it is in my gift then I will do so. You, in return, will do no harm."

~~~~

The cab ride from Manchester Airport was bumpy and hot. The windows were closed to keep out the spray from the trucks heading for Liverpool docks after another spring shower turned into a minor monsoon.

Joe and Kathleen sat on the rear seats, hanging on to the straps for dear life as the Manchester cabbie swung through the traffic. It was a good, fixed fair – sixty quid – so the sooner he got back within the Manchester city limits, the quicker he could get another one and clock up a proper day's earnings. That's what he loved about the airport: good long-distance fares. His best was to Carlisle, for two hundred and twenty quid. Now that was a day and a half.

~~~~

Lady Bell took them to her bedroom. "You'll find what you need here," she explained. "He's a typically messy chap and there'll be plenty of it lying around." Anna knew what would yield the best results and headed straight for the bathroom. She'd asked to borrow a few sealable freezer bags and put the comb in one and the toothbrush in the other.

"He was due a new one, let's be honest," admitted Caroline wistfully.

CHAPTER SEVENTEEN

The Russians had left the evening before, their jet taxiing quietly to their slot on the western runway at John Lennon, perfectly set where the Mersey is at its widest to minimize noise pollution. It turned north up the river, offering a view of the city's new downtown skyscrapers, built before the boom petered out. Adaksin paid no heed: he would never return and his mind was on how he might limit the risk of news of his disloyalty leaking from those other than the Brits. He had no doubt that they'd keep the file in the locker, but if they could have compiled such a thing in the first place, who else might have done so? Where had the tip-off come from and who had given the Brits the access they needed? He had a mole in his organization and there would be much torture and bloodshed ahead until his paranoia abated. First on his list was the hapless Pugin.

Bell had called a review the following morning with his legal and public affairs teams. Now the Russians were off the scene that just left the matter of the rag-tag and bob-tail bunch of alcoholic, sexually incontinent and Mafioso Yanks to sort out. He didn't quite know how to categorise Anna Heuston and he'd formed a sneaking regard for her abilities throughout this bloody mess, truth be told.

"We're putting this to bed team and I want your ideas on how," Sir Meredith opened.

Middlewood jumped straight in, balls metaphorically aching after the thorough shafting they'd administered to the Russians. He wanted more action and his testosterone count was sky high.

"They had nothing but the flimsiest of pretexts when this whole episode began and they've gathered no further evidence since," he suggested, his tone hinting at his mood. "Our archives are clean and apart from a rather unfortunate body count over in Brooklyn there's nothing else to suggest that there's truth in the story. We play hardball now and we send them packing back to New York. They don't have the resources to take us on and when we promise to unleash hell, they'll baulk and go home."

Bell nodded and looked towards Godber. She was unconvinced: "Whatever the evidential issue, they have a weight of media and public sympathy behind them. Theresa Madden's life story has now become a cause célèbre and whilst we may think we can close this off legally, there'll be a raft of investigative journalists for decades raking over this story. It's just too meaty. Perfect ingredients: innocence, love, deception, cunning aristocrats, a disinherited love child and generations of hurt. You get the picture. This story doesn't die if we pay off our antagonists. It'll run and run whatever we agree. That's the beauty behind the whole game they played," and she knew who the architect of it all was, too.

"So how do we close this off? What do we do to give this a happy ending? We can't admit liability when no-one can pin it on us," said Sir Meredith.

"Yes they can, darling. In fact we just have."

Lady Caroline Bell strolled into her husband's board room, his PA Mo scurrying after her with an apologetic look. Bell held up his hand, stopping Mo in her tracks, before waving her off. Behind Caroline came the Jewish lawyer and that rather tidy little PR girl. What had they found, he wondered.

"There's one piece of evidence you could never kill off, fake or hide away, dear. Your DNA," and with that she threw two images on his desk, both DNA structures, like large bar codes. He looked up at her for an explanation.

"Oh darling, tell me the penny has dropped. Your DNA, here," she said, exasperated, pointing at the left hand bar code, "and Kathleen Fabrini's, nee Madden, here," as she stubbed her finger on the image provided by Roz.

"See the similarities? No? Blimey, Merry, are you really that dim?" His team sat, not for the last time in this mad episode, open-mouthed.

"Barrington Bell is your great-grandfather. And he's Kathleen Fabrini's, too. Which makes Kathleen your cousin, albeit several times removed. Theresa Madden's letter is the truth, or at least the bit about her having Barrington's child was. And now that we have established that fact an army of Mrs Godbers couldn't persuade the rest of the world that the other claims in the letter aren't also. So the question facing you lot is not how you make the story go away, but how you now turn it to your advantage," and she shot a look to Godber as if to say 'you're the PR girl, you fix it.'

"But, but," spluttered Sir Meredith, "how on earth did you get my DNA?"

"Your comb darling, and a little help from a few friends in the School of Tropical Medicine. You're not the only one well connected there," she said, referring to her own fundraising work for one of Liverpool's most prestigious institutions. She'd pulled a few strings, obviously, and there was silence as Bell took in what was before him.

It was Anna Heuston who broke it. She seemed to be making a habit of that, he thought.

"I can see a very neat solution to this," she opened. My, my, what a fucking surprise, thought Godber, who was beginning to tire of being upstaged by this slip of a thing who couldn't be older than, what, twenty seven? Cow.

"Sir Meredith," she said, appealing directly to him, "you want to be able to say that you are the architect behind our solution and that, as you demonstrated with the offer of your jet and hospitality, you have always been as keen to see justice served as the next man. It was just that you needed evidence, of course – you wouldn't be much of a businessman if you had just rolled over. And so you volunteered your DNA to bring the issue to a close. It was you, in fact, that suggested the settlement and Bell Group's long term partnership with the Madden Academies. You, personally, will announce this with Kathleen in a joint press conference in New York and the political and public relations gains for your businesses based in the States will be substantial. Neat, don't you think?"

"And what settlement would that be, young lady?" asked Sir Meredith.

"The one we are about to hammer out," said Goldstein.

~~~~

They met Kathleen and Joe on the steps of the Cunard Building just after they'd fallen out of their cab and, once the tears and hugs were over, Anna brought them to order.

"Guys, have we got some shit to tell you. C'mon, let's go for a coffee."

"Sod that," said Joe. "You're in my town now. We're going for a pint," and with that he flung his arm out and a passing hackney cab pulled in sharply down Water Street.

They settled into Brahms, one of the stunning mahogany parlours in the Philharmonic, Liverpool's most ornate pub and only three hundred yards from the Hahnemman Hotel. We can stagger back, said Joe, to laughter. A waitress came in, took their order and left them to it.

"We've done you a deal," said Roz, who, like Anna, had managed to keep tight-lipped until they got to the pub, focusing the conversation on Joe and Kathleen's travails in Brighton Beach.

"What sort of deal? What do you mean?" asked Kathleen.

"It's all over. We signed for you. Or rather, I signed for you, as your lawyer."

"And I witnessed it for you, as your publicist," smiled Anna.

"Ladies, what on earth are you talking about?" grinned Kathleen.

"Your grandfather, Sean Madden, was Barrington Bell's first son,"

explained Anna. "We've proven it with DNA from Sir Meredith Bell no less."
Kathleen looked stunned, as did Joe.

"We'd issued a subpoena in New York which gave us access to the company's archive but they'd cleared the whole thing out. A very professional job. Not a shred of evidence about the deal that Theresa had written about," explained Anna. Joe thought back to his internet searches with Cindy. What was it they'd said? It was like she'd been redacted from history.

"But then I found something," said Anna. "I was going through the company's original memorandum and articles of association."

"What's that?" Kathleen interrupted.

"It's like a founding charter that sets out how the company is to be run and who can and can't do what amongst the shareholders and bosses. Anyways, they'd clearly started the whole show with a dynasty in mind because the charter said that the first born son would always inherit. Sean was that first born by a whole three years and it made no distinction between legitimate or illegitimate, although the convention of the day would have interpreted it only one way. Still, it gave us grounds for argument. If we could prove the DNA link then we'd have a strong bargaining chip and could play it rough if we needed to."

Katherine's mind raced at the possibilities of where this was headed. Had she inherited the whole shooting match? Surely not.

"If we'd gone to the courts on the point of inheritance it's likely that they would have argued that you had to interpret the charter as the court of the day would have done so, which would have been to deny the bastard and give title to the child born within wedlock. Harsh days, when viewed from our perspective, but there'd have been plenty of precedent in that regard," explained Roz.

So I'm not a multi-billionaire then, thought Kathleen, smiling at the absurdity of it all.

"But there are plenty of precedents showing that among that class of people the illegitimate child would have been provided for handsomely. A trust fund, a large house for the mother, fully expensed with servants and the like. People like that became minor aristocracy in their own right in Britain. So we conceded the point of inheritance to show our reasonableness and pressed the case for the dowry," explained Roz.

"They wanted a quick solution and Anna had outlined a rather brilliant plan that left them winners all ways up, apart from the money I wanted to wring out of them. But the PR upside was huge and Sir Meredith saw a way out of all this, which bought me a bit of headroom to be, well, ballsy. Give me a sniff of victory and I'll drive it home until I'm sure the other side are tied up like a Thanksgiving turkey."

Kathleen was bursting at this point. Just. Tell. Me. It was written all over her face but they'd rehearsed this, clearly, and it would be bad manners to interrupt. Manners mattered in her way of things and she wasn't about to break that golden rule.

"You are now CEO of the Madden Academies," said Roz. "That was her idea," she said, nodding to Anna, who shifted on her seat a little and smiled, shyly.

"It has an endowment of one hundred million pounds in cash – that's about a hundred and sixty five million US dollars at today's prices – and a fifteen per cent share in the four shale gas drilling zones operated by Bell Resources off St. John's in Newfoundland. Sir Meredith Bell is chairman and will appoint three major CEOs as non-executive directors to your board to help with the roll-out and management of your academies across American and British inner-cities, starting first here in Liverpool and then onwards."

Kathleen sat stunned, tears streaming down her face. She rubbed them away roughly with her right hand, smudging her make-up, then nodded and grinned inanely as her dream unfolded before her.

"Once the gas starts flowing the Academies' share of the annual profits should be around forty five million pounds a year for twenty three years. We've managed to ring-fence that so that they can't manipulate the costs in the business to depress your share, so you can rely on it, exchange rate variances aside. Oh, and your salary as CEO is nine hundred thousand dollars a year, partly to recompense you for the creative idea behind the Madden Method, but also because you ought to have some sort of share of your great-grandmother's legacy. She talked about that in her letter, remember."

Kathleen hugged her friend Roz then held Anna's face in her hands before planting a big kiss on her forehead. She said nothing. What was there to say that wouldn't sound trite? She wanted to hear the rest of the story and share hers, too, particularly about how Joe saved her life. The priest or ex-priest, she wasn't sure which, had earned a shot at redemption, especially from Anna whom she sensed was a bit cool on the man because of his past. But all that aside, she just swelled with pride and happiness.

The waitress came in with their order: a whisky and soda for Roz; a chardonnay for Anna; a gin and tonic for Kathleen and a pint of Guinness for Joe. He looked at it, settled beautifully, the contrast between the white creamy top and the dark ruby body a thing to behold.

He held it up to them all to admire. "'Tis a thing of beauty," he said, and they agreed it was, the laughter and tears flowing readily.

CHAPTER EIGHTEEN

It was quite a session in the Philharmonic and, good as his word, Sir Meredith Bell had Edwards drop him off for an hour on his way back to his hotel so that he could join his erstwhile foes for a couple of drinks. He queued with the early evening crowd to get his round in and found himself needing to catch up, the others being a few drinks ahead of him, so he ordered himself a Scotch to go with his pint of Cains.

He'd ensure that, when the announcement about the deal was made, the press would know that it was concluded over a pint, just as he'd offered a few days and half a lifetime ago.

Bell found himself drawn in to their easy company, this odd group of misfits, all fighters in their own way and, like Bell, all with their own stories to tell about human frailty. They ended up staggering the three hundred yards down Hope Street to the Hahnemann Hotel together and he smiled when he saw Joe and Anna take the stairs as one, the ex-priest's arm gently around Anna's waist. He made a mental note to ask the housekeeper the next day if one of their rooms had been unused, then took himself off to the Skyline Suite and a good night's sleep. He'd earned it, he felt.

THE END.

Buy the sequel now:
The Colony – www.amazon.com/author/tompaver

Also available in the Redemption series:
The Blood Puzzle (Redemption, book 3)
The Sanctuary Stone (Redemption, book 4)

From 1st November 2012:
Take the Soup (Redemption, book 5)

Follow Tom on twitter: @TomPaverAuthor
Learn more about Joe Delahunty & Anna Heuston at www.tompaver.com
Email Tom at: tp@tompaver.com

With thanks to my editor, Dr Arline Wilson, for her advice, encouragement and support.

For Rory and Elizabeth and their amazing mother, Helen.

Printed in Great Britain
by Amazon.co.uk, Ltd.,
Marston Gate.